"YOU LIED TO ME, BYRON!"

"I couldn't think of any decent way to tell you."

"Of course not. Decency isn't your style." She tilted her chin up, hanging on to the last shreds of her dignity. "Does Cliff know about us?"

"He knows you don't like me."

"But I never indicated..."

Byron grinned. "You aren't as good at hiding your emotions as you think, Miss Gates. But you can relax. He doesn't know why you dislike me so much. I haven't told him anything."

Nora exhaled at the blue autumn sky. "I could strangle you, Byron." She looked back at him. "And that's only the half of it."

"I'm sure," he said. His tone was neutral, but she saw the lust—the damned amusement—in his eyes.

"Don't you get any ideas, Byron Sanders Whoever. You don't mean any more to me than a bag of dried beans."

"Remember your fairy tales, Nora." Byron smiled. "Jack's beans turned out to be magic."

Special thanks and acknowledgment to Joanna Kosloff
for her contribution to the concept for the Tyler series.

Published May 1992

ISBN 0-373-82503-X

WISCONSIN WEDDING

WISCONSIN WEDDING

CARLA NEGGERS

Harlequin Books

TORONTO • NEW YORK • LONDON
AMSTERDAM • PARIS • SYDNEY • HAMBURG
STOCKHOLM • ATHENS • TOKYO • MILAN
MADRID • WARSAW • BUDAPEST • AUCKLAND

TYLER

TYLER

American women have always used the art quilt as a means of expressing their views on life and as a commentary on events in the world around them. And in Tyler, quilting has always been a popular communal activity. So what could be a more appropriate theme for our book covers and titles?

WISCONSIN WEDDING

This unique variation of the Wedding Ring Tile quilt includes the vivid lines of a Wisconsin Star inside each circle. On the frontier, women used scraps of leftover fabric to create art, just as they found moments of joy in shared communal labor.

Dear Reader,

Welcome to Harlequin's Tyler, a small Wisconsin town whose citizens we hope you'll soon come to know and love. Like many of the innovative publishing concepts Harlequin has launched over the years, the idea for the Tyler series originated in response to our readers' preferences. Your enthusiasm for sequels and continuing characters within many of the Harlequin lines has prompted us to create a twelve-book series of individual romances whose characters' lives inevitably intertwine.

Tyler faces many challenges typical of small towns, but the fabric of this fictional community created by Harlequin will be torn by the revelation of a long-ago murder, the details of which will evolve right through the series. This intriguing crime will culminate in an emotional trial that profoundly affects the lives of the Ingallses, the Barons, the Forresters and the Wochecks.

Renovations have begun on the old Timberlake resort lodge as the series opens, and the lodge will also attract the attention of a prominent Chicago hotelier, a man with a personal interest in showing Tyler folks his financial clout.

Marge is waiting with some home-baked pie at her diner, and policeman Brick Bauer might direct you down Elm Street if it's patriarch Judson Ingalls you're after. Nora Gates will make sure you find everything you need at Gates Department Store. She's helping Liza Baron prepare for her wedding, but is having great difficulty handling the unexpected arrival of the groom's brother! So join us in Tyler, once a month for the next ten months, for a slice of small-town life that's not as innocent or as quiet as you might expect, and for a sense of community that will capture your mind and your heart.

Marsha Zinberg
Editorial Coordinator, Tyler

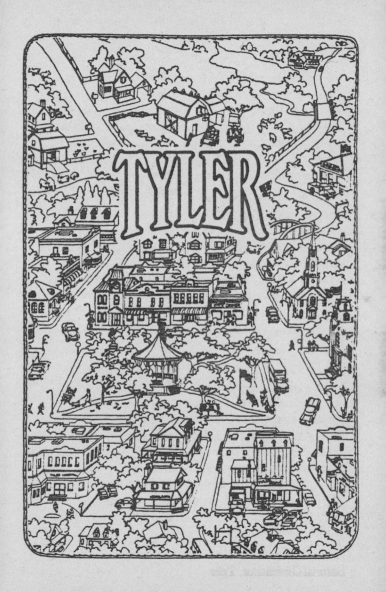

TYLER

CHAPTER ONE

WITHIN THE SEDATE, mahogany-paneled president's office of Pierce & Rothchilde, Publishers, Byron Forrester pitched a sharp-pointed dart at the arrogant face of his latest traitorous author. The dart nailed Henry V. Murrow smack in the middle of his neatly clipped beard. Byron grinned. He was getting pretty good at this! Now if Henry had been in the office in person instead of in the form of an eight-by-ten glossy publicity photo, Byron would have been a happy man. Only that morning Henry had called to notify him that he'd just signed a mega-deal with a big New York publisher.

"For what?" Byron had demanded.

"A technothriller."

"What, do you have a dastardly villain threatening to blow up the world with a toaster? You don't know anything about advanced technology. Henry, for God's sake, you haven't even figured out the tele-graph yet."

"Research, my boy. Research."

Pierce & Rothchilde didn't publish technothrillers. Its specialties were expensive-to-produce coffee-table books, mostly about art, geography and history, and so-called literary fiction. Some of the latter was deadly stuff. Byron found Henry's books depressing as hell.

Technothrillers. From a man who'd been utterly defeated by the locks on Byron's sports car. "How does one exit from this contraption?" he'd asked.

Now he was calling himself Hank Murrow and planning to make a bloody fortune. Probably had shaved his beard, burned his tweeds, packed his pipe away in mothballs and taken his golden retriever to the pound.

"I wonder how much the fink's really getting."

Byron aimed another dart. Henry—*Hank*—had said seven figures, but Byron didn't believe him. He'd yet to meet a writer who didn't lie about money.

A quiet tap on his solid mahogany door forced him to fold his fingers around the stem of the dart and not throw it. He really wanted to. Henry had offered to send him a copy of his completed manuscript. Byron had declined. "It'll be more fun," Henry had said, "than anything that'll cross your desk this year." A comment all the more irritating for its probable truth. Byron had wished the turncoat well and gotten out his darts.

Without so much as a by-your-leave from him, Fanny Redbacker strode into his office. Trying to catch him throwing darts, no doubt. She regularly made it clear that she didn't think her new boss was any match for her old boss, the venerable Thorton Pierce. Byron considered that good news. His grandfather, whose father had cofounded Pierce & Rothchilde in 1894, had been a brilliant, scrawny old snob of a workaholic. He'd vowed never to retire and hadn't. He'd died in that very office, behind that very desk, five years ago. Byron, although just thirty-eight, had no intention of suffering a similar fate.

"Yes, Mrs. Redbacker?" he said, trying to sound like the head of one of the country's most prestigious publishing houses.

Mrs. Redbacker, of course, knew better. Stepping forward, she placed an envelope on his desk. Byron saw her eyes cut over to Henry Murrow's dart-riddled face. Her mouth drew into a straight line of disapproval.

"It's tacked to a cork dartboard," Byron said. "I didn't get a mark on the wood paneling."

"What if you'd missed?"

"I never miss."

She inhaled. "The letter's a personal one addressed to you and Mrs. Forrester." Meaning his mother. Byron wasn't married. Mrs. Redbacker added pointedly, "The postmark is Tyler, Wisconsin."

Byron almost stabbed his hand with the dart, so completely did her words catch him off guard. Regaining his composure, he set the thing on his desk. Fanny Redbacker sighed, but didn't say anything. She didn't have to. It had been three months, and Byron still wasn't Thorton Pierce. He didn't even look like him. Where his cultured, imperious grandfather had been sandy-haired and blue-eyed and somewhat washed out in appearance, Byron took after the Forresters. He was tall, if not as tall as the Pierces, and thick-boned and dark, his hair and eyes as dark as his father's had been. For a while everyone had thought that despite his rough-and-ready looks Byron would step neatly into his grandfather's hand-tooled oxfords.

But that was before he'd ventured to Tyler, Wisconsin, three years ago. After that trip, all bets were off.

"Thank you, Mrs. Redbacker."

She retreated without comment.

Byron had forgotten his annoyance with Henry Murrow. Now all he could think about was the letter on his desk. It was addressed to Mr. Byron Forrester and Mrs. Ann Forrester, c/o Pierce & Rothchilde, Publishers. At a guess, the handwriting looked feminine. It certainly wasn't Cliff's.

"Oh, God," Byron breathed.

Something had happened to Cliff, and now here was the letter informing his younger brother and mother of the bad news.

Nora... Nora Gates had found out who Byron was and had decided to write.

Not a chance. The letter wasn't big enough to hold a bomb. And the scrawl was too undisciplined for precise, would-be spinster Eleanora Gates, owner of Gates Department Store in downtown Tyler, Wisconsin. She was the *last* person Byron wanted to think about now.

He tore open the envelope.

Inside was a simple printed card inviting him and his mother to the wedding of Clifton Pierce Forrester and Mary Elizabeth Baron the Saturday after this in Tyler.

A letter bomb would have surprised Byron less. There was a note attached.

Cliff's doing great and I know he wants to see you both. Please come. I think it would be best if you just showed up, don't you?

Liza

A hoax? This Liza character had neglected to provide a return address or a phone number, and the invitation didn't request a reply. The wedding was to take place at the Fellowship Lutheran Church. To find out more, presumably, Byron would have to head to Wisconsin.

Was that what Liza Baron wanted?

Who the hell was she?

Was Cliff getting married?

At a guess, Byron thought, his brother didn't know that Miss Liza Baron had fired off an invitation to the sedate Providence offices of Pierce & Rothchilde, Publishers.

Byron leaned back in his leather chair and closed his eyes.

Tyler, Wisconsin.

A thousand miles away and three years later and he could still feel the warm sun of a Midwest August on his face. He could see the corn standing tall in the rolling fields outside Tyler and the crowd gathered in the town square for a summer band concert. He could hear old Ellie Gates calling out the winner of the quilt raffle, to raise money for repairing the town clock.

First prize was a hand-stitched quilt of intersecting circles. Byron later learned that its design was called Wisconsin Wedding, a variation on the traditional wedding ring design created by Tyler's own quilting ladies.

And he could hear her laugh. Nora's laugh. It wasn't her fake spinsterish laugh he heard, but the laugh that was soft and free, unrestrained by the peculiar myths that dominated her life.

He'd gone to Tyler once and had almost destroyed Nora Gates. He'd almost destroyed himself. And his brother. How could he go back?

Please come....

Byron had waited for years to be invited back into his older brother's life. There'd been Vietnam, Cambodia, a hospital in the Philippines, sporadic attempts at normality. And then nothing. For five years, nothing.

Now this strange invitation—out of the blue—to his brother's wedding.

A woman named Alyssa Baron had helped the burned-out recluse make a home at an abandoned lodge on a lake outside town. Was Liza Baron her daughter?

So many questions, Byron thought.

And so many dangers. Too many, perhaps.

He picked up his last dart. If he or his mother—or both—just showed up in Tyler after all these years, what would Cliff do? What if their presence sent him back over the edge? Liza Baron might have good intentions, but did she know what she was doing in making this gesture to her fiancé's estranged family?

But upsetting Cliff wasn't Byron's biggest fear. They were brothers. Cliff had gone away because of his love for and his loyalty to his family. That much Byron understood.

No, his biggest fear was of a slim, tawny-haired Tylerite who'd fancied herself a grand Victorian old maid at thirty, in an era when nobody believed in old maids. What would proper, pretty Nora Gates do if he showed up in her hometown again?

Byron sat up straight. "She'd come after you, my man." He fired his dart. "With a blowtorch."

The pointed tip of the dart penetrated the polished mahogany paneling with a loud *thwack,* missing Henry Murrow's nose by a good eight inches.

The Nora Gates effect.

He was probably the only man on earth who knew that she wasn't anything like the refined, soft-spoken spinster lady she pretended she was. For that, she hated his guts. Her parting words to him three years ago had been, "Then leave, you despicable cad."

Only Nora.

But even worse, he suspected he was the only man who'd ever lied to her and gotten away with it. At least so far. When he'd left Tyler three years ago, Nora hadn't realized he'd lied. And since she hadn't come after him with a bucket of hot tar, he assumed she still didn't realize he had.

If he returned to Tyler, however, she'd know for sure.

And then what?

"MISS GATES?"

Nora recognized the voice on the telephone—it was that of Mrs. Mickelson in china and housewares, around the corner from Nora's office on the third floor. For a few months after Aunt Ellie's death three years ago, the staff at Gates Department Store hadn't quite known how to address the young Eleanora Gates. Most had been calling her Nora for years, but now that she was their boss that just wouldn't do. And "Ms. Gates" simply didn't sound right. So they settled, without any discussion that Nora knew about, on Miss Gates—the same thing they'd called her aunt. It was as if nothing had changed. And in many ways, nothing had.

"I have Liza Baron here," Mrs. Mickelson said.

Nora settled back in the rosewood chair Aunt Ellie had bought in Milwaukee in 1925. "Oh?"

"She's here to fill out her bridal registry, but...well, you know Miss Baron. She's grumbling about feudalistic rituals. I'm afraid I just don't know what to say."

"Send her into my office," Nora said, stifling a laugh. Despite her years away from Tyler, Liza Baron obviously hadn't changed. "I'll be glad to handle this one for you."

Claudia Mickelson made no secret of her relief as she hung up. It wasn't that Nora was any better equipped for the task of keeping Liza Baron happy. It was, simply, that should Liza screech out of town in a blue funk and get Cliff Forrester to elope with her, thus denying its grandest wedding since Chicago socialite Margaret Lindstrom married Tyler's own Judson Ingalls some fifty years before, it would be on Nora's head.

Five minutes later, Mrs. Mickelson and the unlikely bride burst into Nora's sedate office. Mrs. Mickelson surrendered catalogs and the bridal registry book, wished Liza well and retreated. Liza plopped down on the caned chair in front of the elegant but functional rosewood desk. Wearing a multicolored serape over a bright orange oversize top and skinny black leggings, Liza Baron was as stunning and outrageous and completely herself as Nora remembered. That she'd fallen head over heels in love with the town's recluse didn't surprise Nora in the least. Liza Baron had always had a mind of her own. Anyway, love was like that. It was an emotion Nora didn't necessarily trust.

"This was all my mother's idea," Liza announced.

"It usually is." Nora, a veteran calmer of bridal jitters, smiled. "A bridal register makes life much easier for the mother of the bride. Otherwise, people continually call and ask her for suggestions of what to buy as a wedding gift. It gets tiresome, and if she gives the wrong advice, it's all too easy for her to be blamed."

Liza scowled. There was talk around town—not that Nora was one to give credence to talk—that Liza just might hop into her little white car and blow out of town as fast and suddenly as she'd blown in. Not because she didn't love Cliff Forrester, but because she

so obviously did. Only this morning Nora had overheard two members of her staff speculating on the
potential effects on Liza's unusual fiancé of a big
wedding and marrying into one of Tyler's first families. Would he be able to tolerate all the attention?
Would he bolt? Would he go off the deep end?

"Well," Liza said, "the whole thing strikes me as
sexist and mercenary."

Liza Baron had always been one to speak her mind,
something Nora admired. She herself also valued di-
rectness, even if her own manner was somewhat more
diplomatic. "You have a point, but I don't think that's
the intent."

"You don't see anybody dragging *Cliff* down here
to pick out china patterns, do you?"

"No, that wouldn't be the custom."

It was enough of a shock, Nora thought, to see Liza
Baron with a catalog of Wedgwood designs in front of
her. But if Liza was somewhat nontraditional, Cliff
Forrester— Well, for years townspeople had wondered if they ought to fetch an expert in posttraumatic stress disorder from Milwaukee to have a
look at him, make sure his gray matter was what it
should be. He'd lived alone at Timberlake Lodge for
at least five years, maybe longer. He'd kept to himself for the most part and, as far as anyone knew, had
never hurt anyone. Nora had long ago decided that
most of the talk about him was just that: talk. She
figured he was a modern-day hermit pretty much as
she was a modern-day spinster—by choice. It didn't
mean either of them had a screw loose. Cliff, of

course, had met Liza Baron and chosen to end his isolation. Nora had no intention of ending hers.

"If I were in your place," she went on, "I'd consider this a matter of practicality. Do you want to end up with three silver tea services?"

Liza shuddered. "I don't want *one* silver tea service."

Nora marked that down. "When people don't know what the bride and groom want, they tend to buy what *they* would want. It's human nature. It's to be a big wedding, isn't it?"

"Mother's doing. She's got half of Tyler coming. Cliff and I would have been happy getting married by a justice of the peace without any fanfare."

That, Nora felt, wasn't entirely true. Cliff no doubt dreaded facing a crowd, but would do it for Liza—and for her mother, too, who'd been his only real friend for years. But in Nora's estimation, Liza Baron relished being the center of attention again in Tyler. It wasn't that she was spoiled or snobby; she was still getting used to having finally come home to Tyler at all, never mind planning to marry and stay there. It was more that she wasn't sure how she was supposed to act now that she was home again. She needed to find a way to weave herself into the fabric of the community on her own terms. The wedding was, in part, beautiful vivacious Liza's way of welcoming the people of her small hometown back into her life. As far as Nora was concerned, it was perfectly natural that occasionally Liza would seem ambivalent, even hostile. In addition to the stress of a big church wedding, she was also coping with her once-tattered relationship with her mother, and all the gossip about the Ingalls and Baron families.

And that included the body that had turned up at the lake. But Nora wasn't about to bring up that particular tidbit.

She discreetly glanced at the antique grandfather clock that occupied the corner behind Liza. Of the office furnishings, only the calendar, featuring birds of Wisconsin, had changed since Aunt Ellie's day.

"Oh, all right," Liza said with great drama, "I'm here. Let's do this thing. The prospect of coping with stacks of plastic place mats with scenes of Wisconsin and a dozen gravy boats does give one pause."

Gates carried both items Liza considered offensive. Nora herself owned a set of Wisconsin place mats. She used them for picnics and when the neighborhood children wandered into her kitchen for milk and cookies. Her favorite was the one featuring Tyler's historic library. She didn't tell Liza that she was bound to get at least one set of Wisconsin place mats. Inger Hansen, one of the quilting ladies, had bought Wisconsin place mats for every wedding she'd attended since they first came on the market in 1972. Nora had been in high school then, working at Gates part-time.

They got down to business. "Now," Nora explained to her reluctant customer, "here's how the bridal register works. You list your china, silverware and glassware patterns, any small appliances you want, sheets, towels, table linens. There are any number of variables, depending on what you and Cliff want.''

Liza wrinkled up her pretty face. She was, Nora saw, a terribly attractive woman. She herself was of average height and build, with a tendency to cuteness that she did her best to disguise with sophisticated— but not too chic—business clothes and makeup. She didn't own a single article of clothing in pink, no flowered or heart-shaped anything, no polka dots, no T-shirts with pithy sayings, damned little lace. No se- rapes, no bright orange tops, no skinny black leg- gings. She preferred cool, subdued colors to offset her pale gray eyes and ash-blond hair, which she kept in a classic bob. Liza Baron, on the other hand, would look wild in anything. Cast them each in a commer- cial, and Judson Ingalls's rebellious granddaughter would sell beer, Ellie Gates's grandniece life insur- ance.

''Nora, Cliff doesn't want anything. He'd be happy living in a damned cave.''

But, as Nora had anticipated, in the quiet and pri- vacy of the third floor office, with its window over- looking the Tyler town square, Liza Baron warmed to her task. She briskly dismissed anything too cute or too simple and resisted the most expensive patterns Gates carried. She finally settled on an elegant and dramatic china pattern from England, American sil- ver-plate flatware, a couple of small appliances, white linens all around, Brazilian knives and a special re- quest to please discourage can openers. The stemware gave her the worst fits. Finally she admitted it was Waterford or nothing.

"Go for it," Nora said, amused. She tried to picture Cliff Forrester drinking from a Waterford goblet and found—strangely—that she could. Had someone said he was from a prominent East Coast family? Like most people in Tyler, Nora knew next to nothing about the mysterious, quiet man who lived at rundown Timberlake Lodge.

Liza slumped back in the delicate caned chair. "Is it too late to elope?"

"People would still buy you gifts."

Their work done, a silence fell between the two women. Despite her busy schedule, Nora was in no hurry to rush Liza out. The young woman had gone through a lot in the past weeks, and if the rumors circulating in the shops, restaurants and streets of Tyler were even remotely on target, she had more to endure. Falling in love with an outsider had certainly been enough to stimulate gossip, even undermine Liza's beliefs about what she wanted out of her life. In Nora's view, that right there was enough reason to steer clear of men: romance caused change.

It was as if Liza had read her mind. "You've never been married, have you, Nora?"

"No, I haven't. I like my life just the way it is."

Liza smiled. "Good for you. Have you ever been tempted?"

Nora's hesitation, she was sure, was noticeable only to herself. "Nope."

"Well, I certainly don't believe a woman has to be married to be happy or complete."

"But you're happy with Cliff."

"Yes." Her smile broadened. "Yes, I am."

Indeed, falling so completely in love with Cliff Forrester had already had an unmistakable effect on one of Tyler's most rebellious citizens. Liza Baron, however, seemed much more willing to embrace change than Nora was. She seemed more at peace with herself than she had when she'd first blown back into town, if a little rattled at the prospect of a big Tyler wedding.

Nora shrugged. "Romance doesn't have a positive effect on me, I'm afraid. It makes me crazy and silly...I lose control."

Liza's eyes widened in surprise, as if she'd never imagined Nora Gates having had anything approaching a romance, and she grinned. "Isn't that the whole idea?"

"I suppose for some, but I—" Nora stopped herself in the nick of time. What was she saying? "Well, I'm speaking theoretically, of course. I've never...I'm not one for romantic notions." A fast change of subject was in order. "How're the renovations at the lodge coming?"

"Fabulously well. Better than I expected, really, given all that's gone on. You should come out and take a look."

"I'd love to," Nora said, meaning it. As if marriage and her return to Tyler weren't stressful enough, Liza had also come up with the idea of renovating

Timberlake Lodge, a monumental project Nora personally found exciting. Unfortunately, the work had led to the discovery of a human skeleton on the premises. Not the sort of thing one wanted percolating on the back burner while planning one's wedding.

"Anytime. And thank you, Nora."

"Oh, you don't need to thank me—"

Liza shook her head. "No, I've been acting like a big baby and you've been so nice about it. The store looks great, by the way. Your aunt would be proud, I'm sure. You've added your own touches, but retained the flavor and spirit everyone always remembers about Gates. When I think I'm living in the boondocks, I just walk past your windows and realize there is indeed taste and culture here in Tyler." She hesitated a moment, something uncharacteristic of Judson Ingalls's youngest grandchild. "Ellie Gates was quite a character. She's still missed around here."

"She is," Nora agreed simply.

"Well, I should be off." Liza rose with a sudden burst of energy. "I guess I'll go through with this big fancy wedding. If nothing else, Tyler could use a good party right now."

Now Liza Baron was sounding like herself. Nora swept to her feet. "You're probably right about that. I suppose you haven't heard anything more from the police?"

Liza shook her head. "Not a word."

Without saying so outright, they both knew they were talking about what Nora had begun to refer to as the Body at the Lake. The *Tyler Citizen* reported every

new and not-so-new development in the case, but the
rumors were far more speculative. Given her owner-
ship of Tyler's only department store, her member-
ship on the town council and her circumspect nature,
Nora was privy to considerable amounts of local gossip, which she never repeated. Certainly *anyone* could
have been buried at the long-abandoned lodge.
Someone from out of town or out of state could have
driven up, plucked a body out of the trunk, dug a hole
and dropped it in. But townspeople's imaginations
were fired by the idea that the body was that of Tyler's
most famous—actually, it's only—missing person,
Margaret Alyssa Lindstrom Ingalls. People said Liza
was a lot like her flamboyant grandmother. Bad
enough, Nora thought, that Liza had to cope with
having a dead body dug up in her yard. Worse that it
could be that of her long-lost grandmother.

"I'll continue to hope for the best," Nora said diplomatically.

Liza's smile this time was feeble. "Thank you."

But before she left, she spun around one more time,
serape flying. "Oh, I almost forgot. Cliff specifically
wanted me to ask if you were coming to the wedding.
You are, aren't you?"

"Well, yes, I'd love to, but I've never even met
Cliff—"

"Oh, he's seen you around town and admires your
devotion to Tyler and . . . how did he put it? Your balance, I think he said. He says if he has to endure a
huge wedding, he should at least have a few people
around who won't make him feel uncomfortable."

Liza's eyes misted, her expression softening. She looked like a woman in love. "God knows he's trying. He's still uneasy around people—I guess you could call this wedding a trial by fire. Not only will half of Tyler be there, but there's a chance his family'll come, too."

"I didn't realize he had any family."

"A mother and a brother." Liza bit the corner of her mouth, suddenly unsure of herself. "They're from Providence."

"Providence, Rhode Island?" Nora asked, her knees weakening.

"Umm. Real East Coast mucky-mucks."

Byron Sanders, the one man who'd penetrated Nora's defenses, had been from Providence, Rhode Island. But that had to be a coincidence. That wretched cad couldn't have anything to do with a man like Cliff Forrester.

"Are they coming?" Nora asked.

Liza cleared her throat hesitantly. "Haven't heard. From what I gather, our wedding's pretty quick for a Forrester, so who knows?"

"Cliff must be anxious—"

"Oh, no, I don't think so. He hasn't had much to do with his family since he moved out here. Nothing at all, in fact. He takes all the blame, but I don't think that's fair. He didn't tell them where he was for a couple of years, but when he did finally let them know, he told them to leave him alone. But they could have bulldozed their way back into his life if they'd really wanted to." She grinned. "Just like I did."

"But Cliff did invite them?"

"Well, not exactly."

Nora didn't need a sledgehammer to get the point. "You mean *you* did? Without his knowledge?"

"Yep."

Now that, Nora thought, could get interesting.

"I guess we'll just have to see how it goes," Liza added.

With a polite, dismissive comment, Nora promised Liza that she and her staff would steer people in the right direction when they came to Gates hunting for an appropriate wedding gift. Liza looked so relieved and happy when she left that Nora felt much better. Why on earth was she worrying about Byron Sanders, just because he and Cliff Forrester were from the same state? Rhode Island wasn't *that* small. No, that weasel was just a black, secret chapter in her life.

She tucked the bridal register under her arm to return to Claudia Mickelson. She did love a wedding—as long as it wasn't her own.

CHAPTER TWO

"I DON'T KNOW how Liza Baron can even *think* about getting married with this body business unresolved."

Inger Hansen's starchy words stopped Nora in her tracks. It was two days after Liza had sat in her office grumbling about feudalistic rituals while thumbing through a Waterford crystal catalog. As was her custom on Thursdays, when she gave piano lessons, Nora was moving toward Gates Department Store's rear exit shortly before five. She usually didn't leave until six.

Inger, the most imperious member of the Tyler Quilting Circle, went on indignantly, "That could be her grandmother they found out there."

Martha Bauer held up two different shades of off-white thread. It was just a show; she'd been buying the same shade for thirty years. "Well, I do wish they'd tell us something soon," she said with a sigh. "Don't you think they've had that body up at the county long enough to know *something?*"

"I understand that the body's a skeleton already," Rose Atkins, one of the sweetest and most eccentric elderly women in Tyler, said. "Identification must be a difficult process under such circumstances. And it would be terrible if they made a mistake, don't you think? I'd prefer them to take their time and get it right."

Nora agreed, and found herself edging toward the fabric department's counter. Stella, the fabric clerk and a woman known for her sewing expertise, was occupied sorting a new shipment of buttons. Nora didn't blame her for not rushing to the quilting ladies' assistance; they knew their way around the department and would likely chatter on until the store's closing at six.

Inger Hansen sniffed. "In my opinion, the police are dragging their heels. No one wants to confront the real possibility that it's Margaret Ingalls they found out at the lake."

"Now, Inger," Rose said patiently, "we don't know for sure it's Margaret. The body hasn't even been identified yet as male or female."

"Oh, it's Margaret all right."

Martha Bauer discarded the wrong shade of off-white thread. "And what if it is?" She looked uncomfortable and a little pale. "That could mean..."

Inger jumped right in. "It could mean Margaret Ingalls was murdered."

"My heavens," Martha breathed.

"I never did think she ran away," Inger added, although in all the years Nora had known her she'd never given such an indication. "It just wasn't like Margaret to slip out of town in the cloak of darkness."

Rose Atkins inhaled, clearly upset by such talk, and moved to the counter with a small, rolled piece of purple calico she'd found on the bargain table. "Why, Nora, I didn't see you. How are you?"

"Just fine, Mrs. Atkins. Here, let me take that for you."

Off to their left, Martha Bauer and Inger Hansen continued their discussion of the Body at the Lake. "Now, you can think me catty," Inger said, "but I, for one, have always wondered what Judson Ingalls knew about his wife's disappearance. I'm not accusing him of anything untoward, of course, but I do think—and have thought for forty years—that it's strange he's hardly lifted a finger to find her in all this time. He could certainly afford to hire a dozen private detectives, but he hasn't."

"Oh, stop." Martha snatched up a spool of plain white all-cotton thread in addition to her off-white. "Margaret left him a note saying she was leaving him. Why should he have put himself and Alyssa through the added turmoil of looking for a wife who'd made it plain she wanted nothing more to do with him? No, I think he did the right thing in putting the matter behind him and carrying on with his life. What else could he have done? And in my opinion, that's not Margaret they found out at the lake."

Inger tucked a big bag of cotton batting under one arm. "Of course, I don't like to gossip, but whoever it was, I can't see Liza Baron and that recluse getting married with this dark cloud hanging over their heads. You'd think they'd wait."

"Oh, Inger," Martha said, laughing all of a sudden. "Honestly. Why should Liza put her life on hold?

Now, would you look at this lovely gabardine?"
Deftly she changed the subject.

Nora took two dollars from Rose Atkins for her
fabric scrap. As had been the custom at Gates since it
opened its doors seventy years ago, Nora tucked the
receipt and Rose's money into a glass-and-brass tube,
which she then tucked into a chute to be pneumati-
cally sucked up to the third floor office. There the
head clerk would log the sale and send back the receipt and any change. None of the salesclerks handled any cash, checks or credit cards. The system was
remarkablely fast and efficient, contributing an old-
fashioned charm to the store that its customers seemed
to relish.

"Everybody's gone to computers these days," Rose
commented. "It's such a relief to come in here and not
have anything beep at me. Have you seen those light
wands that read price stickers?" She shuddered; the
world had changed a lot in Rose Atkins's long life.
"You've no plans to switch to something like that,
have you?"

"None at all."

That much Nora could say with certainty. In her
opinion, computers didn't go with Gates's original
wood-and-glass display cases, its Tiffany ceilings, its
sweeping staircases and brass elevators, its gleaming
polished tile floors. Tradition and an unrivaled reputation for service were what set Gates apart from malls
and discount department stores. As Aunt Ellie had
before her, Nora relied on value, quality, convenience
and style to compete. At Gates, Tyler's elderly women

could still find a good housedress, its children could buy their Brownie and Cub Scout uniforms, its parents could find sturdy, traditional children's and baby clothes. The fabric department kept a wide range of calico fabrics for Tyler's quilting ladies. There was an office-supply department for local businesses, a wide-ranging book section for local readers, a lunch counter for hungry shoppers. Nora prided herself on meeting the changing needs of her community. As far as she was concerned, tradition was not only elusive in a fast-paced world, it was also priceless.

The tube returned, and she slipped out Rose's change and receipt.

"Have you seen much of Liza Baron since she's come home?" Rose asked.

"She came in a couple of days ago to fill out her bridal registry," Nora replied. "But other than that, no."

Rose's eyes widened, no doubt at the prospect of wild, rebellious Liza doing anything as expected of her as filling out a bridal registry, but, a discreet woman, she resisted comment.

Behind her, Inger Hansen did no such thing. "I can't imagine Liza would want to do anything so normal. She's so much like her grandmother. You don't remember Margaret Ingalls, Nora, but she was just as wild and unpredictable as Liza Baron. It's odd, though. Your great-aunt and Margaret managed to get along amazingly well. I have no idea why. They were complete opposites."

"Ellie was always extremely tolerant of people," Martha Bauer put in.

"Yes," Inger said. Even tart-tongued Inger Hansen had respected and admired Ellie Gates.

"I'm sure it'll be a wonderful wedding," Nora said, half-wishing she hadn't delayed her departure to serve the quilters. Liza Baron and Cliff Forrester's upcoming wedding was indeed the talk of the town, but it was having an effect on Nora that she couldn't figure out. Was it because Cliff was from Rhode Island?

No. She'd put Byron Sanders out of her mind months and months ago. If the wedding was unsettling her it had to be because of the ongoing mystery of the identity of the body found at Timberlake.

Stella scooted behind Nora. "Here, Miss Gates, let me help these customers."

Nora backed off, and with Inger Hansen wondering aloud how Liza could have ended up with that "strange man living out at the lake," ducked out the rear exit.

Even if Liza Baron had been a fly on the wall during the past fifteen minutes, she wouldn't have cared one whit what the quilting ladies were saying about her and Cliff—she'd marry whenever and whoever she wanted. Liza had a thumb-your-nose-at-the-world quality that Nora appreciated. Nora wondered if *she* was ever the subject of local gossip. Not likely. Oh, her latest window display always received plenty of attention, and the time she'd added a wheelchair ramp to one of the entrances had gotten people talking about accessibility and such. And folks had talked when, after much soul-searching and calculating how few were sold, she'd ceased to stock men's overalls. But nobody, she was quite certain, talked about *her*. Her personal life.

"That's because it's dull, dull, dull."

But wasn't that exactly what she wanted?

The crisp, clear autumn air lifted her spirits. It was getting dark; the streetlights were already on, casting a pale glow on the bright yellow leaves still clinging to the intrepid maples that lined the perimeter of the parking lot. The feeling that life was passing her by vanished as quickly as it had overtaken her. *This* was life, at least hers. Small-town Midwest America. So it wasn't Providence, Rhode Island. So it wasn't wandering place to place with an elitist East Coast photographer who neither understood her nor the community she cared about. She belonged in Tyler. It was her home, and if it was Byron Sanders's idea of hell, then so be it.

He was a cretin anyway.

Coincidence or not, Cliff Forrester's own Rhode Island origins had gotten her thinking about the rake who'd almost ruined her life. For two days running now. She couldn't make herself stop.

Well, she had to. Rhode Island might be a small state, but the chances of Tyler's town recluse and a sneaky photographer having any knowledge of each other were remote. And Byron Sanders wasn't from any "mucky-muck" East Coast family.

He also knew to keep his size elevens out of Tyler, Wisconsin.

But he'd been her one love, and he remained her one secret. *No* one knew they'd been lovers. Not even Tisha Olsen over at the Hair Affair, who knew everything that went on in Tyler, or the quilting ladies, whose combined knowledge of the town's social history went all the way back to its founding during the great German immigration to Wisconsin 140 years ago. As far as everyone in Tyler was concerned, Nora was just like her great-aunt, the memorable Ellie Gates.

Only she wasn't. And she knew it.

So did Byron Sanders.

She was so preoccupied that she arrived at the doorstep of her 1920s house before she even realized she'd come to her tree-lined street. She'd inherited the house from Aunt Ellie. They'd lived together from the death of Nora's parents in a boating accident on Lake Superior when she was thirteen until Aunt Ellie's death three years ago, not long after Byron Sanders had moved on. In the house's quiet rooms and in Aunt Ellie's quiet life, Nora had found peace and stability and hope.

She'd had the wide clapboards repainted last summer in the same cream color Aunt Ellie had chosen back in 1926. The trim was pure white. It was almost Halloween, but the porch swing was still out, the flower boxes planted with bright yellow mums.

With the house having been shut up all day, Nora left the front door open to catch the afternoon breeze while she went back to the kitchen. It was still thirty minutes before her first student arrived. Time enough for a cup of tea.

She'd made a few changes to the interior of the house, softening some of Aunt Ellie's relentless formality. She'd covered the furniture in pale neutrals and had added cotton throw rugs, Depression glass, quilted pastel wall hangings. There were two small bedrooms upstairs, one downstairs, a small library, a living room and a dining room that she'd converted into a music room, shoving the gateleg table up against the wall to make room for a new baby grand.

Nora, however, hadn't changed a thing in the kitchen. Its white cabinets, pale gray-blue walls and yellow accents didn't need changing so far as she could see. Her friends said she should get a microwave, but she hadn't yet succumbed. Before she died, Aunt Ellie had purchased a toaster oven. It still worked fine.

After putting on the kettle for tea, Nora sat at the kitchen table and looked out at her darkening yard. The bright leaves of the sugar maple had already fallen to the ground. Lately, birds had taken to fattening themselves at her bird feeders. Soon it would be completely dark. Winter wasn't far off.

She sighed. She loved autumn; she even loved winter. So why was she hovering on the edge of depression?

She fixed a proper tea: Earl Grey tea leaves, her English porcelain pot, her matching cup and saucer, milk in a tiny milk glass pitcher. A sterling silver spoon. Homemade butter cookies from her favorite bakery. She put everything on a teak tray, which she carried out to the music room.

And nearly dropped it all on the floor.

Moving with the speed and silence of a panther, Cliff Forrester took the tray from her and set it one-handed on the gateleg table. "I didn't mean to startle you," he said.

In his five years in Tyler, those were the first words Nora remembered his ever saying to her. She'd bumped into him on occasion at the hardware store, but Liza Baron's fiancé had made clear he didn't want to be disturbed at Timberlake Lodge. He wanted to be left alone. To heal his wounds and chase his demons or do whatever it was he did. Nora had heard all the rumors and possibilities. He was a tall, dark man. He didn't look like . . . how had Liza put it? Like his family were East Coast mucky-mucks.

"It's quite all right," she said, sounding stuffy even to herself. "I was expecting a piano student."

"You play?"

"Mmm, yes."

His brow furrowed. "I didn't know."

How could he have known? They'd never even officially met until now. "Would you care for a cup of tea? I made more than enough. I always end up having to throw out half the pot."

He shook his head. "No thanks."

And then he smiled. Nora found it an unsettling experience, but she couldn't pinpoint why. She felt no attraction to Liza's lover. It wasn't *that* at all. Then what? *Men in general,* she thought, disgusted with herself. *Tall, dark men from Rhode Island in particular.*

Too darned much thinking, she added to herself.

"Are you all right?" Cliff Forrester asked.

She nodded. "Perfectly."

"I gather you know who I am."

"Cliff Forrester. Yes, I think everyone in town knows."

The corners of his mouth twitched in an ironic smile. "I guess so. Look, I won't keep you, Miss Gates."

"Nora," she corrected.

"Nora, then." His dark eyes probed her a moment. "I came by because of Liza. She was grateful for the way you treated her the other day."

"I'd do the same for any of my customers, Mr.—"

"Cliff. And I think you would. Liza and I are..." He paused, seeming awkward, even pained. "We want this to work."

Nora thought she understood what he was trying to say. The Body at the Lake, the wedding, Alyssa Baron, Judson Ingalls, Liza's return to Tyler, the incessant gossip, long-lost Margaret Ingalls—it was a lot. And then there was Cliff Forrester himself. A recluse. A man uncomfortable around even small crowds. A man, it was said, afraid that something, someone, would trigger a bad memory and he'd crack. Hurt himself. Worse yet, hurt someone he cared about.

"Is there anything I can do?" Nora asked, instinctively wanting to help.

He seemed to relax, at least slightly. "If there's anything you can think of to help Liza through this thing, I'd appreciate it. She doesn't want to alienate anyone. She's trying."

Wasn't that what Liza herself had said about him? Nora found their concern for each other touching. This, she thought, was what love and romance were about. Two people coming together as individuals, not asking the other to change, not demanding perfection, not expecting fantasies to come true. Just loving and accepting each other and perhaps growing together.

"I wouldn't be interfering?"

"No."

He was, she thought, a man who knew his own mind. "Then I'll see what I can do."

His smile was back, or what passed for one. "Thank you."

"No need. It won't be long before Liza feels at home again in Tyler. She has family and friends, Cliff. They'll be here for her."

"I'm glad you already are," he said, and before she could respond, he was out the door.

Nora debated a whole two seconds, then went after him, catching him on the front porch. "Cliff?"

He turned, and there was something about him as he stood against the dark night—something both dangerous and sensitive—that hinted at his pain and complexity. Liza Baron hadn't solved all his problems. Nora suddenly wished she'd just sat down and drunk her tea instead of following him out. But what to do about it now?

She licked her lips. "Um—Liza mentioned that you're from Rhode Island originally. I was...well, I knew someone from Rhode Island once." She sounded ridiculous! "It was a while ago, but I—"

"Who?"

She swallowed. She'd never said his name aloud, not in public. "A guy by the name of Sanders. Byron Sanders."

Cliff Forrester remained stock-still on her porch step, staring at her through dark eyes that had become slits. Nora chose not to dwell on all the more lurid rumors about him.

"He's a photographer," she added quickly. "He did a series a few years back on Aunt Ellie. It was printed in one of the Chicago papers—"

"I'd like to see it."

"Well, I have a copy in my library—"

"Get it."

His words were millimeters shy of being an order, but there was a curious intensity to his tone, almost a desperation, that Nora detected but couldn't explain. Cursing herself for having brought up that cretin's name, she dashed to her study, dug out the scrapbook and ran back to the porch. Cliff Forrester hadn't moved.

She showed him the spread Byron Sanders had done on Aunt Ellie just weeks before she died. Picking the winner of the quilt raffle. At her desk in her old-fashioned office. In her rose garden. In her rocking chair on her front porch. In front of the department store she'd started, on her own, in 1924. Nora had every photograph memorized. It was as if each shot captured a part of Aunt Ellie's soul and together recreated the woman she'd been, made her come to life. Whatever his shortcomings as a man, Byron Sanders was unarguably a gifted photographer.

"This Byron Sanders," Cliff Forrester said, tight-lipped. "Is he a friend of yours?"

"No!"

His eyes narrowed. "Did he hurt you?"

She shook her head. Through Byron Sanders, she'd managed to hurt herself. She took full responsibility for her own actions. Which didn't mitigate her distaste for him. "No. I just remember he's from Rhode Island and wondered if you knew him."

"No," Cliff said. "No, I don't know Byron Sanders at all."

THE WAY BYRON FIGURED it, he was dead meat. If Nora Gates didn't kill him, his brother surely would. Slumped down in the nondescript car he'd rented in Milwaukee, he watched Cliff head toward the center of town. He looked grim. Byron felt pretty grim himself. His jaw had begun to ache from gritting his teeth. He forced his mouth open just enough to emit something between a sigh and a growl.

No, I don't know any Byron Sanders at all....

It was all Byron had heard, but it was enough. His return to Tyler wasn't going to be all sweetness and light. Nora was already on the lookout for him, and now his brother had to have figured out that he'd been to Tyler before. Not a good start. When Nora found out that he'd lied, he'd be lucky to get out of town with all his body parts intact. When Cliff found out he'd sneaked into Tyler three years ago to make sure he was all right *and* had lied, he'd be—

"You're dead meat, my man," he muttered to himself.

He took heart that Cliff didn't fit any of the images that had haunted him for so long. He wasn't scrawny, scraggly, bug-infested or crazy. He looked alive and well and, other than that crack about his younger brother, reasonably happy. For that, Byron was grateful.

He loosened his tight grip on the steering wheel. Coming to Tyler ten days early had been his mother's idea. He'd phoned her in London, where she was visiting one of Pierce & Rothchilde's most prominent, if not bestselling, authors, one who'd become a personal friend. Anne Forrester was a strong, kind woman who'd endured too much. She'd lost a husband and had all but lost a son.

"But this note," she'd said, "leaves more questions unanswered than answered."

"I know."

"Do you suppose he really wants us there?"

"There's no way of knowing."

For years, Cliff had maintained that he didn't dare be around his family for fear of inflicting more pain on them. He didn't trust himself, not just with his brother and mother, but with anyone. So he'd left.

Withdrawn from society. Turned into a recluse at an abandoned lodge on a faraway lake in Wisconsin. His absence, on top of her husband's horrible captivity and death in Cambodia, had been particularly difficult for Anne Forrester, but she was made of stern stuff and disliked showing emotion. She blamed herself to some degree for having let Cliff go to Cambodia to try and do something for his father. Blamed herself for not being able to do something to ease the pain of his own ordeal in Southeast Asia.

"You have no idea who this Liza Baron is?" his mother had asked.

"The Barons are a prominent family in Tyler." Byron had chosen his next words carefully. "I remember meeting an Alyssa Baron. She's the woman who sort of took Cliff under her wing. Liza could be her daughter."

Anne Forrester didn't speak for the next two minutes. Although the call was overseas long distance, Byron hadn't rushed her. She needed to regain her balance. Rational and not prone to jealousy, she nonetheless had had a difficult time facing the fact that Cliff had allowed another woman to at least try to help him, where he'd only run from her. Even if Alyssa Baron was on the periphery of Cliff's life, she was at least in a small way part of it. His mother wasn't. But that, Byron knew, was precisely the point: far away, Cliff couldn't cause his mother—or his brother—further pain and suffering. Or so he thought.

"Maybe there's hope yet," she said finally, in a near whisper. "Oh, Byron, if he's happy...if he's *trying*..."

"I know, Mother."

"I can't get out of here until at least the first part of next week. What's your schedule like? I'm not sure we should both barrel in on Cliff for the wedding if we're not entirely certain he wants us there." She was thinking out loud, Byron realized, and he didn't interrupt or argue. "Unless there is no wedding and this is Cliff's way...well, that would be ridiculous. Not like him at all. He'd never play a trick like that on us, would he?"

"No," Byron had said with certainty.

"Would this Liza Baron?"

"I wouldn't think so."

"It's just all so...sudden. What if someone's using the wedding as a ploy to get us out there? You know, upset the applecart and see what happens?"

"It's a possibility," Byron had allowed, "but not a serious one, I would think."

Anne Forrester sighed heavily. "Then he *is* getting married."

In the end, Byron had agreed to go to Tyler ahead of time and play scout, find out what he and his mother would be walking into in ten days' time. None of the myriad excuses Byron could think of to keep him in Providence would have worked, so he didn't even bother to try. The truth was he'd do anything to see his brother again, even go up against Nora Gates. Hell, they were both adults. She'd just have to endure his presence in Tyler and trust him to keep quiet about their "tawdry affair" three years before.

She'd only, he recalled, talked like a defiled Victorian virgin when she was truly pissed off.

He'd half hoped she'd forgotten all about him.

Of course, she hadn't. Eleanora Gates wouldn't forget anything, least of all the man who'd "robbed" her of her virginity. She'd conveniently forgotten that she'd been a more than willing participant. And he hadn't told her he'd thought he loved her.

He exhaled slowly, trying to look on the positive. The shattered man his brother had been for so long— too long—seemed mostly a bad memory. For that, Byron was thankful. But Nora...

Before he could change his mind, he popped open his seat belt and jumped out of the car. She'd already gone back inside. Except for the masses of yellow mums, the front porch was unchanged from his last visit, when Aunt Ellie had still reigned over Gates Department Store. She'd been a powerful force in Nora's life. Maybe too powerful. Ellie had sensed that, articulating her fears to Byron.

"The store will be Nora's," she'd told him. "It's all I have to give her. But I don't want it to become a burden to her—it never was to me. If it had, I'd have done something. I never let my life be ruled by that store. Nora knows, I hope, that I won't roll over in my grave if she decides to sell. The only thing that'll make me come back to haunt her is if she tries to be anyone but herself. Including me."

A perceptive woman, the elder Eleanora Gates. Byron remembered feeling distinctly uncomfortable, even sad, although he'd only known the eccentric Aunt Ellie little more than a week. "What's all this talk about what will happen after you're gone?"

Gripping his hand, she'd laughed her distinctive, almost cackling laugh. "Byron, my good friend, you and I both know I'm on Sunset Road."

It was her self-awareness, her self-acceptance, that had drawn Byron to the proprietor of Gates Department Store—what he'd tried to capture in his photograph series on her. Aunt Ellie had been a rare woman. Her grandniece was like her—and yet she wasn't.

The front door was open.

Byron's heart pounded like a teenager's. Three years ago, Ellie Gates had greeted him with ice cold, fresh-squeezed lemonade and a slice of sour-cherry pie. What could he expect from her grandniece?

A pitcher of lemonade over his head? A pie in his face? Nora Gates didn't forget, and she didn't forgive.

Hard to imagine, he thought, reaching for the screen door, that she hated him as much as she did. She didn't even know who he was.

"Well, my man," he said to himself, "here's mud in your eye."

And he pulled open the screen door, stuck in his head and called her name.

CHAPTER THREE

"NORA," HE CALLED softly, only half-fearful for his life now that he was putting it on the line. "Nora, it's Byron."

He left off the Sanders and judiciously didn't add the Forrester. First things first. Remembering the screen door had a tendency to bang shut, he closed it behind him. Nora didn't come screaming out of some dark corner. So far, so good.

The small entry hadn't changed. To his right, the cream-colored stairs wound up to the second floor under the eaves. Three steps up, where the stairs made a right-angle turn, a window seat was piled with chintz-covered pillows, musty-looking library books and a well-used afghan. It was the sort of spot where Nora would like to curl up with a murder mystery on a rainy Sunday afternoon. Her idea of bliss. Until he'd come around, anyway. Then, for a little while, she'd preferred to curl up with him.

Calling her name again, Byron moved carefully into the living room, which had changed. The neutral colors, the informality, the American art—they were Nora's touches. Aunt Ellie's tastes had been more Victorian. She'd have been comfortable in the formal parlor of the Pierce family's Providence town house. Nora would have been stifled, even if the late-eighteenth-century mansion had been in Tyler. Of course, Byron had learned early on not to point out the differences between Eleanora Gates the older and Eleanora Gates the younger. Nora much preferred to hear of similarities.

The living room was separated from the dining room by a curved archway. There Nora had added a baby grand piano, definitely her own touch. He vividly recalled Aunt Ellie's happy amazement that her grandniece had any musical ability whatever. *"Didn't get that from me. Do you play piano, Byron?"*

He did. So did Cliff. There'd been years of required lessons. He hadn't touched a piano in ages. Wondering if he were completely mad instead of just half, he played a C-major scale, right-handed, one octave. As he'd expected, the piano was perfectly in tune. He added his left hand and went up another octave, then down two octaves, chromatically. All that drilling when he was a kid came back to him.

"Ricky?"

It was her voice. Even as his heart lurched, Byron snatched his fingers from the keyboard and readied himself for skewering.

"You really *have* been practicing, haven't you?" She sounded pleased and delighted, a mood due to end as soon as she caught sight of who was playing scales in her dining room. "That was wonderful! You're lagging a bit in the left hand, but—" She stood under the archway. "Oh, no."

Short of a knife at the throat, it was the sort of greeting Byron had expected. He moved back from the piano. "Hello, Nora."

If she'd changed, he couldn't see it. She was still as trim and quietly beautiful as she'd been three years ago, her hot, secret temper smoldering behind her pale gray eyes. She must have been upstairs changing. She had on purple tennis shoes, narrow, straight-legged jeans and an oversize purple sweatshirt—neat and casual, but nothing she'd ever wear to the store. She was, he thought, a very sexy woman, all the more so because she didn't try to be.

He didn't fail to notice how she'd balled up her hands into tight fists. Apparently he still possessed the uncanny knack for bringing out the aggressive side of her nature—which she'd deny.

And he didn't fail—couldn't fail—to remember how very much this woman had once meant to him.

"You really are a bloodsucker," she said through clenched teeth. "Did you come here to photograph us small-town folk all aflutter over the Body at the Lake?"

"The what? Nora, I don't know what you're talking about."

"Always so ignorant and innocent, aren't you, Byron?" If her voice had been a knife, he'd have been cut to thin slices. But that was her way, at least with him, of repressing emotions she distrusted even more than anger—emotions like fear, love, passion. "Well, this time I happen to believe you. I think you're here for an even more despicable reason: Liza Baron and Cliff Forrester's wedding.''

Byron almost choked. So she'd figured it out. She knew who he was. Now there'd be no explaining, no chance to plead his case . . . just his marching orders. Get out and don't ever come back. Damned without a trial.

But Nora went on in her chilly voice, ''Another Rhode Island boy's getting married, and with his being a recluse from a big East Coast family, you thought you'd nose around. You're a leech, Byron Sanders. Pure and simple.''

A bloodsucker and a leech. He was getting the point. First, she hadn't forgotten him. Second, she hadn't forgiven him. Third, she didn't know his photography days were over and he was president of Pierce & Rothchilde, Publishers. And fourth, she didn't know he was Cliff's brother. He had a chance— if a slim one—of getting out of Nora's house intact after all.

And an even slimmer chance of making her understand why he'd done what he had three years ago.

''Nora, I'd like to talk to you. Do you have a minute?''

''I don't have a *second* for you, Byron Sanders. If you think you can march into Tyler and into my life and expect anything but a frosty welcome, you've got your head screwed on upside down. Now get out before I . . .'' She inhaled deeply, and her eyes flooded— which had to irritate her—and he could see the pain he'd caused her. "God, Byron, how could you come back here?"

Might as well get started by coming clean. "I was invited to Cliff's wedding."

"You were *invited?* By whom? Why?"

She was looking at him as if he'd just told her Cliff and Liza had invited a gorilla to their wedding. Byron didn't appreciate her incredulity, but he realized he'd set himself up three years ago to have Nora hate him. He could have told her everything. About Cliff, their father, his own demons—he hadn't done enough, hadn't saved his father, hadn't saved his brother, hadn't been able to stop his mother's suffering. Probably Nora would have been sympathetic. But she'd had her own problems—Aunt Ellie's impending death, what to do about the store, and about staying in Tyler. And there'd been Cliff. Three years ago staying in Tyler hadn't been a option for Byron, any more than leaving it had been one for Nora. He'd come uninvited into a world where his brother had finally found stability. Byron couldn't destroy that stability. It wasn't the only reason he'd left, but it was an important one.

Still, he hadn't explained any of this to Nora. He'd told her he was moving on, let her think he was nothing more than an itinerant photographer, a bit irresponsible, wont to loving and leaving women. So she'd called him a cad, a bloodsucker, a leech and the rest. Because at the time that had been easier—for him and for her—than admitting they'd broken each other's hearts. Three years later, he'd chased away the worst of his demons, but he wasn't about to risk hurting Nora Gates again. If she needed him to be a cad, fine.

"This is just a courtesy call, Nora. I'm trying to be nice—"

"The hell you are."

"You know," he said calmly, "for a woman who prides herself on being something of a Victorian lady, you have a sharp tongue."

She raised her chin. "I want you out of my house."

Byron sighed, leaning one hip against the edge of her piano. "Nora, you have an attitude."

"Byron," she mimicked, "*you* have a nerve barging into my house after what you did to me."

"What *I* did to you?" he repeated mildly.

She got the point and flushed clear to her hairline, almost making him believe she was a maiden lady. "What we did to ourselves," she corrected. "Now get out."

He switched tactics. Not that he wanted to prolong this scene and have her attempt to forcibly remove him, but he did have a nonrefundable return ticket to Providence for the Sunday morning after the wedding. If he was to survive until then, he needed to neutralize Nora Gates as a potentially explosive force.

Of course, the truth wasn't going to help that process. "Look, Nora, I know it must seem presumptuous of me to walk in here after all this time, but I knew if I rang the doorbell you'd never let me in."

"I never said you were stupid."

So far, reason wasn't working with the woman. "Then we'd have ended up having this discussion on the porch," he added, "which I know you wouldn't want. As I recall, you'd prefer to be a receiver of gossip than a subject of gossip—"

It was a low blow. He could see his words scratch right up her spine. "Leave, Byron. Slither out of my house and out of Tyler the same way you slithered in. I can't imagine that Cliff Forrester needs a friend like you."

Probably he didn't, but they were brothers, and that was something neither of them could change. "I haven't seen him in five years."

That wasn't strictly true. He'd seen Cliff three years ago. From afar. They hadn't talked. Byron had sensed that Cliff wasn't ready yet, might never be, and for his brother's sake he'd left.

Nora's clear, incisive gray eyes focused on him in a way that brought back memories, too many memories. Of her passion, of her anger. Of how damned much they'd lost when he'd left Tyler. "Did he invite you?" she asked, her tone accusatory.

"In a manner of speaking."

"What's that supposed to mean? No—no, don't tell me." She dropped her hands to her sides, then pointed with one finger toward the front door. Her precious self-control had abandoned her. "Out, Byron. Right now. You're worse than a cad. I don't know what your game is, but I'm not going to let you crash Cliff and Liza's wedding. Cliff's pulled himself together after an ordeal probably none of us in Tyler can imagine. He's *happy*, Byron. You are not going to play games with the man's head. You both might be from Rhode Island and maybe you do know his family or something, but you're not his friend. I know you're not. Cliff didn't even invite his own mother and brother to his wedding—Liza did. He doesn't even know about it, and if you tell him…" She gulped for air. "By God, I'll come after you myself. So you go on and leave him alone." She took a breath. "And leave me alone, too."

Byron had debated interrupting three or four times, but had kept his mouth shut. "Nora," he began reasonably, "you don't understand. I . . ."

"Out!"

"I didn't come here to bother you or Cliff."

"Now, Byron. Now, or I swear I'll—"

She didn't finish, but instead grabbed a huge book of Beethoven sonatas from the gateleg table. She heaved it at him. Byron ducked. The book crashed into the piano, banging down on the keys, making a discordant racket. Nora was red-faced.

Clearly this was no time for revelations destined only to make her madder. Byron grinned at her. "Bet you haven't lost your temper like that since I was last in Tyler."

"You're damned right I haven't!"

Then a big blond kid was filling up the doorway behind her. "This guy bothering you, Miss Gates?"

Byron could see her debating whether to sic the kid on him. *Yeah—throw him in the oven, will you?* But she shook her head tightly, and said even more tightly, "Not anymore."

This time, Byron took the hint. As he walked past Nora and through the living room, he heard the kid make the mistake of laughing. "Gee, Miss Gates, I guess you're stronger than you look. That book's *heavy*."

"Chromatic scale, Mr. Travis. Four octaves, ascending and descending. Presto."

Byron decided not to hang around. But he had no intention of leaving Tyler. There was his brother to see, Cliff's fiancée to meet, a body at a lake to learn more about. And there was Nora Gates herself. Piano player, department store owner, would-be Victorian old maid. She was a woman of contradictions and spirit, and as he walked back to his rented car, it occurred to Byron that the past three years had been but a pause—a little gulp—in their relationship. It wasn't finished. There'd been no resolution. No final chord.

At least, he thought, not yet.

NORA DIDN'T CHARGE Ricky Travis for his lesson. In fact, for the first time since she'd had pneumonia six years ago, she cut a lesson short.

"You okay, Miss Gates?" Rick asked.

"I'm fine, just a little distracted."

"That guy—"

"I'm not worried about him. Don't you be, either."

He shrugged. "If you say so. I'll have the Bach down by next week. Promise. It's just hard with it being football season."

"I understand. It's not easy being both a talented musician and a football player at this time of year. But you've had a good lesson, Rick. It's not you. I'm just . . . well, it's been a long day." She rose from her chair beside the piano. "I'll see you next week."

"Sure thing, Miss Gates."

With Rick gone, the house seemed deadly quiet. Foregoing Bach and Beethoven, Nora put on an early Bruce Springsteen tape and tried to exorcise Byron Sanders from her mind.

She couldn't.

She hadn't forgotten a single thing about him. He was as tall as she remembered. As strongly built and lithe, and every bit as darkly good-looking. His eyes were still as blue and piercing and unpredictable—and as dangerously enticing—as the Atlantic Ocean.

It would have been easier, she thought, if there'd been things she'd forgotten. The dark hairs on his forearms, for example, or his long, blunt-nailed fingers. But she'd remembered everything—the warmth of his eyes, the breadth of his shoulders, the way he had of forcing her not to take herself too seriously, even how irritating he could be. *Especially* how irritating he could be.

How had he learned about Cliff and Liza's wedding? It wasn't a secret, but how had an East Coast photographer heard that a Wisconsin couple was getting married? Maybe he *did* know Cliff—but Cliff had said he didn't know a Byron Sanders. Perhaps Byron knew the Forresters, the mother and brother Liza had taken the liberty of inviting. Nora wondered if she should warn Liza about Byron.

Singing aloud with Bruce, she made herself another pot of tea and dug in her refrigerator for some leftovers for supper. If Sanders had shown up *before* Cliff had, she'd have pressed Liza's reticent fiancé a little harder about his fellow Rhode Islander.

Well, she thought, pulling a bit of brown rice and chicken from the fridge, *someone* was lying.

She made a tossed salad and warmed up her dinner. Really, what a terrific old maid she'd make. A pity the term was démodé.

The Spinster Gates.

It sounded deliciously forbidding. She turned off Bruce and tried to put her former lover—*arrgh, why couldn't he be less appealing?*—out of her mind. Sitting at her kitchen table, she found herself staring at her hands. They were ringless, still soft and pale. She remembered Aunt Ellie's hands in her final days: old, spotted, gnarled. Yet they'd possessed a delicacy and beauty that suggested she was a woman who'd lived her life on her own terms, a life that had been full and happy. She'd relished her family, she'd had many friends. She'd been generous and spirited and frugal, a model of independence and responsibility.

Once, over a similar supper of leftovers, Nora had asked Aunt Ellie if she ever got lonely. "Of course," she'd replied immediately, in her blunt, unswerving way. "Everyone does. I'm no different."

"But... I meant, did you ever wished you'd married?"

She'd shrugged, not backing away from so personal a question. "At times I've wondered what it might have been like, but I've no doubt a married woman at times wonders what would have become of her if she hadn't married. But I have no regrets, any more than your mother had regrets about having married your father. I know and have known many wonderful men. I just didn't care to marry any of them."

"What about children?" Nora had asked.

Aunt Ellie had laughed. "My word, Tyler's filled with children. Always has been. You know, I believe sometimes when you don't have children of your own you're better able to appreciate other people's. You can do things for them and with them that their parents simply can't. You can enrich their lives. You don't worry about the same things. To be honest, Nora, I've never had the urge to bear children myself. I know that's hard for some people to believe, but it's the truth. But I've enjoyed having children in my life."

Indeed she had. Even before she'd come to live with Aunt Ellie when she was thirteen, Nora had loved her visits to the twenties house a few blocks from Gates Department Store. They'd bake cookies, go to museums, arts and crafts festivals, libraries. Aunt Ellie had taught her how to manage money and had instilled in her a sense of independence and confidence that continued to stand her in good stead.

She was stronger than she'd been three years ago, Nora reminded herself. She'd had time to adjust to the loss of Aunt Ellie and to becoming sole owner of Gates. She knew herself better. She knew that if Aunt Ellie had never yearned in any real way for marriage and children, she herself occasionally would. Every now and then, a man would even come along who tempted her.

She would survive Byron's reappearance in Tyler.

Once, of course, she'd figured out what he was up to.

Feeling a little like Agatha Christie's Miss Marple, Nora finished her supper and made her plans.

AFTER HASTILY REMOVING himself from Nora's house, Byron parked in the town square, put a quarter in the meter—which miraculously allowed him a full hour to mosey around—and found his way to the Tyler Public Library. It was located in a particularly beautiful, if run-down, turn-of-the century home. Given his own upbringing in a Federal-period town house and a center-chimney cottage on Nantucket Island, Byron found the preponderance of Victorian, Craftsman and Prairie architecture in Tyler refreshing.

Inside the library, which was old-fashioned and in desperate need of renovation, he tried not to draw attention to himself as he made his way to a stack of recent copies of the *Tyler Citizen*. He sat at an oak table in a poorly lit corner. Deliberately and patiently, he skimmed each edition of the daily paper, backtracking several weeks until he found the front-page article announcing the discovery of a skeleton at Judson Ingall's Timberlake Lodge. The grisly discovery had been made when local construction chief Joe Santori and his crew struck the body with a backhoe while doing some excavation work; Cliff Forrester, the lodge caretaker, was called onto the scene. Apparently Liza Baron, Judson's granddaughter, was also up at the lodge at the time. According to the paper, Judson himself hadn't stepped foot on the property since his wife left him more than forty years ago.

Liza Baron.

Byron rolled the name around on his tongue and tried to remember. But no, he didn't recall a Liza Baron from his first visit to Tyler. He remembered Judson Ingalls, though. A taciturn, hardworking man, he was one of Tyler's leading citizens, owner of Ingalls Farm and Machinery. As Byron recalled, Judson's wife had been a Chicago socialite, unhappy in a small Wisconsin town.

Now why had he remembered that little tidbit of Tyler lore?

"Aunt Ellie," he whispered to himself.

In their long talks on her front porch, Ellie Gates had told Byron countless tales of the legions of friends she'd had over her long, full life. She'd mentioned Judson Ingalls's wife. "Margaret was a fish out of water here in Tyler, but we became friends, although she was somewhat younger than I. I'm afraid she didn't have too many friends here in town. A pity. She was such a lively woman. Of course, some of that was her own doing—but it wasn't all her own doing. In a small town, it's easy for people to develop a wariness of strangers, of outsiders." And she'd paused to give him a pointed look, as if she knew he was another outsider who'd fallen for a Tyler resident. "It's also easy for out-of-towners to act on their prejudices and figure a small town has nothing to offer, including friends."

Ellie Gates had believed in tolerance. She'd been an opinionated woman herself and forthright in stating her views, but she appreciated fresh thinking, a good argument and people's right, as she liked to put it, "to be wrong."

Her grandniece and sole heir was a good deal more stiff-necked. Nora Gates much preferred to deal with people who agreed with her.

Flipping back through the newspapers, Byron caught up with all the current Tyler news, as well as fresh developments regarding the body. He gathered that its presence at Timberlake Lodge had fueled much speculation in town. Without directly stating as much, the paper gave the clear impression that some townspeople believed the body was that of Margaret Alyssa Lindstrom Ingalls herself. Now all the authorities had to do was get busy and confirm that fact, and prove how she'd ended up buried at her husband's lodge.

So for the past five years, Byron thought, his one and only brother had been living right on top of Tyler's greatest unsolved mystery. Given all the horrors Cliff had witnessed in Southeast Asia, how had he reacted to finding a dead body under his feet? He'd come to Tyler to escape death and destruction.

He'd fallen in love, was what he'd done.

Byron shrugged. There was a certain logic in that, he supposed.

At one point, the *Citizen* had printed a grainy picture of Liza Baron, for no solid reason Byron could figure out except that she was Judson Ingall's grand-daughter and had finally come home. So this was the woman his brother planned to marry. She was attractive in a dramatic, grab-you-by-the-short-hairs way. Byron guessed that she would be bold and direct with her loves and hates.

A few days later, the paper had dredged up an old photograph of Margaret Ingalls. Apparently she'd been quite the party animal. Putting the two photos side by side, Byron saw a strong resemblance between grandmother and granddaughter.

There was no picture of Cliff. No quotes from him, as there had been from Joe Santori, about having discovered the body. "Cliff Forrester couldn't be reached for comment," the paper said. Which might have meant anything from they couldn't find him to he'd chased them off with a shotgun.

Byron suddenly wished he hadn't agreed to sneak into Tyler and play scout for his mother—or for himself. He'd done that once, completely on his own, with disastrous results. There were too many unknowns. Cliff's being involved with a Tyler woman Byron had anticipated. And he'd have to have been a complete idiot not to know he was in for a fight with Nora Gates. But a dead body? A dead body that could belong to the grandmother of his future sister-in-law?

Best, he thought, to hold off for a bit before phoning his mother in London and reporting the news.

But that wasn't what was really eating at Byron and he knew it.

He was bothered by the big unknown, the one that had gnawed at him for three long years. How would he react if he ever saw Nora Gates again?

He shoved the newspapers back where he'd found them and left the library, walking quickly to his car. It was fully dark now. Cold. There was a stiff breeze. The square was quiet. Byron already had his car door open, but he shut it softly. He had another five minutes on his meter.

After crossing the street, he walked down to Gates Department Store, a fixture on Tyler's square since Ellie Gates had opened the three-story building in the Roaring Twenties, using an unexpected inheritance from an uncle back East. People had been surprised she'd risked her money on a business venture instead of putting it safely in the bank so she could lead a ladylike life. They'd doubted she'd be able to stay in business, never mind make enough profit to fill three floors with merchandise, or attract enough customers from Tyler and surrounding communities to support a full department store. But she'd proved them wrong, her sense of style, service and tradition finding a large and loyal following.

Gates closed at six o'clock, except for Thursdays and Fridays when it stayed open until nine. Its widow displays were often mentioned in Wisconsin travel guides, regional magazines and newspapers, a "must see" in Tyler. They were Nora's brainchild. Aunt Ellie had done the usual perfunctory displays, but not her grandniece. Nora's were elaborate and creative, playing on the history and charms of her corner of the Midwest.

The current display featured Halloween, complete with witches, pumpkins, black cats and skeletons, but also a touch of whimsy: two figures, a boy and girl, dressed as children of Swedish immigrants, bobbing for apples in a wooden bucket; a puppy stealing a caramel popcorn ball from an overflowing bowl; a cheerful-looking ghost peering out of a closet. It was a montage of scenes that were warm, nostalgic, funny, spooky. Busy owner of Gates or not, Byron thought, Nora had to have been personally responsible for such an imaginative window.

A gust of Canadian air went right through his slouchy jacket and chamois shirt. But instead of moving along the street, Byron remained in front of the department store window, staring at the children bobbing for apples, trying not to remember....

A hot, muggy August afternoon, his first in Tyler. Byron hadn't come to Wisconsin to take pictures. For him, then, photography was only a hobby. He'd come to see his brother. Cliff had retreated from society two years before and Byron wanted to reassure himself that his brother was alive, functioning, living a life he needed to live, on his own terms. For Cliff's sake, Byron had come to Tyler unannounced, on the sly, without fanfare. He didn't want to do anything— *anything*—to upset the precarious balance his brother had established for himself. But if Cliff needed him, if he was in any danger of hurting himself or anyone else, Byron felt he had to know. If necessary, he would have intervened.

His first stop in Tyler had been the square, his first stop on the square, Gates Department Store. He'd wanted to get a feel for the town in which his brother had taken up residence, if as a recluse.

Nora had been in the window, working on a back-to-school display that featured Tyler's original settlers heading across the fields to their one-room schoolhouse. Already Byron had been feeling a little better about where his brother had landed. Tyler, Wisconsin, wasn't a weird, gritty, hole-in-the-wall town where he'd find Cliff living in some gutter. It was picturesque and homey, a real community, with farms, businesses, schools, a hospital, a sense of history and pride. The people ran the gamut from the working poor to the well-to-do; it wasn't just an upper-class or a working-class town. Those things mattered to Byron, although, even now, he couldn't have said why.

Nora had worn her hair longer then. With a thick braid trailing down her back, and wisps of ash-blond hair poking out, she'd looked as old-fashioned and fresh-faced as her nineteenth-century figures.

She'd spotted him and smiled politely. He could tell she'd already pegged him as a stranger.

That night, pretending to be a free-lance photographer, he'd had dinner with her and Aunt Ellie at their twenties house a couple of blocks from the square. Things had snowballed from there. Although still technically the sole owner of Gates Department Store, Ellie Gates was ninety and in failing health, and left

most of the day-to-day management up to her grandniece. And, to his delight, Byron had discovered that
Nora was hardly an eighteen-year-old kid. In fact, she
was thirty, unmarried and determined to stay that way.
He'd admired her independence, her spirit, her energy, her devotion to her hometown and her sense of
humor and tolerance. He hadn't, however, expected to
fall in love with her.

He hadn't guessed she was a virgin. And she hadn't
told him until the last moment, in the tent at the lake
outside town where he'd camped. Afterward, she'd
insisted she had no regrets. It might not even have been
a conscious lie. Byron's own regrets had nothing to do
with making love to Nora Gates, of having loved her
and dreamed of having a life with her, but everything
to do with having himself been so damned blind to
what was going on in her life. He'd been preoccupied
with his own problems—Cliff, their father, his own
pain and guilt over their suffering. He hadn't seen,
until it was too late, that Nora Gates was letting go of
the last person she had in the world, a woman who'd
meant everything to her. That Aunt Ellie was ninety
and had never pretended she'd live forever wasn't the
consolation Byron, in his blindness, had anticipated.
She had been a force in Nora's life, and Nora had been
trying to find a way to carry on without her.

They'd picked a hell of a time to fall in love.

Two weeks after that first night together, he'd left
Tyler, knowing Nora thought him, incorrectly if not
unreasonably, a cad and a heel and a scurrilous East
Coast rake. Nora Gates was as inventive in her insults

as in her window displays, only a good deal less charming. But he'd known her anger toward him had been, in a peculiar way, a relief to her. A consolation. She'd fallen—blindly, temporarily—for the wrong man. In her odd world, that was better than having fallen for the right man.

"This isn't your first trip to Tyler," a quiet, familiar voice said next to him.

Byron turned slowly, and for the first time in five long years, he faced his brother. Cliff seemed to have materialized out of the darkness. For a moment, Byron wondered if he was just imagining him. But the lines in his brother's face were too real—the dark, narrowed eyes, the touches of gray in his hair. He was a different man from the one Byron had known, neither the eager, determined young man who'd gone off to Southeast Asia after their father nor the broken, potentially explosive man who'd tried, and failed, to come home. This Clifton Pierce Forrester was grownup, changed by the suffering he'd witnessed and endured, but whole at last. With a photographer's visual acuity and a brother's instincts, Byron made his assessment and was confident he was right.

He also knew his brother was royally pissed off.

"Cliff," he said, barely able to say more.

"Yeah." Cliff remained rigid and unmoving, performing his own assessment of his younger brother. "You came to Tyler to spy on me. You've done it before."

Byron neither confirmed nor denied the accusation. "I'd like us to talk, Cliff."

"Nora said you called yourself Byron Sanders."

"It's the name I used professionally," he said with heroic equanimity. "I used to take photographs."

Cliff's hardened face remained expressionless. "Nora asked me if I knew a Byron Sanders. I figured she meant you."

"And you said you didn't."

"That's right."

"Why not?"

"Because I wasn't sure I do know you."

Byron nodded. He and Cliff had always, at minimum, been honest with each other. If everything else had changed, the tough honesty between them hadn't.

Then Cliff added, in a voice so low his words were almost lost to the wind, "And because you're my brother."

"Nora," he whispered in the dark of a moonless summer night. "I love the sound of your name." Slowly, purposefully, he moved his palms across her bare breasts, already inflamed by his touch. "I love the feel of you." And he kissed her, running his tongue along the sharp edges of her teeth, into the secret corners of her mouth. "I love the taste of you."

She was nearly delirious with wanting him. She'd never realized such aching passion was possible, not for her. It made her forget everything but him. Pressing her hands against his strong hips, she drew him to her, moaning at the feel of the rough hairs of his chest against her, the taut muscles of his abdomen, his long, long legs.

"I want to feel you inside me," she whispered.

"Are you sure?"

"Yes," she breathed.

"There'll be no going back. We can stop, but you won't ever be—"

She smiled. "A virgin again?"

But he was serious.

She pressed him harder. "Love me, Byron."

Nora awoke sweating and panting—not, in her opinion, a moment too soon. She snatched up the water glass she kept by her bed and took a huge gulp. Water dripped down the sides of her mouth and spilled onto her sheets.

"Whew," she said, and laughed a little.

It had only been a dream. *Thank God.* She switched on the small pottery lamp on her antique nightstand. She was alone in her brass bed, cozy under her down quilt and Egyptian-cotton sheets. She wasn't in a musty old tent making love to Byron Sanders.

Feeling awkward and embarrassed, although there were no witnesses to her dream, she flipped on her radio to a predawn classic jazz program. Benny Goodman's clarinet playing filled the silence. She fluffed up her pillows and leaned against them, knowing she'd never get back to sleep. She didn't want to sleep if her subconscious was going to betray her like that again.

She didn't want to dream about that man.

"Dream, my foot," she muttered.

Unfortunately, it had been a memory.

Benny Goodman hit a high, clear, impossible note. Nora threw back the covers and jumped out of bed. It was chilly in her room. Just as well. A good shot of cold air was what she needed. She wasn't one to turn up the heat until the pipes were in danger of freezing. Not bothering with a robe, she headed for her bathroom down the hall, where she allowed herself the luxury of a space heater. She turned the water on in the tub to let it get good and hot, then switched on the shower. Of course, after that dream, she should probably take a cold bath.

So far she was failing miserably as Miss Marple, and not only because Agatha Christie's intrepid heroine would never have had such a steamy dream. Before heading to bed, Nora had disguised her voice, pretending she was from back East, and had checked all the obvious places in and around Tyler where Byron Sanders might have decided to rest his untrustworthy head. He wasn't registered anywhere. Had he pitched his reeking tent on private property? Well, if he was in Tyler, she'd find him. He wasn't going to do anything—not one single thing—to disrupt Cliff Forrester and Liza Baron's wedding.

"It's not your problem, you know," she said aloud to herself. "Aunt Ellie always warned you against meddling."

Nora could hear her great-aunt at her most imperious. "Meddling," she'd said on numerous occasions, "is too often one of the great temptations of the single woman."

But Nora knew Byron Sanders. He wasn't nearly as upright and honest and sensitive as he came across on first impression. How could she stand back and let him work his charms on an unsuspecting Cliff and Liza? *They'd* end up in a spread in a Chicago newspaper.

If any two people could take care of themselves, she knew, it was those two. But still, it was her *duty* to find out what the weasel was up to.

And she would. Come morning, she'd track him down, for sure.

CHAPTER FOUR

BYRON SAT on a battered Adirondack chair in a clear-
ing along the shore from Timberlake Lodge, the sun
sparkling so brightly on the water it hurt his eyes. He'd
planned to stay in a motel in the next town, but Cliff
had found him an old tent at the lodge and let him
pitch it on an out-of-the-way stretch of lakefront.
With hardly a word, Cliff had disappeared for the
night. He'd reappeared shortly after sunup, bearing
stale doughnuts and a thermos of piping-hot black
coffee, more from duty, Byron suspected, than from
a desire to be nice.

Now Cliff was standing on a rock, staring out at the
lake. Byron drank from the thermos cup and dipped
his plain doughnut into the coffee to soften it. Even as
kids, Cliff hadn't been picky about food. Byron
wasn't, either, but he did prefer fresh doughnuts.

So far, neither had had much to say. Byron had
opted against trying to explain his trip to Tyler three
years ago—one attempted explanation in the past
twelve hours had already backfired. And from Cliff's
reaction to seeing his younger brother in town, Byron
guessed Miss Liza hadn't yet confessed she'd shot off
an invitation to her future in-laws. Byron wasn't go-

ing to step into that particular pile of warm Wisconsin dung. Nor did Cliff initiate any conversation. How had he come to fall in love? What had his life been like the past five years? What were his plans now that he was getting married? Answers would have to wait. Byron was patient. It was enough, for now, that he and his brother were together by a beautiful lake on a cool, bright morning in Wisconsin.

"Are you going to tell me about you and Nora Gates?" Cliff asked without turning around.

Byron sipped his coffee, feeling it—or guilt—burn a path to the pit of his stomach. He'd never told anyone about his brief, fiery, insane affair with Nora Gates. He'd promised her. She'd insisted on calling it, derisively, his "fling."

Cliff interpreted his brother's silence in his own way. "This isn't good, Brother."

"No."

Looking around at Byron, Cliff asked, "Does she hate your guts?"

"Apparently."

"Because of the photos?"

"That's one reason."

"I can't imagine Nora Gates hating anyone," Cliff said thoughtfully, "but when she asked about you..." He sighed. "Dammit, Byron, did you break that woman's heart?"

"That woman," Byron said, popping a soaked piece of doughnut into his mouth, "doesn't have a heart capable of breaking. Don't let her fool you. She needs your sympathy about as much as a badger does.

You know what she eats for breakfast, don't you? A five-pound bag of nails. Guaranteed. Check it out yourself."

Cliff frowned. "She's not that kind of woman."

"That, Brother, is what she wants everyone in Tyler to believe. She has the tongue of a witch."

Overhead, in the distance, he could hear the seemingly chaotic honking of a flock of Canada geese. Winter was coming to Wisconsin. The geese knew when to clear out. Pity, Byron thought, he lacked their good sense.

His brother's mouth twitched in what Byron decided passed for a smile these days. "Do you care about her?"

"Cliff, I have to warn you, you're treading on thin ice even bringing up the subject. What did or didn't happen between Nora and me three years ago is between us. I can't talk about it. If I did, she'd hunt me down like a rabid weasel and put me out of her misery."

His brother's smile almost blossomed, then faded abruptly. It seemed suddenly as if he'd never smiled before and never would again.

"Are you and Nora friends?" Byron asked.

"Not in any normal way."

And Cliff's eyes, hinting of the years of pain and self-imposed isolation and loneliness he'd endured, reached Byron, reminding him that his brother had come a long, long way from where he'd been five years ago, ten years ago. And there was healing still to be done—for him, for Byron, for their widowed mother.

Had Liza Baron made his tortured life a thing of the past? But if Cliff encouraged Byron to talk, listened intently, he avoided himself as a topic of conversation. Cliff was guarded about his upcoming marriage, the life he'd been leading, where he planned to go from this point, even the body that had been dug up not too far from where they now sat. Byron knew he needed to continue to be patient.

And he wanted to hear Cliff's views on Nora Gates. It was crazy, he thought, but there it was.

"You could say," Cliff went on, looking out at the glistening lake, "that Nora's one of the people in Tyler I've admired from afar. Until yesterday afternoon, I'd never even spoken to her. But I've seen her around town, heard about her from time to time from Alyssa Baron, read about her in the newspaper. She's her own person. She sits on the town council and is active in various local charitable organizations. She has strong views on certain issues and she's direct, but she manages to be gracious at the same time. People listen to her, even when she's saying something they don't want to hear, because they know she cares about them and Tyler."

Byron knew his brother spoke the truth, but couldn't help recalling that saintly Nora Gates had thrown a book of Beethoven sonatas at him. If she'd had any kind of arm, she'd have knocked him out.

"I doubt she takes to liars," Cliff added.

The geese were directly overhead, flying in picture-postcard formation against a sky as clear and blue as any Byron had seen, from Maine to Florida to Cali-

fornia to Alaska. He could think of worse places to
end up than Tyler, Wisconsin. His mahogany-paneled
Providence office, for one, he decided wryly. He drank
more of his coffee, the warmth of the plastic cup finally penetrating his fingers. It had been a chilly night.
He was used to camping out in every type of weather,
although there'd been something eerie about pitching
his tent not far from where a body had been mysteriously buried for who knew how long. And his memories of Nora Gates, both past and current, hadn't
been conducive to sleep. But it was simpler to blame
the weather.

With the sun climbing higher, sitting outside wasn't
so bad. Anyway, Cliff hadn't invited him into the
lodge.

"I lied to Nora about who I was," Byron said,
"because I was afraid of what would happen if word
got out that Cliff Forrester's brother was in town."

"If I found out, you mean?"

Cliff's tone was deadly calm, even neutral, but
Byron sensed the regret, the guilt, the uneasy resig-
nation. "You did what you had to do, Cliff," he said
carefully. "So did I."

Bending down suddenly, Cliff snatched up a small
rock, straightened and skipped it across the calm lake.
Yards out, it disappeared in spreading concentric circles. "Father taught us that," he said, his back to
Byron. "Remember?"

"I remember."

Cliff turned, his expression harsh and unyielding in
the bright sun, maybe more so than he meant it to be.

But his eyes looked as if they were melting. Byron was almost seared by his brother's torment. "I thought this would be easier."

Byron tossed the last of his coffee into the grass. "Me, too."

"Liza . . ." It was the first time Cliff had mentioned her directly. He turned back to the lake, where the last of the concentric circles had vanished, leaving behind a glasslike surface. "She thinks all things are possible. Sometimes I get to thinking that way, too."

"Cliff—"

"She told you and Mother about us, didn't she?"

"You'll have to talk to her about that."

"She would, you know. She's meddlesome like that—the kind of woman who'd teach a kid to swim by pitching him headfirst into the water." He sighed. "But this time she went too far. I don't know if I'm ready for this."

"That's why I came early. To see if you were. She can't understand what it's been like, Cliff. No one can."

He nodded.

"If you're not ready to see me, I'll leave. Now, today. Mother won't come at all. It's your call."

Cliff was silent. Then he said, "Tell her who you are, Byron."

Back to Nora Gates. Cliff, apparently, would go only so far in articulating his innermost thoughts. Byron smiled thinly. "That might mean the end of me."

"And if you want to stay," Cliff said, his face expressionless, "then stay."

"I'll see how today goes. As for Nora— I'll tell her the truth after the wedding."

"Before."

"She's invited?"

Cliff jumped from his rock, landing as silently as a panther. "Half the damned town's invited."

For a moment, Byron dismissed his troubling thoughts about Nora Gates. She was a strong woman, a survivor. He didn't need to coddle her. He remembered every second of their time together, wishing like hell he didn't. He *had* loved her. And he'd tried, amid his own pain and confusion, to do the right thing, even as he'd lied to her and ended up making her hate him. But through knowing her, through knowing Aunt Ellie, he'd learned that before he could help anyone, commit to anyone or anything, he had first to save himself.

It was his brother, once again, who worried him. "Are you going to make it through this thing?"

"I will. For Liza's sake."

"She wants a big wedding?"

But Byron had stepped over the line. The mask dropped into place, covering up the raw, exposed parts of himself that Cliff preferred to deal with on his own. He looked out past Byron to the lodge. "Company."

"Work crew?"

"Nope." And because the mask was in place, because he was the big brother and didn't need anything from Byron, Cliff managed one of his twitching smiles. "That's Nora Gates's car."

Byron followed his brother's gaze, but could only make out a champagne-colored BMW. Far too racy and expensive for frugal, demure Nora Gates. "Where?"

"The BMW."

"That's no Victorian old maid's car."

Cliff grunted. "And you think you know everything about Nora Gates."

NORA HAD DRESSED conservatively for her trip out to Timberlake Lodge, not for Liza's sake—Liza greeted her in jeans and an oversize Tyler Titans sweatshirt—but for her own. Her reliable double-breasted wide-wale charcoal corduroy jacket, her black wool gabardine trousers and her stark white cotton shirt reminded her that she was smart, successful, responsible and perfectly capable of handling most anything, including the return of Byron Sanders to Tyler. It would not be a repeat of three years ago. She would keep a level head, unsettling dreams or no unsettling dreams.

"Nora," Liza said, obviously surprised. "Well, hi—what on earth brings you out here?"

"I hope I'm not too early. It's such a beautiful morning I thought I'd take a ride out. The place looks great."

"Doesn't it, though? Come on inside— I'll give you the grand tour."

"I'm not disturbing you?"

"Not at all. I was just stewing about this wedding getting out of hand, and Joe Santori isn't around this morning so I can't pester him. Cliff's off somewhere. It's just me and the cobwebs right now."

Liza's infectious cheer helped Nora recover her own steady manner. They climbed onto the old lodge's formidable porch, which overlooked the beautiful lake. The long-abandoned lodge was a grand dinosaur of a place, but Nora, as a member of the Tyler town council, was thrilled to see it being renovated. It was a pity the discovery of a body on the premises had put a damper on things.

"Stay all morning if you want," Liza said. "I've got nothing special planned, except a phone call to my mother tactfully reminding her that it's my wedding, not hers." She smiled guiltily over her shoulder. "She's such a sweetheart, though. We're both under a lot of strain. I keep telling myself she means well—"

"And she just wants you to do the right thing."

Liza's smile broadened into a grin. "Isn't that true of all mothers?"

"I'm sure it is," Nora said softly. Her own mother had been dead for twenty years.

"Oh, drat, me and my big mouth again. I'm sorry, Nora. I forgot—"

"It's all right. Gosh, Liza, I can't get over how much you and Cliff have accomplished in such a short time."

Her small faux pas behind her—Liza Baron wasn't one to beat herself over the head for long—she breezed through the front door into the entry. She seemed cheerful and content, if also somewhat hyper and overwhelmed by all that was going on in her life. Nora thought she could understand. Never mind finding a dead body in your yard, one, no less, that might be that of your long-lost grandmother. Never mind coming back to your hometown to live. As far as Nora was concerned, falling head over heels in love as fast and furiously as Liza Baron had with Cliff Forrester would turn anyone's life inside out. Even if Liza *was* used to doing everything fast and furiously. From her own glaring romantic mistake, Nora was convinced that if there was one area in life where a woman should always act with great deliberation and extreme caution, it was in affairs of the heart. A woman should take her time about falling in love. Shop around. Be careful. Romance was not an area in which to be precipitate. If she was feeling reckless, Nora would head to the racetrack before she would dial Byron Sanders's number.

"Anything in particular that brings you out here, or did you really just seize the moment?" Liza asked.

"I guess I wanted to see how you were doing."

She shrugged. "On the whole, I'm doing great. A little nuts maybe, but I've never been happier."

Something only someone madly in love would say. Nora had felt that way when she'd thought she was in love with Byron Sanders. She'd learned, in the years since, that she could be just as happy out of love, if not happier. It was a matter of perspective and self-discipline. People in love always thought they were happier than people who weren't. In her opinion, that kind of thinking was just . . . hormones.

"Have you ever been up here before?" Liza asked.

Nora pulled herself out of her introspective mood. "I trespassed once or twice when I was a kid—hunting wildflowers, as I recall. And I've canoed by a number of times."

"You and Aunt Ellie used to go canoeing together, didn't you? She was something else. Damn, she used to make my grandfather mad sometimes. But she'd always remain so calm and composed. Granddad told me once that he wanted to get her mad enough to spit nickels, but I don't think he ever succeeded. She just refused to let him get to her. You're a lot like her, Nora. You don't let people get to you, either."

Nora kept her expression neutral and refrained from comment, wondering what Liza Baron would think if she'd witnessed her throwing a book of Beethoven piano sonatas at her ex-lover just last evening. Fortunately, Ricky Travis wasn't a big mouth or the story would have been all over town by now. If his little brother Lars, another of Nora's piano students, had caught her, she might as well have taken an ad out in the *Tyler Citizen* announcing the news. Lars did like to talk.

"Your grandfather must be thrilled with how the lodge is shaping up," Nora said, deftly changing the subject.

"Oh, I think he would be, if we hadn't . . ." She waved a hand awkwardly. "You know."

The Body. Nora nodded sympathetically, sorry she'd brought it up, even indirectly. But Judson Ingalls's lodge, where his wife had had so many of her wild parties in the late forties, was showing fresh potential, new life. No one but Cliff Forrester had lived in the place since Margaret Ingalls had left her husband in 1950. And now, of course, Liza and her daily influx of renovators. Her creative spark was evident in the ongoing work, in the choice of walls she'd had Joe Santori knock down, in the colors she'd chosen, in her attention to detail, even in the way she'd made the spare furnishings and torn-up rooms seem downright homey.

"What do you think of my rug?" Liza asked as they passed over a small Oriental rug in the entry. "Neat, huh?"

"It's beautiful."

"I found it up in the attic when Cliff and I—well, when we were still stalking each other, you might say. I think it's a real Oriental, not a fake. Cliff's not so sure. Look at those colors, though. I don't know if you can get that rich burgundy from a fake. I don't really care, except if it's real, my grandmother might have bought it on one of her infamous shopping trips."

Nora, who treasured her own family heirlooms, was intrigued. Margaret Ingalls was on the minds of just about everyone in Tyler; Nora wanted more insight into the woman Aunt Ellie had believed was rather misunderstood by the townspeople. "Did you ask Judson or your mother about it?"

"No, not yet. Margaret's not the best subject of conversation to bring up right now. And I'd hate Granddad to make me take up the rug just because she might have bought the damned thing—you're never sure how he'll react. You know what an old curmudgeon he can be."

One, however, who adored his irrepressible granddaughter Liza. Nora had never pretended to fully understand the Ingalls family. But Liza seemed reluctant to say anything further about her grandfather.

"And I'd ask Mother," she went on, sighing, "but she hasn't had much of anything to do with the lodge since she was a little girl. Of course, I wasn't even born when my grandmother hit the road—I have to remind myself that she was my mother's mother, not some stranger." She made an exaggerated wince, as if she'd just caught herself doing something naughty. "I'm sorry, I don't mean to bore you with all this stuff. Anyway, it's no big deal. There's so much junk squirreled away around here I got excited when I found the rug, but it's probably just junk, too. Oh, well, I like it, regardless. I'm going to have it cleaned and appraised, but I thought I'd wait until the dust settles around here." She gestured broadly toward a partially destroyed wall as they made their way to the kitchen. "Literally."

Long-lost rugs, sawdust, a rambling, run-down lodge—near chaos seemed to suit Liza Baron, which, Nora thought, was so unlike herself. She preferred order and stability. But in the kitchen, freshly renovated, she saw another side of her new friend, because its unexpected coziness—the rag rugs, the splashes of color, the chipped pottery teapot filled with autumn wildflowers—had to be Liza's doing. She'd added character and charm to what, with its long stainless steel counters and stark white cabinets, could have been an institutional-looking kitchen. Nora could imagine Liza and Cliff having dinner together at the battered pine table. The two of them, she suddenly saw, were completely right for each other.

"Hey, what do you say to a cup of hot coffee on this chilly autumn morning?" Liza offered cheerfully, already pulling two restaurant-style mugs down from an open shelf. "I tried to talk Cliff into building a fire to take the nip out of the air, but he was off like a bat out of hell at the crack of dawn. That man. I'll never figure him out." She grinned over her shoulder, reaching for the coffeepot. "Guess that'll make our life together all the more intriguing."

Nora smiled. "You have a way of jumping head-first into the future, don't you?"

"It's the only way I know how. Cream and sugar?"

"Just black," Nora said absently, sitting down at the table. She herself plotted and plodded and eased her way into the future, tried to predict it as much as possible, relied on short-term and long-term goals.

Liza set the steaming coffee in front of her and sat down. Nora finally became aware of her probing, curious stare. "Is something wrong?" Liza asked.

"No! No, not at all." Nora sat up straight and tried the coffee. "Hazelnut, isn't it?"

"Hope you like it. I only make it when Cliff's not around. He hates it."

"It's lovely. You and Cliff are so different—"

"Yep. Keeps life interesting. Nora..." Liza squinted, her expression a reminder of her astuteness. Given her rebellious, outrageous side, people often tended to underestimate her intelligence. "Nora, did Cliff put you up to coming out here?"

"Actually..."

"I'm not going to get mad. I told you, he thinks highly of you. He's that way—makes up his mind quickly about people."

Nora sighed. Naturally. People generally did think "highly" of her. But wasn't that what she wanted? If she had a choice, she'd prefer to inspire respect, not passion. *Why not both?* That was dangerous thinking, the sort in which she'd indulged when Byron Sanders came to Tyler for the first time.

"Well, yes," she said, "he asked me to give you a hand in whatever way I could, but I was going to do that anyway, especially after I saw you in the store the other day. I gather with everything going on you haven't really had much chance to touch base with your old Tyler friends."

"Not really, no," Liza said, dumping a heaping teaspoon of sugar into her mug of coffee. "My best friend from high school lives in Chicago these days and the rest..." She shrugged. "As you say, there hasn't been time. I suppose a few will turn up at the wedding. Mother handled most of the Tyler invitations. RSVPs keep pouring in...." She trailed off, looking uncharacteristically preoccupied and unsure of herself. "Do you think we're overdoing it? Or at least me? None of this wedding stuff's Cliff's doing—the hoopla, I mean—but I'm trying to pull it off in no time at all. It's a lot to handle."

"Yes, it is, but if a big wedding is what you want," Nora said diplomatically, "then it's what you should have."

Liza groaned, throwing up her hands. "I don't know anymore if it *is* what I want. Maybe I'm trying to please too many people. You know what I mean? Mother's lassoed one of her friends into having a bridal shower for me. Can you imagine? It's supposed to be a surprise, but when I started yapping about how relieved I am there wouldn't be time for that sort of thing, she told me."

Liza shook her head, and Nora refrained from comment as she drank more of the hot, flavorful coffee. She would just let her new friend articulate her worries and frustrations . . . before she found a subtle way to introduce the subject of Cliff's fellow Rhode Islander.

Wrinkling up her face, Liza continued, "I hate the idea of going through with a shower. Every nosy old prune in town'll be there—you know, those women who've never even had a man but feel free to offer advice." She stopped herself all at once, blushing furiously, something not a few in Tyler would have paid to see. "Nora, I'm sorry. I didn't mean—"

"It's quite all right."

"No one *ever* called your aunt Ellie a nosy old prune, and I'm sure it'll be the same for you—oh, God, I'm just making it worse."

But Nora, who'd never minded being compared to Aunt Ellie and who well understood the ramifications of being an old maid, started to laugh, imagining what Liza Baron would have to say if she'd been privy to Tyler's youngest spinster's steamy dream just a few hours ago. Liza stared at her, obviously confused and embarrassed, and then sputtered into laughter, too.

"Look," Nora said finally, really *liking* Liza Baron as a person, "why don't I talk to your mother and find out what she has in store that she wouldn't want you to know? If it's anything dreadful—and I'm sure it isn't—I'll do what I can to spare you any unpleasant surprises. I'll also offer to lend a hand, since this can't be all that easy on her, either."

"Oh, Nora, I couldn't let you go to all that trouble—I was just going to put my foot down with Mother and tell her to cancel."

"What, and spoil everyone's fun?"

"Showers are so—"

"Sexist and mercenary," Nora supplied, recalling Liza's forceful opinions on bridal registries. "Another feudalistic ritual."

Liza's bright, pretty eyes were glistening with amusement. "Right. And I don't intend to have any bridesmaids, either."

"I'm sure that's a perfectly legitimate decision. Traditions sometimes need a fresh look—or even to be abandoned altogether. But I like to look upon bridal showers and bridesmaids not as being about pots and pans and male power and dependence and such, but about sisterhood."

"No kidding?"

"Sure. When these things work, they're a celebration, an affirmation of who we've been as a community of women in the past and the possibilities and hope for what we can become in the future, as individuals, in our roles as wives, mothers, grandmothers, aunts, sisters."

"I'll have to mull that over," Liza said dubiously. "You do have a way of putting a nice spin on things, Nora Gates."

Nora shrugged. "Everyone loves a wedding."

"I know, and I've been thinking of so many of these wedding traditions as a burden—you know I'm a rebel at heart. It's my nature to question everything that's 'expected.' But it's refreshing to consider the meaning behind all these traditions. You *don't* have to talk to my Mother, however."

"But I want to. Really."

Liza narrowed her eyes. "You mean it, don't you?"

Nora smiled. "I wouldn't mislead you on something this important. A bridal shower shouldn't be an imposition and it shouldn't be trivial—it should be fun."

"You're right."

"And a shower would help you get your feet wet—so to speak—before the wedding. You know, see your mother's friends and some of your old friends before you and Cliff—"

"Are waltzed up the aisle," Liza finished, grinning suddenly. "Okay, I get your point." But her grin vanished, her beautiful eyes darkening. "*Do* you think Cliff and I are rushing things?"

"It's not my place to say—"

"I don't mean about falling in love. That's happened. Nothing and nobody can undo that. I mean the wedding. People have hardly had time to adjust to my being home, never mind to my marrying the town recluse. And they don't know Cliff."

"Look," Nora said, comfortable in her role as confidante, "everyone in Tyler knows you do things in a whoosh. A couple of weeks' notice for your wedding is about all anyone who knows you would expect."

Liza downed half her coffee in a big gulp. "You wouldn't do it this way."

"I'm not you, Liza."

But Nora couldn't help thinking—*again*—of Byron Sanders. If their short-lived affair hadn't been a spontaneous whirlwind of lunacy, she didn't know what was. And there'd been a time when she'd thought nothing and no one could have pulled them apart. But that was over, an incident she didn't care to repeat because it *wasn't* her way of doing things. Whirlwind love affairs—even one that endured—were not her style.

She went on, "You need to do what's right for you without—"

"Without getting myself tarred and feathered and run out of town," Liza said good-naturedly. "I'm glad

Cliff got you to come out here. For one thing, it shows he's thinking about me—which I *know*, but it's always nice to have it demonstrated. For another thing, it's a relief not to have to go through these wedding 'traditions' alone. I know I have Cliff and Mother— and Amanda and Jeffery, of course, but—''

"But fiancés, mothers and siblings don't help when what you really need is a friend."

Liza nodded. "Sisterhood, right? Honestly, Nora, from anyone but you that kind of talk'd sound downright radical. Hey, you want to say hi to Cliff? He should be around outside somewhere."

"If I won't be intruding."

"Not at all."

Nora rose to take her empty coffee mug to the sink, as Liza went on, "If you ask me, Cliff needs more intrusion. People in Tyler have been tiptoeing around him for too long, and there's just no need. You know, he'd had almost nothing to do with the human race for years and years until I barreled into his life."

She seemed quite pleased with herself as, standing next to Nora, she dumped out the rest of her coffee. Liza Baron was confident that she and Cliff Forrester were right—*meant*—for each other. Any of the upheaval their romance had caused for him and for herself was well worth the struggle, the change, the need to adapt and adjust.

Three years ago, Byron Sanders could have been smug about having barreled into Nora's life. But there was a difference. Cliff Forrester's life had needed stirring up. Nora's hadn't.

And it still didn't, she thought.

And, she added silently, there was another big difference: Liza Baron and Cliff Forrester loved each other.

"Come on," Liza said, "I'll take you through the back. There's a path down to the lake. I think that's where Cliff went."

They cut through a small sitting room off the kitchen and went out onto the veranda, which offered one of the old lodge's many spectacular views of the lake. With her usual boundless energy, Liza made a beeline to a narrow, beaten path that wound through the overgrown yard down toward the lake, as blue and clear as the autumn sky. The grass, knee-high along the path, was dotted with goldenrod and asters, and there were pale birches, the odd gnarled pine and clumps of sumac. All the more brightly colored leaves—the reds, burgandies and vivid oranges—had fallen to the ground, leaving only those of the more muted colors, yellows and soft oranges, clinging to the trees.

Nora screwed up her courage. "Have you heard from any of Cliff's family or friends in Rhode Island?"

"Oh, I only invited family—just his mother and younger brother. His father's dead. I don't know any of his old friends."

So Byron Sanders *hadn't* been invited to Tyler. The lying fink. How had he found out about the wedding? From the Rhode Island Forresters? The mother or the younger brother must have blabbed to someone who'd blabbed ... well, Byron would be on the receiving end of any manner of gossip and news. He was that way. If the reclusive Cliff Forrester did indeed come from a prominent East Coast family, Byron could have himself quite a coup if he managed to photograph his wedding.

"How long has it been since Cliff's seen his family?" Nora asked casually.

Liza was getting well ahead of her. "Five years at least," she said over her shoulder. "Why?"

"I was just curious. Sorry if I seem nosy—"

"No, that's okay. You don't seem nosy." Liza stopped in the middle of the narrow path until Nora caught up with her, a matter of thirty seconds. Nora was intensely aware of her new friend's scrutiny. "You do seem a little ... I don't know, nervous or something."

"I'm not—"

But Nora stopped, feeling her face drain of all color. Up ahead, probably on the same path, or not bothering with a path at all, two men were walking toward them. One clearly was Cliff Forrester. The other, just as clearly, unless Nora had gone completely off her rocker, was Byron Sanders.

"Hey, there!" Cliff called, waving.

Spotting him, Liza beamed and waved back. A woman in love. "What're you up to? Who's that with you?"

"I can't hear you. Wait there and we'll join you."

Liza frowned, her hands on her hips as she peered down toward the lake and the two men. "That's not one of Joe Santori's crew, is it?"

"I don't think so," Nora said, gritting her teeth.

Then the two men came up over the rise and she could see Byron's dark hair glistening in the sun, the hard edges of his face, his strong, even gait. The prospect of such ignominy, of having to deal with this man again, and in front of two friends—two potential victims of Byron Sanders's wiles and charms—thoroughly unsettled and annoyed Nora.

She thought she saw him smiling.

The cad. Had he just recognized her? Did it amuse him to know he threw her off balance? Did he *enjoy* making her miserable?

I won't give him the satisfaction, she thought.

But as the two men came closer, Nora found herself muttering an oath Aunt Ellie certainly had never taught her.

Liza glanced at her, eyes twinkling. "Gee, Nora, I didn't think you had it in you."

Nora could feel the color returning to her cheeks. "Sorry. I'm just . . . it's possible I know this guy."

"No kidding?"

Then they were approaching and Nora gritted her teeth, saying nothing, refusing even to look at Byron Sanders. She felt his presence, though. It was just that way with her and him—one of those uncomfortable realities, like poison ivy and root canals.

"Hi, Cliff," Liza said. "Who's your friend?"

"He's not a friend."

Nora's eyes shot up. Cliff was looking pointedly at Byron Sanders. Had he found out what a two-faced weasel his fellow Rhode Islander was? Had he—

With a brief, dark glance at Nora, Byron stepped forward, stretching out his hand. "Hello, Liza," he said in his most suave, debonair voice. "It's a pleasure finally to meet you."

"Oh, yeah? Who are you?"

Only Liza.

"My name's Byron," he said, with no detectable catch in his voice. "Byron Sanders Forrester."

Nora's knees when weak.

Liza said, "Then you're..."

"Yes. I'm Cliff's brother."

CHAPTER FIVE

GIVEN THAT SHE HAD an audience, Nora managed to keep her mouth shut and not go for the bastard's throat. She prided herself on her ability to make a quick recovery and hold back her emotions under the most trying circumstances, but this was beyond trying. She knew she must look shocked, pale, stiff, furious. But at least she wasn't in the process of committing a felonious act of violence.

"It's great to meet you, Byron," Liza said, not a little unnerved herself. Nora could see her glancing sideways at her husband-to-be, who hadn't, of course, known his brother was invited to their wedding. "When did you get here?"

"Yesterday."

Byron, Nora observed, was the only one who didn't look as if he wanted to strangle someone. He was used to sticky situations, however, and wasn't a man who could be easily analyzed from his outward appearance.

"Do you need a place to stay?" Liza asked. "Cliff and I have tons of room at the lodge—"

"That's okay. I'll manage."

Her hands locked into fists, Nora struggled to retain her composure. Had Byron squealed to his brother about their affair? There were too many dangers, too many questions.

Cliff moved close to his fiancée. "I promised Byron something to eat."

"Sure," Liza said. "Nora, would you care to join us? We could have an early lunch."

Nora would rather have joined a public snake roasting. "No, thank you." She sounded hoarse and a bit overcome even to herself. She cleared her throat. "I need to get back to the store. It's good to see you, Cliff." She made herself turn to the dark-eyed weasel. "Good to meet you, Mr. Forrester."

Because she was trying to be grown-up and not betray her true feelings, the way she said "Forester" was frosty but not icy-sharp.

Cliff must have noticed. "Come on, Liza. You and I need to talk."

"About what?" Liza asked innocently.

"You know."

Never one on whom subtlety worked with any degree of regularity, Liza frowned. "I don't get it."

With a sigh of love and exasperation, Cliff took her by the elbow and hustled her off.

Nora tried to follow them, but Byron stopped her with one soft-spoken word. "Stay."

In the ensuing silence, Nora could hear the rustling of the breeze in the grass and in the woods beyond the path. She could hear birds, the distant honking of geese and the quiet lapping of lake water on the rocky shoreline nearby. Her ex-lover hadn't made another sound. She would have wondered if he'd slithered off to a sunny rock, but she could see his shadow. She refused to look at him. First she had to get a grip on herself.

Finally, he said, "I couldn't think of any decent way to tell you."

"Of course not. Decency isn't your style."

"I don't blame you for being angry."

He didn't go on, but waited for her to respond. She kept her silence. She couldn't yet allow herself to indulge in a full reaction. She might start screaming or cursing at him. She might jump him. Worse, she might cry. She'd hate that. The absolute worst, however, was not knowing what she'd do. And that was how it had been from the start when she was around this man: she couldn't count on being sensible. She couldn't always predict how she'd react.

"Cliff is . . ." Byron broke off with a grunt of frustration and, Nora guessed, out-and-out irritation. She didn't care. What did he want her to do? Look up at him angelically and say all was forgiven? If he was annoyed with her for her stony silence, with himself for the deep, dark hole he'd dug for himself, then good. She had no sympathy. But he went on quietly, in that gentle voice of her dreams, "Cliff's my only brother, Nora. He's been through a hell I can't even imagine. I had to come back."

"Yes," she said stiffly, in her most holier-than-thou old maid tone. "I suppose so."

"Sanders is my middle name."

It had a nice ring to it. Byron Sanders Forrester. One of your good upper crust East Coast names. No doubt he knew how to sail and play lacrosse. Probably had a pair of horn-rimmed glasses tucked in a tweed coat pocket somewhere.

When she didn't respond, Byron added, "My paternal grandmother was a Sanders. From Boston. Cliff's named for my mother's side of the family— Clifton Pierce Forrester. It's just the two of us. We were raised in Providence. The Pierces have been there almost since the Puritans banished Roger Williams from Massachusetts in 1636 and he came to Narragansett Bay."

By now his tone was only half-serious, but Nora neither smiled nor relaxed. She wished she trusted herself to be as spontaneous as Liza Baron was. But Byron wouldn't charm her. Not this time. "Liza said that Cliff's from a prominent East Coast family."

"That would be the Pierces."

She heard a wry bitterness creep into his voice, prompting her to look at him square in the face. Immediately she wished she hadn't. The man was still, after three years, one handsome devil. If she'd known she'd be seeing him again, she would have prayed to her fairy godmother to turn him into a frog. At the very least, she'd have hoped that she'd take one look at him and ask herself what all the fuss had been about three years ago: how could she have fallen for someone as transparently rotten as he was? He was so obviously wrong for her. Not even sexy. Sort of lazy and worn-out looking.

But that wasn't how she'd reacted. If wrong for her on other counts, the man who'd swept her off her feet three years ago still possessed the roguish sexiness and charm that had drawn her to him so disastrously. She could no longer try to blame bad timing. Aunt Ellie wasn't dying anymore and she wasn't reexamining the choices and assumptions she'd made about her own life. She was stable, satisfied, successful. In a word, she was happy.

And still damnably, irreversibly, it seemed, attracted to Byron Sanders. And not just physically. Their attraction to each other had never been purely physical. She and Byron Sanders, in a very real way, had been kindred spirits and—

She seethed. Byron Sanders *Forrester*. She'd have to remember. She couldn't allow herself to forget that he was a liar, if a dangerously irresistible liar.

He didn't turn away from her, but met her probing gaze straight on. His eyes were as dark as his brother's, with fine, almost imperceptible lines spraying out from the corners. They were memorable eyes. But where she'd once found only unshakable confidence and humor, she now detected hints of pain and regret, hints of complexity. He wasn't *just* a cad or a rake, and she knew it. Perhaps, deep down, she'd always known it.

"They were publishers," he said, still talking about the Pierces. "My great-grandfather and a friend of his founded Pierce & Rothchilde, Publishers, more than a hundred years ago. They moved to their present location in Providence in 1894. The Rothchildes got out of the business in the twenties. Cliff and I are the last of the Pierces.''

And Cliff was a near-recluse, Byron an itinerant photographer. Pierce & Rothchilde was one of the most prestigious publishers in the country. Nora was intrigued by the questions and potential conflicts those facts presented, but she'd already made up her mind. "I don't need to know anything about you or your grandmother Sanders or the Pierces or the Forresters. I really don't."

He sighed. "I know you don't. I guess I just don't know what the hell to say to you."

"Goodbye would be nice."

"All right. Goodbye, Nora."

But it wasn't good enough. Nora got three steps back up the path and knew she needed satisfaction. The man had slept with her and she hadn't even known his real name! She whirled back around, the sun almost blinding her.

"Unless you can uproot a tree," Byron said calmly, "there's nothing handy for you to throw at me."

He was maddening. How did he know what she was thinking? What she was feeling? She tilted up her chin, hanging on to the last shreds of her dignity. "Does Cliff know about us?"

"He knows you don't like me."

"But I never indicated..."

Byron grinned. "You aren't as good at hiding your emotions as you think, Miss Gates. But you can relax—he doesn't know why you dislike me so much."

"What did you tell him?"

"Nothing."

"He just thinks I dislike you because of the series on Aunt Ellie?"

Byron shrugged, his eyes clouding, his expression unreadable. "I don't know what he thinks."

Nora exhaled at the blue autumn sky. "I could strangle you, Byron." But the truth was out, and at least it explained—even excused—his presence in Tyler. It did, in fact, have nothing to do with her. She looked back at him. "And that's only the half of it."

"I'm sure," he said. His tone was neutral, but she saw the lust—the damned amusement—in his eyes.

"Don't you get any ideas, Byron Sanders Who-ever. You don't mean any more to me than a bag of dried beans."

"Remember the fairy tales, Nora. Jack's beans turned out to be magic."

"You're making fun of me."

"I'm not—"

"You never did take me seriously—*my* hopes, *my* dreams, who *I* am. You were only interested in your photography career and a little quick, convenient sex with an unsuspecting small-town woman."

Byron's mouth twitched, but apparently he was smart enough not to smile outright, given that there were uprootable trees in the vicinity. "Nora, it wasn't a little sex, it wasn't quick, that wasn't all there was to our relationship, and you're about as much the stereotypical unsuspecting small-town woman as Cliff and I are the stereotypical East Coast blue bloods."

He paused while she came to a full boil. "I'd like to explain why I lied to you."

"You don't owe me an explanation, and frankly I don't require one." She looked at him for a moment, daring him to respond, but he didn't. What could he say? She was proud of her cool tone. She had to prove to herself that his remarks about their love life wouldn't get to her—at least so that anyone would notice. "All I ask is that you keep what we . . . *were* to each other to yourself."

And she started back up the narrow path, wondering what she would tell Liza. Because now, for sure, she wouldn't become involved with the wedding festivities. She didn't even want to attend the ceremony with Liza's future brother-in-law there. It was just too dangerous. Even if she trusted him—which she didn't—she didn't, in a very different way, trust herself. Seeing Byron Sanders Forrester all dressed up for his brother's wedding just might do her in.

"I owe Cliff the truth," Byron said behind her.

That did it. Nora swung around, marched down to Byron and slapped him hard across the face, just as Katharine Hepburn slapped Humphrey Bogart in *The African Queen,* Aunt Ellie's favorite movie. Before she turned around and flounced back up the path, she noticed the red handprint on Byron's cheek. It just wasn't in her to feel sorry for him. He owed Cliff the truth. What about her? She'd spent three years thinking—

Well, she wouldn't think about Byron Sanders *Forrester* anymore.

"You know," he said, not far behind her, "you always act like an insulted Victorian virgin when you're mad. It's a good defense mechanism. But I don't believe it."

She ignored him.

He had to speak a little louder for her to hear him. Thank heaven Joe Santori and his crew weren't lurking about, eavesdropping. "I think you'd like to do a hell of a lot more than slap my face."

Like what? She almost panicked.

"*I* think," he yelled, "that what you'd like to do right now is skin me alive, and what grates is that you know I know it."

Skin him alive. Yes, that was it. That was just exactly what she wanted to do with him.

She whirled around, stepping backward. "Skin you alive and throw your bones to the wolves, you cad!"

He grinned. He wasn't marching in fast little steps the way she was, but moving deliberately, his long legs eating up the distance between them. She wished she'd worn her running shoes and jeans instead of her conservative businesswoman's outfit. She couldn't see his eyes against the bright sun. Three years ago, they'd told her what he was thinking, even feeling. Or at least she'd thought they had. She'd only seen what she'd wished to see—which wasn't like her. She prided herself on her ability to look life straight in the eye.

"I've never met anyone like you, Nora Gates," he said, still grinning.

She scoffed. "You told me that three years ago."

"Meant it."

"Then it was the one thing you said that you did mean."

"Oh, I said a lot of things I meant. But I don't blame you for being skeptical. Nora, the past is past. Let it go. I don't want my presence in Tyler to be a thorn in your side. You don't need to avoid me. I won't—" He broke off, his dark, dark eyes resting on her. "I won't let what happened three years ago happen again."

She didn't say a word. Could she believe him? Was that what she wanted to hear from him? "What happened and didn't happen wasn't just up to you, you know."

"Oh, really?"

"Byron..."

"No one needs to know that we were lovers three years ago. I just mean that I owe Cliff the truth about why I was in Tyler, what I did, why I left. He doesn't need to know the sordid details about us."

He'd said it so easily. As if being lovers with someone was no big deal. Probably the country was dotted with his ex-lovers. Nora raised her chin. "You're Cliff Forrester's brother. Everyone in Tyler's madly curious about him and his relationship with Liza—she's from one of the town's more prominent families. He's been a recluse out here for years and years. You're going to be well scrutinized."

"I expect so."

"Has it occurred to you that someone might recognize you as the photographer who did the series on Aunt Ellie?"

"It's possible, but—"

"Then not only will people be asking you questions, but they'll be asking *me* questions as well. Did I recognize you? Have I talked to you? Did I know you were really Cliff's brother?" She gulped for air, tense and irritated, just imagining what could be in store for her. "You've put me in one hell of a position."

"I'm sorry," he said.

His apology seemed genuine. What did she want from the man? Any other woman discovering an ex-lover back in town wouldn't go nuts at the prospect of people finding out about their long-dead relationship. It wasn't as if she'd been married to another man when Byron had burst into her life.

"I weighed all the pros and cons when I decided to come to Tyler," Byron said.

"And you came anyway."

"He's my brother, Nora. I had to come."

"Just keep your distance," she told him.

"Okay."

"And don't tell anyone *anything*. I value my reputation in this town."

"Your secret's safe with me."

"Scout's honor?"

He winced at the acid in her tone. "I'm not making fun of you."

"Yes, you are."

"Nora . . ."

"What you are doing, Byron, is belittling me. And I object. Vociferously. You don't have to understand me, but do not belittle me."

He sighed. "Nora, for the love of God, if I took out a billboard and announced that Nora Gates and I fell in love three years ago and it didn't work out, do you honestly think anyone in Tyler would give a damn?"

She squared her shoulders. "I swear, if there was a rock handy the coroner would be examining *two* bodies found at Timberlake Lodge! We did *not* fall in love. We—"

"Okay. I'll put on the billboard that Nora Gates isn't a virgin and I know it because I slept with her. Or should I be more explicit?"

"I'm just saying—" her whole body was on fire! "—that whatever it was we had together, it had precious little to do with love."

"Then it had to do with sex. I'll put that on my billboard."

"Dammit, Byron!"

"Don't 'dammit' me, Nora. Just tell me what you really do want."

"I want you not to exist!"

"No can do."

"Then at least..." She groaned, wondering what she did want. "At least respect me. I don't want my friends and customers—my community, Byron—to know that I... that you..."

"You did. I did. We did. Nora, nobody but you will care."

"That shows how little you know about Tyler."

Byron didn't relent. "Maybe it shows how little you know."

His tone was soft and seductive, so serious she would have thought he cared and understood, but experience had taught her otherwise. "I'll take full responsibility for my actions," she said tightly, "but don't you judge me, Byron *Forrester.* I'm not the one who talked a dying old woman into spending so many of her last days having her picture taken. I'm not the one who cynically swept a vulnerable small-town girl off her feet. I'm not the one who said Tyler wasn't for him and slithered out of town. I'm—" She stopped, staring at him. "What're you looking so incredulous over?"

"You," he said.

"Me? Byron, aren't you *listening?*"

"Yeah. I'm hearing every word, sweets. Just one question—what vulnerable small-town woman did I cynically sweep off her feet?"

Nora called him something that, coming from her, would have raised Liza Baron's eyebrows and dropped the jaws of half the people in Tyler. Aunt Ellie wouldn't have been shocked; it was her favorite thing to call randy neighborhood dogs who ran amok in her bushes.

Byron Forrester just laughed.

It was the same laugh that had awakened her from too many dreams over too many months. A laugh that she hadn't made up, but was real. Byron wasn't a fantasy.

"Relax, Nora," he said. "Lots of women fall for cads."

"I don't."

"You did. At least for a little while."

If she stayed there, she *would* skin him. Or fall for his roguish charms all over again.

"But I promise," he went on, "that I won't tell anyone you were human once for a few weeks. I'll keep your secret, Nora." Then his eyes darkened, and he added, "Until you decide you want to tell the whole world yourself that you're human after all."

Spotting Cliff and Liza out on the lodge's veranda kept Nora from an appropriately physical reaction. She wasn't a violent person. She wasn't even remotely homicidal. She just wanted Byron Sanders Forrester out of her life.

But his brother was about to marry one of Tyler's first citizens.

Byron, Nora thought miserably as she trudged up the path, pretending she hadn't heard that last gibe, would haunt her *forever.*

As BYRON WATCHED NORA in full retreat, a sudden, brisk wind blew off the lake and chilled him to the bone. It was like a parting shot from the owner of Gates Department Store, warning him to keep his distance.

Well, he thought, too late.

"Coffee's ready," Liza Baron yelled from the porch. "Lunch'll be ready in a bit."

Byron was torn. Given his reception, he wished he'd ignored Liza's invitation to the wedding and had waited to hear from Cliff himself. The least he could have done was to have worked up the guts to tell Nora the truth last night. Not that she'd given him the chance. There'd been the book of Beethoven sonatas, the beefy piano student. His own unexpected reaction to a woman he'd slept with for a couple of weeks one past summer—which was how he'd tried, mostly unsuccessfully, to think of her the past three years. Standing in her dining room last night, watching her just now in the cold light of day, he'd remembered how very much he'd loved her. Leaving her with so much unsaid, with all the promise of what they could have been together unfulfilled, had been one of the hardest things he'd ever had to do. And also one of the most important. If he'd stayed, he'd have risked destroying any hope for Cliff.

"What to do, what to do," he mused, watching the sunlight catch the cool shades of Nora's hair, making it shine.

He wondered if he would be doing everyone a favor—including himself—if he just headed back to his campsite, packed up and got the hell out of Tyler.

"Are you coming?" Liza yelled.

"In a minute."

And he trotted back to his musty tent, threw things into his nonexecutive-looking duffel in a flurry of purpose and action. Then came the cry of geese and another chilly gust off the lake, and he collapsed on Cliff's rock and thought, the hell with it. What was waiting for him back in Providence? Another smarmy phone call from another author who actually wanted to make a living at his writing? More dubious looks from Mrs. Redbacker? More mornings tossing darts?

No, he thought. He wanted this time with his brother. He wanted to get to know Cliff Forrester all over again.

And Nora Gates.

He wanted this time with her, too. God help him, but he wanted to get to know her all over again, just to find out if what he was feeling right now was real. If what he'd done three years ago *had* been right for her, too.

He sighed, skimming a rock out onto the lake. What he was feeling right now was regret. For the lies, the choices he'd made, the time lost. And desire. There was no question he was feeling a good dose of desire for the gray-eyed woman he'd loved so many, many months ago.

He was also damned hungry, he thought, climbing stiffly to his feet.

By the time he joined Cliff and Liza on the veranda, Nora was long gone and they had put together a simple but fabulous lunch. There was ham and Wisconsin cheese on locally made sourdough rye bread, sliced fresh tomatoes—the last vine-ripened tomatoes of the season, which Liza herself had tucked away—and leftover cranberry-apple crisp, made, of course with Wisconsin cranberries and apples.

It was almost—but not quite—too cold to eat outside.

"Nora left?" Liza asked.

Byron shrugged, trying to seem neutral on the subject of Nora Gates. "Apparently."

"You two chitchatted quite a while. She knows you?"

"Me?"

"Yeah. She thought she recognized you."

"Did she?" He stabbed a slice of tomato with a fork. "She didn't say anything. Mostly we talked about the geese."

"Uh-huh."

Liza didn't sound convinced. Cliff eyed his brother, then looked away. "I've got a few things I need to get done." Without another word, he took off with his sandwich and a cup of coffee.

If Liza was annoyed by her fiancé's abrupt departure or her future brother-in-law's sidestepping her questions, she gave no indication. She did not, Byron decided, have a suspicious, devious mind. He already found himself admiring her energy and optimistic nature, and it was easy to see how much she was in love with his older brother.

Unfolding her long legs from under her on her wicker chair, she planted her feet on the newly painted veranda floor. "So, Byron," she said, "do you think your brother's going to string me up for sending you and your mother that invitation?"

"Did he say he would?"

She grinned. "No, but I got the drift."

"I'd have warned you I was coming, but you didn't include an address or number—"

"Intentionally. I figured I'd just strike the match and see if I could start a fire. You want some more coffee?"

She was, obviously, a woman who didn't look back. "No, thanks, this is fine."

"Cliff didn't tell me he saw you last night."

She spoke without defensiveness or anger. She was a confident woman, too, and sure of Cliff's love for her. Whatever Cliff's reasons for ducking out, they had nothing to do with his relationship with Liza Baron. That was rock solid. Byron had been concerned his brother might have fallen for a woman who'd pity him and indulge his isolation, who'd coddle him and exacerbate his problems. Liza Baron, however, was clearly not that kind of woman.

"We needed to talk first," Byron said.

"Have you?"

"Some. Not enough."

Liza nodded. "I guess you two seeing each other for the first time in so many years must be about as unsettling as my coming back to Tyler to live and all. And it's gotta be a lot tougher."

Byron didn't speak. It *was* tough to see Cliff—and Nora—and not know how it would turn out.

"How come you're here so early?" Liza asked baldly.

"Let's just say I'm on an advance scouting mission."

Liza slapped what must have been another tablespoon of spicy mustard onto her sandwich. "In case Cliff was marrying some fruitcake or had gone nuts altogether?"

Byron smiled. "Something like that."

"Well," she said, jumping to her feet, "we're both probably crazy as hell, but not in the way most people think. Byron..." She paused, suddenly serious. "Byron, I'm worried about Cliff—that I'm making him bite off more than he can chew at one time. Mother says I need to go easy, but then she so obviously wants this big wedding—and then *I* go and meddle in Cliff's relationship with his family. I mean, not too many weeks ago he was living up here like a damned timber wolf."

"I can leave," Byron said.

"No, that'd be the worst thing you could do. The horse is already out of the barn, as the saying goes. I mean, you're here, Byron." She looked in the direction Cliff had gone and said, almost to herself, "I ache for him sometimes." Then she turned to Byron and smiled, her eyes shining with tears. "And he hates it."

"What do you want me to do?"

"For starters, move out of that damned tent. Looks terrible to have you camping out at the lake. People will think you're another recluse like Cliff and the whole damned Forrester family's nuts. We've got to find you a regular place to stay until the wedding."

"I don't mind camping—"

"*I* mind. The gossip mill in this town's grinding me and my family to pieces enough without having my future brother-in-law washing his face in the lake. Can you imagine the morning of the wedding? This is going to be one fancy shindig, you know. It just won't do to have you show up smelling like a musty old tent."

Byron laughed; Liza did have a way about her. "I won't stay here with you two, so don't even try that one on me again. In fact, I wasn't planning to stay at all. The wedding's not until next Saturday." He thought of his nonrefundable ticket and his Yankee soul almost rebelled, but he added, "I'll come back."

Liza frowned, scrutinizing him. "Business to tend?"

"No, but—"

"Then stay. Unless," she said, obviously well aware she wasn't being told everything, "there's some compelling reason you can't."

The reason had just gone screaming back to town. No, Byron thought, not screaming. Not Nora. She did everything purposefully, deliberately. He'd bet she'd never gone over the speed limit in her life. The one time she'd been out of control had been with him, which was why she hated his guts. And also because he'd behaved rather badly toward her, but that was another matter.

His momentary distraction had given Liza enough time to come up with an impulsive idea. "Hey—why don't I ask Nora to put you up? She's anxious to give me a hand, and from what I hear she's a great hostess. She lives alone, so she loves to have company."

Byron didn't believe it necessarily followed that one who lived alone loved to have company, but he didn't disabuse Liza of that point. "Nora Gates, you mean?" he asked as innocently as he could, considering he'd not *that* long ago slept with the woman.

Nevertheless, he wasn't an altogether inefficient liar. "I could never ask her—"

"I could. Leave everything to me."

"People could get the wrong idea—"

"Good!" Liza was grinning, warming to her solution. "It'd do Nora's reputation a world of good to have a little dirty talk circulating about her. Gosh, people have already started calling her Aunt Ellie. You never knew her, but she's a legend in Tyler. She started Gates Department Store. Nora takes after her, but she's...I don't know, she's *not* Aunt Ellie. It was just the two of them for so many years, and now Nora's alone...." Her voice trailed off, as she nodded to herself. "Yeah, I like this idea. I'll let you know what she says."

And she was off, serape flying. In another minute, Byron heard her white T-bird roar to a start.

"She's tough when she latches on to an idea," Cliff commented, coming onto the veranda.

Byron set his empty cranberry-apple-crisp plate on the lunch tray. "Nora will choke on her teeth when Liza asks her to put me up."

Cliff raised his dark eyes to his brother. "Don't be too sure. I saw the way she looked at you. What went on between you two three years ago?"

"Doesn't matter. Right now she'd like nothing better than to have my head stuffed and mounted on her dining room wall."

Cliff gave a small smile. "Not your head, I think."

"Very funny." But his brother was perhaps more astute than Byron wanted to admit. Nora Gates could have forgiven any number of transgressions, any number of things he might have done to her. But he hadn't done any number of things. He'd made love to her. With her. He groaned just thinking about it. "It won't work, Cliff. You and Liza don't need me here. I shouldn't have come back until I knew for sure you were ready."

"I'm ready. Liza knew before I did." Cliff plopped down in her chair. "The question is, are you?"

Byron didn't answer. "Why didn't you stay for lunch?"

"Needed to think. Things are just shy of getting out of hand around here. I needed to get a grip. The wedding's enough of an ordeal...the crowds..." Expressionless, he looked out at the lake. "I didn't expect you. Even less you and Nora." He looked at his brother. "I had no idea you were here three years ago."

"You weren't supposed to."

"You were protecting me?" he asked bitterly.

Byron shook his head, wanting to explain, but Cliff had already jumped to his feet and was heading off the veranda. "I don't want to argue," Byron said.

"Then don't. Come on, I'll show you around the lodge."

Byron didn't budge. "What about Nora? Cliff, she'll never agree to put me up. Liza will want to know why—"

"Liza can be very persuasive when she wants something." Cliff smiled that twitching smile. "Look at me."

"What is it about Tyler that breeds such women?"

"Long, hard winters, I think."

"You don't believe Nora will turn Liza down?"

Cliff shook his head. "If nothing else, she'll want to save face."

"Well, you're crazy."

"So people say."

But Clifton Pierce Forrester, Byron could now see, was not in any way, shape or form mentally unbalanced. Which wasn't to say that his years of suffering and isolation hadn't taken their toll. So had the recent activity around him—the people activity. Byron guessed that a part of his brother wanted to bolt, and perhaps only his overwhelming love for Liza Baron was keeping him from finding another place to hide, retreating from the world he and Liza were building for themselves.

Instinctively, abruptly, Byron knew that Cliff needed him to stay in Tyler. Just as, three years ago, he'd known that Cliff had needed him to leave. No, not just leave. Never to have come at all. It was a fine distinction, but one that mattered. Whether Cliff would see that or not, Byron wasn't prepared to say.

He found himself giving in, nodding. "Okay—let's have the grand tour of where you've been hiding all these years."

"Not hiding," Cliff said. "Healing."

CHAPTER SIX

IT WAS LATE OCTOBER in Wisconsin and night came early. Too early as far as Byron was concerned. Parked outside Nora Gates's house, he checked his car clock. It wasn't even seven yet. He had the whole damned evening still ahead of him.

"She said she'd be glad to have you over," Liza had told him victoriously upon her return to the lodge. She hadn't even been gone an hour. "You're to be at her house for dinner at seven sharp. See, didn't I tell you? Gosh, she's just the *nicest* woman."

Byron had wondered if he were Nora's intended main course. Roasted publisher. He knew writers— and a few editors—with Pierce & Rothchilde who'd share such a fantasy.

He thought Nora Gates was a lot of things, but *nice* wasn't among them.

His brother had been no help. "You and Nora have things you need to settle. Maybe it's a good idea to throw you two together for a while."

Byron had laughed. "Cliff, that's like throwing a spider and a fly together to see if they'll get along. They just won't. It's a matter of nature."

"Who's the fly and who's the spider?"

Byron left his gear—which Cliff had shoved at him when he'd told him to go, confront Nora like a man, not a fly—in his rented car. The wind had kicked up and it was damned cold on Nora's pretty tree-lined street. He walked up onto the front porch. It was such a peaceful place. Why the hell was he looking for booby traps? *You made her hate you. Now reap what you sowed.*

A tall, skinny boy, probably about thirteen, was shuffling out the door. "I promise I'll do better next week, Miss Gates. I haven't had much time to practice with it being footfall season."

"Lars," Nora said, "you're not on the football team."

From the looks of him, Byron thought, he never would be. "I know," the kid said, "but I watch practice every chance I get. I want to go out for the team next year."

"We all have a variety of interests, Lars," Nora, still out of view, said patiently. "The trick is to find a balance that works. You're wasting your parents' money and your time—and, I might add, a considerable amount of natural talent—if you don't practice."

"Right, Miss Gates, I understand. I'll do better."

As Lars came out onto the porch, Nora moved into the doorway, holding open the screen door. She had on charcoal-gray corduroys and a roll-neck charcoal-gray sweater. With her hair swept up off her face, she looked controlled, in charge of her world and very, very attractive. "I hope you do because—" She spotted Byron and straightened up, stiffening noticeably. "Oh, you're here."

All in all, it was the sort of greeting he'd expected.

"Who're you?" the kid asked boldly.

"My name's Byron Forrester."

"He's my houseguest," Nora put in, without enthusiasm. "Byron, this is Lars Travis, one of my piano students."

The kid's eyes had lit up. "Gee, Miss Gates, I had no idea— I mean, everybody in town thinks you don't . . . that you'd never . . ."

"Mr. Forrester is in Tyler for Liza Baron and Cliff Forrester's wedding next Saturday," Nora said, spots of color high in each of her creamy cheeks. "With Timberlake Lodge being renovated, I agreed to have Byron stay here. He's Cliff's brother. Now, Lars, don't get any ideas."

"No, I won't, Miss Gates. I just was surprised because I didn't think you knew any men."

And he scampered off the porch, all bony arms and legs, before Nora could strangle him.

She watched the kid go with narrowed eyes. "I'm doomed. Lars has the biggest mouth in town next to Tisha Olsen and maybe Inger Hansen, and he has very peculiar ideas about me. You'd sometimes think I'm not human."

"Isn't that what you want people to think?" Byron asked casually.

She transferred her piercing gaze to him. "You're not going to make this any easier, are you?"

"You didn't have to take me in."

"I realize that."

"Then why did you? If it's just because you didn't want to disappoint Liza, you can damned well forget it. Nora...dammit, I'm tired of thinking you've got a stiletto tucked somewhere and are going to do me in at any moment. I came to Tyler three years ago, I fell for you, you fell for me, I neglected to tell you my real name, and now I'm back. I can't change history."

"I'm not asking you to," she said softly, "and I didn't agree to take you in just so I wouldn't disappoint Liza." She smiled mysteriously. "And I don't have a stiletto hidden on me."

"A blowtorch?"

"Too big."

"Nora..."

"Come inside, Byron. It's getting cold out. Where are your bags?"

"Nora, I won't stay if you—"

"I'm doing this for myself, Byron," she said, cutting him off. "Not for you, not for Liza, not even for Cliff. Nobody manipulated me or talked me into anything. If you'll recall, I do know my own mind. Now, I've got dinner in the oven."

She walked briskly past him down to the street and reached into the passenger seat of his car, pulling out his disreputable-looking duffel. She made a face. When he was traveling on behalf of Pierce & Roth-childe, he took matching monogrammed bags. Mrs. Redbacker insisted. Nora would have approved.

She carried the duffel back up onto the porch as if it were something dead and smelly she'd found out on her street. Byron didn't offer her a hand. Some things Nora Gates just preferred to do herself.

"You'll have to move your car," she said.

"Neighbors might talk?"

"The street sweepers are doing a special leaf pickup tomorrow."

"Nora..." He leaned against a porch column. "Thanks."

In the harsh light of the porch, he could see the tiny lines at the corners of her eyes and where her raspberry lipstick had worn off, but she looked better than she had three years ago. Not as gaunt, not as uncertain of her own future. He'd have told her so if it wouldn't have infuriated her to have him notice such things. She liked to think men only respected her. And mostly they did. But sometimes they thought about her in other ways, too. Anyway, he did.

He held open the screen door for her. She didn't complain. "I'm putting you in the front bedroom upstairs," she said. "It gets nice morning sun."

"I was expecting the torture chamber."

She shot him a look, but he thought he detected a hint of amusement in her pale eyes. "A pity I don't have one."

"Going to skewer me in my sleep?"

"I'm not going near you in your sleep," she said, dashing inside before he could see if she'd blushed. Not that there was much chance of that. Their lovemaking didn't embarrass her nearly as much as it ticked her off, challenging her most cherished beliefs about herself. She *wasn't* another Aunt Ellie.

She dumped his bag on the bottom step leading upstairs. It was heavier than it looked, and she was breathing hard, as much from the tension of having him there, he felt, as from exertion. "I'll get dinner on the table. You can find your way?"

"I remember," he said in a low voice.

"Maybe," she said starchily, "it would be better if you didn't."

"No. It wouldn't."

His sincerity seemed to have no discernible impact on her. She marched off to the kitchen, leaving him to fend for himself. The front bedroom was the guest room and always had been, from the time Aunt Ellie had had the house built. Nora had moved into the back bedroom overlooking the gardens and yard when she was thirteen. It was where she and Byron had made love, after Aunt Ellie had gone into the hospital. She'd made it home to die. By then, Byron had left Tyler.

The guest room hadn't changed, the senior Eleanora Gates's fussier taste in evidence. The curtains were filmy lace, the bed a four-poster with a lace dust ruffle, lace coverlet, lace pillow shams. There was a tiger-maple bureau with a matching mirror, and an Oriental rug of vivid roses and blues.

Byron couldn't resist: he went across the hall and had a peek. Nora obviously had moved downstairs, and her old room was completely different. It was as if she'd wanted to exorcise the girl she'd been there, the woman she'd become. She'd installed two twin beds, covered with utilitarian quilts, and painted chests, a painted trunk and a children's table and chairs set up with teddy bears at a tea party. Nora had said she'd make a great aunt. Apparently not having any nieces and nephews of her own hadn't stopped her. What had Liza said? People in town were already starting to call her Aunt Ellie. That was fine, if it was what Nora wanted.

He thought better of tossing his duffel up on the lacy bed and instead shoved it into the closet, which had potpourri sachets hanging from hooks. He'd unpack later, if at all. If worse came to worst, he'd find himself a park bench.

Down in the kitchen, Nora had set the table with a simple but tempting meal of roast turkey breast, baked acorn squash and tossed salad. Byron could smell apples baking in the oven. His stomach flip-flopped on him; he hadn't had anything like this in his life in years. Ever since his return to Pierce & Rothchilde three months ago, he'd found himself relying on Providence restaurants and take-out gourmet.

"You didn't have to go to any trouble on my account," he said.

"I didn't. I always make proper meals for myself, and I set the table every night. Just because I live alone doesn't mean I don't lead a civilized life."

"Whoa, there. Don't forget that I live alone, too."

"In a tent," she sneered.

Byron raised a brow. "You've been keeping track of me?"

"The store carried your last book. Naturally I couldn't resist a peek at your bio—which I presume wasn't *all* lies?"

A year ago, he'd had a slender volume of his photographs published by a small press—he'd refused to pull any strings at Pierce & Rothchilde. The distribution was nil and there wasn't a chance that it would have been accidentally or casually picked up by a department store with a small book section. It would have had to have been special-ordered. But giving that Nora was putting him up—and had a carving knife in her hand—Byron decided not to press the issue.

"It wasn't any of it lies," he said, sitting in the chair she pointed at with her knife.

"Your name—"

"I used Byron Sanders as a pseudonym, that's all. It's a common practice."

"The bio said you'd spent the previous two years crisscrossing the country and some of Canada and Mexico, living out of your van and a tent."

"Pretty much true."

She set down her knife and laid slices of steaming turkey on a small platter, which she set in the middle of the table. "Byron Sanders is 'pretty much' your own name, too, but it hardly tells the whole story."

"Do you ever let anything go?"

"Seldom."

"By 'pretty much' I only mean that I also had the family place in Providence." He lifted half an acorn squash, dripping with butter and brown sugar, onto his plate. "My mother's away frequently, and it's...

spacious.'' Telling her it was a mansion, he decided, would further undermine the myths Nora had created about him and would not, given the timing, be wise. "So it's not as if I had no place to go but my van and tent."

"I see. Can't let life get too tough, huh?"

He frowned. "Nora, if you don't lighten up you're going to get indigestion. And give me indigestion while you're at it."

But she smiled suddenly, her entire face brightening. It was the way he most liked to remember her, when she was at her most captivating. He'd never really understood what made Nora Gates smile. "Byron, I was kidding. A bit sensitive about this family place, hmm? Must be something. But I don't care if it was designed by Charles Bulfinch, has the best view of the Atlantic in Providence and is the next fanciest thing to the Ritz on the East Coast. As Aunt Ellie used to say, it makes no never mind to me."

Byron chose not to tell her how damned close she'd come to describing the Pierce house on Benefit Street in Providence, Rhode Island.

Her expression turned serious. "The book...your photographs were wonderful, Byron. I mean that."

"Thank you."

Despite its modest sales, his book had won a couple of prestigious awards, individual photographs other smaller rewards. His subject had been fathers and sons. He'd traveled from small town to big city, in search of the extraordinarily ordinary. And he'd found it, time and time again. His work, his years of being on the road, neither a Pierce nor a Forrester, had helped him make himself whole again.

"When you came to Tyler," Nora said, sitting across from him, "you weren't a professional photographer, were you?"

"I'm still not."

"Then what did you...what do you do for a living?"

She asked the question as if she already knew she wouldn't like the answer. Anyone else, Byron thought, would have squirmed having to face those incisive eyes. But Nora Gates didn't intimidate him; none of the little ways she kept people at a comfortable distance—or men, anyway—worked with him.

Which still didn't mean she'd like his answer.

"I was president...I *am* president of Pierce & Rothchilde, Publishers."

She didn't throw anything. She just leaned back, fork in hand, and narrowed her eyes at him.

"What are you doing?" he asked.

"Trying to picture you in pinstripes."

"Oh, pinstripes are much too racy for P & R."

"But..." She scooped a piece of squash onto her plate, stabbed some turkey. "Then I assume you have a business background or some sort of training."

He nodded matter-of-factly. "A Harvard M.B.A. Being the great-grandson of Clifton Rutherford Pierce—P & R's founder—hasn't hurt any, either."

She inhaled, and he could see her revising her thoughts. First, she'd had to adjust to his being the younger brother of the reclusive man up at Timberlake Lodge. Now she had to adjust to his not being the disreputable, uneducated, incorrigible heel of a photographer she'd imagined he was three years ago. Mostly it *had* been her imagination; he'd never told her all that much about himself. He hadn't lied so much as omitted pertinent details.

"You quit to do your book?" she asked.

"I took a leave of absence after I came to Tyler."

"For how long? I mean, are you going back?"

"I have gone back," he said.

"So you're president of one of the most prestigious publishing houses in the country?"

There was no way around it. "Yes."

"Well," she said, and muttered something about having forgotten the cranberry sauce. She got a small bowl from the fridge and sat back down, changing the subject to the fate of the Tyler Titans, the high school football team, in their latest game, and how Ricky and Lars Travis were both talented pianists but so different. Finally, she looked at him and said, "Harvard, huh?"

"Yep."

"Well, that makes everything easier."

"How so?"

"You're not the man you were three years ago. You're someone else. You're Byron Sanders Forrester, East Coast blue blood, amateur photographer, president of Pierce & Rothchilde, Publishers—I don't know. You're just not the Byron I saw staring at me in Gates's window that summer. I guess..." She paused, swallowing a piece of turkey. "I guess in a way that Byron doesn't exist."

He leaned back. "Nice try, Nora."

"I beg your pardon?"

"It won't work. You can't erase me. You can't press a damned delete button and just eliminate me." He pushed back his chair and leaned over the table, so that he could almost feel her breath on him. "I am the same man who slipped your bra off that night in the tent. It was lace—it had a front clasp. I'm the same man who kissed the little mole on your stomach. I'm the same man who went skinny-dipping with you in that swimming hole in the stream—"

"Stop!"

"I'm the man who made love to you, Nora Gates."

She jumped to her feet. "Leave the dishes. I'll—"

"I'm not a dead file you can just clear out of your cabinet."

"I'll do them when I get back. I take a fitness walk most evenings."

He turned around in his chair so he could see her sneak across her kitchen. "I'm not somebody you made up one summer."

She smiled coolly, distantly. "Make yourself at home— I won't be long."

She was already at the kitchen door. Byron tilted his chair back on two legs. "You know," he said, not cool, not distant, "you should be thanking your lucky stars I do exist. In fact, you're damned lucky I turned up in Tyler again."

Only her eyes—as always—betrayed her intensity.
"I fail to see why."

"Because, Miss Gates," he said, "you're trying to become something you're not."

"And what, pray tell, is that?"

"Your Aunt Ellie."

He could see her swallow. "You're wrong."

"Am I?" he asked gently.

"Yes." She looked away. "Anyway, we're not discussing me. Three years ago, you tried to be something you weren't. Don't try to resurrect Byron Sanders now. It won't work."

"I don't know," he mused, setting his chair back down on four legs. If she wouldn't talk about Aunt Ellie, he couldn't make her. "That haughty way you talk...I think you've been spending too much time rereading Jane Austen and the Brontë sisters."

"You can be such a jerk, you know that?"

"That's better. Thought you might call me an 'incorrigible rake' or a 'dastardly fellow'—"

He didn't see it coming. He was still thinking Jane Austen when he noticed the cookbook flying through the air; she'd snatched it from a shelf by the door and launched it before he could react. It missed by far fewer inches than the Beethoven had.

Byron laughed, reassured. He'd thought for a second that mentioning Aunt Ellie had only reminded Nora that she wasn't behaving the way she figured she ought to behave. But if she was back to throwing things, she was at least letting her emotions, however raw, rip. "Look at it this way—my being here will improve your aim."

And she was off, wishing out loud that her life *did* have a delete button so she could send him into the electronic ether. Byron was unreasonably glad that she at least wasn't neutral on the subject of her ex-lover.

Suddenly he was ravenous. Reaching across the table he grabbed Nora's plate and finished off her dinner. Then, half to annoy her, half because he'd been taught to be a proper guest, he did up the dishes.

But that wasn't the only reason he did them. Washing the dishes was one way of staking out territory in whatever relationship they were to have in the days until Cliff and Liza's wedding—and beyond. He wasn't just Nora's guest. He wasn't an old friend. And he sure as hell wasn't somebody who hadn't *existed* one August three years ago. He was a man who'd loved her, and there was no way either of them could deny it.

There was no way, either, he thought, scrounging in her kitchen drawers for aluminum foil, that he could deny it would be all too easy to fall in love with Nora all over again. What was it about the woman?

He found the foil, then tripped over the book she'd pitched at him. It was a low-fat, low-everything cookbook. Snatching it up, he grumbled aloud that there wasn't *anything* about that unforgiving prude that should attract a solid, reasonable, nonself-destructive man such as himself. Was she just a challenge to him? Did he want her only because she'd made herself so damned unattainable?

"You are out of your mind, my man," he muttered. "You've no business wanting that gray-eyed witch."

But then he could see those gray eyes fill with unspoken pain, with loss and grief, and love, when he'd mentioned Aunt Ellie, and nothing, he knew, would ever be simple or easy when it came to his feelings for Nora Gates.

AFTER HER TENSE and over-long day, Nora returned from her brisk three-mile walk relaxed, if also tired and cold and a bit chastened. She could warm her hands in a pan of dishwater and soothe her soul with a good book and an early lights-out. But Byron had already done the dishes. He'd even slipped her cookbook back into its slot on the shelf. Looking at its torn cover reminded her of her fit of anger, but that was over now. She wouldn't let him get to her like that again.

She found him in the study, where he had a fire going in her brick fireplace. He was sitting on the carpet in front of the fire, his long legs stretched out in front of him, just staring at the flames. He seemed unaware that she'd come in.

"Thank you for doing the dishes," she said.

He glanced up at her; she hadn't moved from the doorway. "You don't have to thank me. How was your walk?"

"Invigorating." She licked her lips, suddenly unsure if she should go any further. She'd done some thinking on her walk. A lot of thinking. "I haven't been very grown-up about your being back in Tyler. I mean, throwing things *is* a bit puerile...."

"Puerile? Haven't heard that word in years. Look, Nora, I don't mind honest emotion—in fact, I'm glad you can be yourself when you're around me. And you'd never get so out of control as to hurt me...."

She almost smiled. "You always have been an optimist. I do admire that about you—and your sense of humor. Most of the time, anyway." She cleared her throat, wondering if launching down the perilous path of being amiable with Byron had been a smart idea. But here she was. "You've made it clear that your lying about your name had nothing to do with me—that things you didn't tell me three years ago were ... well, you know. It's over. I see no reason why we can't go on from here and at least be civil to each other."

"I haven't thrown anything at you."

He did know how to upset her equilibrium. "That's true, but you can't deny that you've deliberately tried to provoke me."

"Okay. I won't deny it."

"Byron..." She sighed, breaking off. "Never mind. I've had a long day. If you don't need anything from me, I'd like to turn in, do some reading."

"Jane Austen?"

"Byron ... !"

He smiled. "Sweet dreams, Miss Gates."

She did not have sweet dreams. She dreamed about him again. Aunt Ellie was still alive, grinning her toothy grin as Nora and Byron made dinner together, laughing and chopping carrots as if the three of them were a happy, if unorthodox, family. Spinster businesswoman, orphaned niece, wandering photographer. The dream made no sense. It took place in the present, although Aunt Ellie had been dead for three years, and she'd seemed to like Byron, enjoy his company, although how could she? He'd lied to her, too. But the discrepancies didn't strike Nora until she woke up with a start, heart pounding, for the dream had ended—abruptly—with Byron kissing a silver band on Nora's finger.

"Perish the thought."

It was rather like coming to amid a nightmare in which one was tumbling from an airplane without a parachute.

Throwing on her chamois bathrobe, she was out in the kitchen before she remembered that part of her dream was true: Byron *was* back in Tyler. And in a fit of madness, she'd agreed to have him as her houseguest.

"Oh, Lord."

He had a pot of coffee on already and was digging in her refrigerator, plaid shirttail hanging out over jeans that after years of wear fit comfortably over the muscular contours of his hips and legs. He was barefoot. He grinned a good-morning over his shoulder, and she saw that his hair was still tousled from sleep. His jawline was a sexy shadow of dark beard. He looked every bit the rakish photographer, but she quickly adjusted her image. He was the president of an East Coast publishing house. He'd been born with the proverbial silver spoon in his mouth. To him, Gates

Department Store—Aunt Ellie's labor of love, her dream, her creation—was probably quaint. Nora realized, with a pang, that she didn't know this man—that she had no right to hate him.

"Eggs for breakfast?" he asked.

"I don't eat eggs and you don't need to make me breakfast."

"Egad, what's this? Eggs in a bottle?"

"It's an egg substitute. Byron, I don't permit houseguests to rummage at will in my refrigerator."

He pushed aside her liquid egg substitute as if he'd found a moldy leftover. "What do you usually eat in the morning?"

"Oatmeal and raisins. Now out—"

"Okay." He rose, making her kitchen seem smaller with his size and the sheer force of his presence. Nora wasn't used to having anyone around in the morning, not even a cat. When she had guests, she kept them out of the kitchen until she had breakfast ready. "Oatmeal it is. No raisins, though. You use brown sugar?"

She shook her head. He hadn't buttoned his shirt all the way and what buttons he had done up were crooked. It was impossibly sexy. She could see curls of dark hair poking out. "I'll cook," she said.

"Nope. You sit. It's Saturday morning and I've put you through hell the past two nights." He laughed. "Bad choice of words. 'Yesterday and the previous evening' sounds less scandalous, hmm? I won't judge your nights."

"Are you making fun of me?"

He poured her a cup of coffee and set it on the table, although she'd yet to sit down. "Never."

"Ha."

"You take your coffee black, right?"

"I'm surprised you remember."

He looked at her. "You shouldn't be."

At that, it was either sit or get out of there so she could collapse in private. She couldn't stand around feeling out of place in her own kitchen. She tried the coffee. It was strong enough to pave a driveway, probably exactly what she needed. Byron got out the oatmeal, measuring cups, a pan. He studied the carton, frowning.

"Recipe's on the inside of the top now," she said.

"Ahh. Haven't made oatmeal in a while."

"You eat eggs every morning?" Then she remembered his background. "Oh. I suppose you have a housekeeper."

"No housekeeper, and I don't eat eggs every morning. I'll often grab a bagel or a muffin or just make toast."

In his tent, the morning after they'd first made love, they'd shared little boxes of cereal. They'd cut the boxes open with his jackknife and poured the milk inside and eaten with plastic spoons. It had been the most romantic breakfast Nora had ever had. Sometimes she wished she could forget it.

"What're you doing today?" he asked.

"I'll stop by the store. Then I have some errands to run. You?"

"I need to see Cliff—he's got to be rattled with all that's going on."

"This business with the body can't have helped matters. I wish the Tyler police department would tell us *something*. The rumors...well, they're unpleasant."

Byron's pot of water had come to a boil. He dumped in a couple handfuls of oatmeal, stirred, contemplated the pot, then dumped in a bit more. Nora had made oatmeal hundreds of times, and although she did have the recipe for a single serving memorized, she measured every time.

"Would you tell me what the rumors are?" he asked.

"I hate to repeat gossip."

"That's why everyone tells you everything."

"Not everyone. Those who expect some little tidbit in return tell me nothing. Gossip is a currency for some people." But that wasn't anything Byron didn't know, or cared about. She was just babbling because it was morning, she'd dreamed about him, and he was making oatmeal for her in her own kitchen. "You want to know because of Cliff?"

Byron nodded, and while he kept an eye on the cooking oatmeal, stirring it occasionally, Nora told him what she knew people were saying around town about the Body at the Lake. That it could be Margaret Ingalls. That Judson might have known more than he was letting on. That she'd been murdered. That she'd never run away.

"If nothing else, people say she wouldn't have abandoned Alyssa the way she supposedly did," Nora said.

"That's Margaret's daughter?"

"And Liza's mother."

"Considering what Cliff's been through," Byron said, dumping scoops of oatmeal into two pottery bowls, "this all could cause him to have a relapse. It could stir up nightmarish memories for him."

"Nightmarish memories of what?"

He stared at her. "You don't know?"

She shook her head. "Byron, nobody in Tyler knows anything about Cliff. Lots of people thought he was certifiable until Liza came back. Not a few wonder if—" She stopped herself.

"If Liza's making a mistake?"

"It's just talk."

Byron nodded. "With the added strain of a big wedding and my being here, our mother planning to show up..."

His voice trailed off, but Nora, abandoning thought of getting him to tell her what exactly Cliff Forrester had endured, finished for him. "You're afraid Cliff could throw in the towel—find another Tyler in which to hide."

"I think he's afraid of it, too. Yesterday he started to give me a tour of the lodge, but he couldn't finish. He...he just walked away and started chopping wood. Posttraumatic stress disorder isn't always predictable."

"But he loves Liza."

Byron looked at her. "Exactly."

Nora frowned. "I don't get it."

"I know you don't." He plopped a bowl of oatmeal in front of her. "Come on, let's change the subject and eat breakfast."

He sat across from her with his box of brown sugar. She fetched the raisins. Then, sitting back down, she suddenly couldn't stand it anymore. "Byron . . . your shirt. It's buttoned crooked."

He smiled and reached across the table. "Your robe," he said a little hoarsely, touching its frayed neckline, "is coming undone."

At first she assumed he meant the fabric was getting frayed and worn, but then she realized he meant the tie. It had sagged into her lap, her robe falling open, exposing the filmy pale mauve lacy nightie she'd secreted from the lingerie department after a Valentine Day sale. Her salesclerk had speculated that it hadn't been sold because it was just too racy for Tyler women.

"I think I will try a little brown sugar on my oatmeal," she said.

And Byron Sanders Forrester had the gall to laugh.

CHAPTER SEVEN

WITH ITS SAGGING SHUTTERS and peeling paint, Timberlake Lodge looked downright spooky under the gathering clouds. The wind had picked up. Gusts kicked up dust and fallen leaves. Even for October it was cold. Cliff's truck was parked outside, but not Liza's T-bird. Byron could smell the lake in the fresh country air. He knocked on the front door and waited, the cold penetrating his jacket and navy mock turtleneck. Lunch on the veranda today would be out of the question.

There was no answer. Given the size of the place, Byron wondered whether anyone inside would hear his knock. He tried the door, which was unlocked, and pushed it open. Such liberties were getting to be a bad habit.

No cookbooks or Beethoven sonatas came flying out at him, but that wouldn't be Cliff's style.

"You don't understand, Byron. I could hurt someone."

"Who?"

"You. Mother. I just don't know. I don't... I can't trust myself anymore."

Byron had tried to reassure him. *"I know you, Cliff. You'd never lay a hand on Mother. As for me— I can hold my own with you, big brother. You don't have to worry."*

His brother's eyes had never seemed so impenetrable. *"How can you know me? I don't know myself. That's the whole point, Byron. I just don't know anymore what I would or wouldn't do. That's why you can't trust me. It's why I have to leave."*

"Let me visit."

"No."

"Cliff, don't shut us out."

"I have no choice."

For two years, Byron had kept out of his brother's life. Then, three years ago, he'd come to Tyler, just to see him, and he'd known Cliff had made the right decision, at least for himself. His only hope was time. Yet, even now, with him on the verge of marrying, Byron wasn't sure his brother wanted him back in his life.

When no one answered his call, he shut the door and walked back down the porch, ignoring the blustery wind, the sprinkle of rain, the wrenching in his gut. Being back in Tyler reminded him all too vividly of how close he'd come three years ago, of how much he'd lost. He'd had so much in his grasp—his brother, a woman he'd loved, stability. And he'd let them go. Cliff, Nora, Tyler itself. He'd left thinking they were gone forever. He'd missed his chance, even if he'd had no choice but to leave.

"Hey, Brother."

He spun around, and there was Cliff, leaning on an ax handle. Sweat poured off him despite the cold, and there were wood chips in his hair. Byron noticed the holes in his jeans, the bald spots in his chamois shirt. His brother the recluse. But even as kids, Cliff had worn whatever was handy.

"I was just giving up on you," Byron said.

His brother's dark eyes flickered. "Not you, Byron. You'd never give up on me." He pulled out a folded black bandanna and wiped the sweat off his forehead. "Liza's off to town. She's got some woman sewing a wedding dress for her. You know, she makes a show of hating all these wedding traditions, but I think deep down she's having a ball."

"You?"

Cliff shrugged. "Seeing her happy is important to me. I'll do what I need to do." He swung the ax onto his shoulder. "Come on, let's take a walk."

The prospect of an imminent rainstorm didn't seem to bother him. For all Byron knew, his brother hadn't started sleeping in the lodge until Liza arrived. They headed out across the driveway toward the lake. The occasional sprinkles had increased to a fine mist.

"How're you and Nora getting on?" Cliff asked, leading the way.

"I lived through the night."

He hadn't slept much, however. He'd lain amid the lace and fluff thinking about how sexy and beautiful Nora had looked standing on the study threshold. Freshly showered with her almond-scented soap, he'd stared wide-eyed at the ceiling and let himself remember every detail of the first time they'd made love, in his tent too long ago. He'd let himself remember how much he'd loved her. How painful it had been to leave. Yet how could he have stayed? Even Aunt Ellie had understood his dilemma. And for the first time, Byron thought he himself truly understood if not what his brother had been through, at least the suffering he'd endured when he'd come home that one time and known he couldn't stay.

"Cliff—she has good reason to hate me."

They'd come to the lake, its waters gray and choppy, a warning of the impending storm. Cliff started along a narrow, rocky path that wound along the shoreline. "I figured as much."

"I promised never to tell anyone what happened between us three years ago."

"Then don't."

Byron sighed. "Thanks. I thought you might insist."

"Nope. I might be something of a hermit, Brother, but I'm not a fool."

Cliff turned off the path and walked out onto a decrepit boat dock, one with more boards missing or rotting than intact and solid. Byron followed, stepping where his brother had stepped. Fat drops of rain struck him on the head and hand. Cliff didn't seem to notice. He squinted, looking out at the lake.

"If you hurt her... break her heart again..." His jaw set and he glanced over at Byron. "That wouldn't sit too well with me."

Byron wondered where his brother got his ideas about Nora Gates, considering he'd never even spoken to her until the night before last. Other than Aunt Ellie, Byron bet he knew Tyler's would-be spinster better than anyone. And if he'd broken her heart three years ago, he'd also made it more tolerable for her by giving her reason to hate him.

"Hell, Cliff," he said, avoiding articulating his true mixed-up feelings, "Nora isn't about to let herself fall for anyone. She's got her heart under lock and key. So far as I can see, I did her a favor by leaving Tyler when I did. Ask her yourself. I'll bet she'll tell you the same thing."

Cliff shook his head. "Then you're both deluding yourselves."

"Everyone in town knows she doesn't want anything to do with romance—"

"Doesn't matter. Until a few years ago—" Cliff looked again at his brother "—presumably when you came to town, Nora Gates was sure of herself, knew where she was going, what she wanted out of life. The past few years, she hasn't been the same and I don't care what anybody says. You could look at her and tell she'd lost some of her spark, some of her sense of purpose. Not a lot. She's a survivor. But you could tell she'd had a look at the dark side of life."

Meaning me, Byron thought. "Nah, Cliff, I don't buy it. She's been grieving for her aunt. She'd lost the last close relative who really cared about her. Of course she's been floundering a little. If Aunt Ellie were still alive and I'd hit the road—hell, Nora would have set off fireworks in her front yard."

Cliff looked unconvinced. "Did you leave before or after Aunt Ellie died?"

"Before."

His brother was silent.

"It's what Nora wanted."

"So she'd say."

"Don't underestimate her, Cliff. She knows her own mind. Besides, I thought you didn't want to know the details. If she finds out you've guessed we... that we had something going..."

"She'll have your head."

"And more," Byron added.

Cliff smiled his almost-smile. "She forgets you're my brother. I know you. You were bound to fall for a woman who'd scare the hell out of you." He gave Byron a pointed look. "And naturally you wouldn't notice until it was too late."

Meaning, Byron thought, that Cliff knew he and Nora had made love because Byron was too damned stupid to *not* have made love to her. A change of subject was in order. "Rain's picking up."

"We need it," Cliff said. He swung his ax down off his shoulder, standing it on its head and leaning on the handle, his toes hanging over the edge of the dilapidated dock. "You left three years ago on account of me?"

Byron almost lost his balance at the guilt in his brother's voice, the deeper meaning of his question. He shook his head, being as frank and truthful as he possibly could. "I know what you're saying and no, Cliff—God, no. I don't know how the hell I can explain this, but when I came to Tyler, I saw you only a couple of times and—"

"You spied on me."

"Yeah, sort of."

Cliff squinted out at the lake. "You used to do that when we were little kids. I'd go off with a friend, and next thing I knew, we'd find you up some tree with your binoculars."

"Spies were big in those days. When you caught me, there was hell to pay."

"Lesson didn't take."

Byron grinned. "You didn't always catch me."

His brother didn't look at him. "So you came to Tyler, spied on me and decided I was a brick short of a load."

"No," Byron said, serious now. "What I decided, Cliff, was to respect your wishes and leave you alone. I didn't count on the rest."

"Nora."

"And Aunt Ellie."

"The pictures," Cliff said, understanding. "Nora showed them to me the other night. They're good, Byron. More than good. Not that you need me to tell you."

"It's always nice to hear." Byron, too, found himself staring out at the lake, part of it lost now in the mist and increasing rain. So far, his jacket wasn't soaked through, but his jeans were damp, his hair starting to drip. "Taking those pictures ... knowing

Aunt Ellie, knowing she was dying—and Nora, seeing how much she was grieving... Then you, living alone up here..." Byron looked up at the sky as the rain came harder now, pelting his face. "It was too much. I had nothing to give to anyone. I was empty, Cliff. Just empty."

"Not empty," Cliff said hoarsely. "Hurting too much yourself."

"I wanted to whisk her off and live happily ever after, but... hell, I couldn't make Aunt Ellie young again, I couldn't undo what you'd seen and done in Cambodia, I couldn't bring Dad home. I've never felt so damned helpless. Maybe that's what I needed, to really feel that emptiness, acknowledge that I had my own demons to confront. I don't know. I was so damned afraid of doing the wrong thing—making Aunt Ellie's last days worse, sending you over the edge, making Nora incapable of carrying on alone. It was hell."

Cliff nodded. "I know. It's a lot easier to hurt people and see them hurting if you don't care about them. Byron, you left because you needed to become whole again yourself."

"That's what Aunt Ellie said."

"She was right."

Byron shook his head. "I should have been stronger. I hadn't seen the things you'd seen, I wasn't dying, I wasn't losing the woman who'd taken me in after my parents were killed. God, Cliff, I failed you all."

"That's what Dad said in the end," Cliff said softly, rain streaming down his face, among his tears. "The villagers told me. He set high standards for himself, too. It was painful, knowing how much he'd done, how hard he'd tried, that he'd died thinking he should have done more. Byron, you did your best. Now let it go."

"I could have gone to Southeast Asia with you."

"No."

"If we'd gone together—"

"It wouldn't have made any difference to Dad or to me. And what would Mother have done? Let it go, Byron. For God's sake, don't torture yourself over what you didn't do."

"Have you let go of what you saw, what you did?"

Cliff hesitated, then answered, "It's a part of me. It no longer controls me."

Byron moved shakily off the dock, choosing his steps carefully. He could hear Aunt Ellie, feel her gnarled, cold hand squeezing his. *You have to know who you are, Byron, before you can give yourself to anyone.*

Slipping on the wet, soggy wood, he jumped onto a rock, then onto firm ground, Cliff right behind him. "You didn't explain any of this to Nora?" his brother asked.

"She had enough problems of her own without taking on mine, too."

"What if she wanted to?"

"She didn't. She's leading the life she's always wanted to lead."

"You're sure about that, are you?"

"She is. That's what counts."

"What about you? Are you leading the life you want to lead?"

Byron left the path. The rain was coming down hard now, and he opted for the shortest route between two points, one being where he was, the other being his car. Suddenly he wanted to be alone. "It seemed right to get off the road. I've done some things I'm proud of at P & R. Mostly, though, the job's incredibly routine."

"And you don't fit in."

"Hell, I don't fit in anywhere," he said without rancor.

"Come on," Cliff said, clapping one hand on his brother's shoulder, "let's go back up to the house, get a cup of hot coffee. I know right now you probably are itching to be alone, but that's the last thing you need. Trust me on that one, Brother. Maybe Liza will be back. She's guaranteed to cheer us up."

Byron smiled. "It's good to see you happy."

"Yeah." His brother's dark eyes danced. "It's even better to be happy."

As Cliff had predicted, Liza's T-bird was parked crookedly in the driveway behind the battered truck her grandfather let him drive. She had rock and roll playing on the kitchen radio, the volume turned up high, and was scooping dollops of orange dough into muffin tins. A big pot of coffee was already in the works. She announced pumpkin muffins would be ready in twenty minutes, then, looking around at the rain-soaked brothers, she shook her head.

"You two been talking serious, nasty stuff, huh? Well, shake it loose. Byron, you can get yourself a towel and dry off, and I'll pour you a cup of coffee in my special travel mug, which I most definitely want back."

"You kicking my brother out?" Cliff asked.

Liza grinned. "Sending him on a mission."

Byron was getting suspicious.

"I saw Nora at Barney's just down the road. She rode her bicycle and it's raining cats and dogs out now— I'd have offered her a ride myself, but I'd already blown past her before it registered that it was her out there among the pumpkins and her BMW wasn't with her. Anyway, Byron, you can go fetch her back here for coffee and muffins."

Cliff sat at the table, looking amused. "Liza can be very dictatorial."

"I'm in a rented car," Byron said, thinking that he had to be the last person Nora Gates would want to have rescue her from the rain.

Liza waved off both their remarks as she scraped the last bit of dough from her wooden spoon with her finger. "Oh, so what? Look, Nora doesn't have her head screwed on straight today if she's off hunting pumpkins on a bicycle. And never mind the rain, how's she going to carry pumpkins back in town on a bike?"

Cliff didn't answer and Byron chose not to, seeing how he wasn't, as far as Liza Baron was aware, supposed to really know the somewhat eccentric owner of Gates Department Store.

"Unless what they're saying in town is true," Liza said, popping the muffins into the oven.

Byron's eyes met Cliff's, but neither man spoke.

Liza was having a great time for herself. "Martha Bauer—she's doing my dress for me—says she saw the photographer who did the picture series on Aunt Ellie at the library the other night. Then Tisha Olsen reminded her that his name was Byron Sanders. Then Ricky Travis's little brother, Lars, said something to somebody who told Inger Hansen who told Martha that Nora has a man staying at her house. From his description, Martha figures it was her photographer. Then *she* talked to somebody else—I hope I've got this all straight—who remembered seeing Nora and some man who fit Byron's description having lunch together a few years ago, but who'd dismissed it, thinking he had to be a salesman or something, given that Nora would never be caught dead *dating* a man."

Without a word, Cliff got up, pulled open a drawer and got out two towels, one of which he handed to Byron. The other he used to wipe his face as he watched his finacée.

Byron swallowed hard. "So people are gossiping about Nora?"

"Oh, my, yes," Liza said delightedly. "Lordy, I missed lots of good stuff while I was away. Now everybody's got it figured out."

"Got what figured out?" Cliff asked.

She grinned. "That Byron and Nora were lovers!"

A HALF MILE from Barney's, which had the most extensive selection of pumpkins in or around Tyler, Nora was drenched to the bone and shivering and absolutely certain she'd lost her mind. What had she been thinking when she'd climbed on her bike to go pumpkin hunting in the rain? Even if it hadn't been raining then, she'd known it *would* rain. She listened to the radio weather report every morning.

She recognized Byron's rented car in her handlebar mirror and hoped she was the last person he'd expect to see, bicycling in the rain with a pumpkin tucked under one elbow and a flimsy camouflage poncho whipping out behind her in the wind. Her sweatshirt, turtleneck, bra, underpants, jeans—everything was soaked. And even as small as her pumpkin was, it felt like a lead weight and made steering more difficult and the ride home even more torturous. But she had her pride. She'd gone to Barney's for a pumpkin, and by God, she'd go back with a pumpkin.

She tucked her head inside her poncho hood, but Byron's car pulled up just ahead of her. Unless she wanted to get run over, she had no choice but to stop.

Byron rolled down his window. "Forget your car?"

"No, I—I planned it this way."

"A bike ride with a pumpkin in the driving rain, forty-mile-an-hour winds and fifty-degree temperatures?"

If it was fifty out, she was home under her down comforter. "You don't have to believe me."

"I lie to save my skin, you lie to save face. It's the fundamental difference between us. Want a ride?"

Rain was pouring off her nose. "No, thank you."

Byron frowned, looking handsome if not entirely dry himself. "My instincts tell me to let you drown or freeze—whichever comes first—but I have orders to bring you back to Timberlake Lodge for coffee and pumpkin muffins."

How tempting. Maybe Cliff would build a fire. Liza could lend her dry clothes. But she shook her head. "I have more errands to run."

"Like that? You'll get a reputation."

She would, too. It was the Byron Sanders Forrester effect. "Liza sent you? I wondered if she spotted me." A strong gust of wind blew the rain hard into her face and almost knocked her off her bicycle. *I'm nuts,* she thought. *Completely bonkers.* "I've got to run along."

Byron sighed. "Nora, quit cutting off your nose to spite your face and get in the damned car."

"My bicycle—"

"Leave it in the ditch. You can come back for it later."

"Someone will steal it."

"In this weather? Besides, you couldn't get three bucks for that bomb at a flea market. How old is it?"

"I don't know— Aunt Ellie picked it up for me at a garage sale when I first came to live with her. It was pretty old then."

The driver's door swung open, and Byron got out of the car, grumbling. "I can't believe I'm discussing how old this rusting hunk of junk is while you're out here freezing your lovely behind off. Now, in the car."

She tilted up her chin, her poncho hood falling down her back, not that it had been doing any good. Her hair was dripping. "I won't have you order me about."

"Then consider it a plea. Liza won't give me coffee and muffins if I come back without you."

"Horrors."

"Come on, Nora."

"As you wish, but— Byron, I think my fingers are stuck."

He covered her frozen hand with his, its warmth immediately penetrating the stiff, purple fingers practically glued to her handlebar. She let him take her pumpkin. She began to shiver uncontrollably as she pried her fingers loose. Byron didn't let go of her hand.

"I feel like an idiot," she said, coughing.

"It's that kind of day."

She peeled off her poncho before getting into the car; Byron balled it and shoved it on the floor in back. "I must smell like a wet dog," she said when she climbed next to him in the front.

He smiled. "Just so long as you don't have fleas. Be tough to explain to the rental car folks."

"If you don't mind—coffee and pumpkin muffins sound great, but I'd prefer just to go home."

The rain was coming down now in sheets, and her bicycle crashed over in the wind. Byron collected it and jammed it in the back seat of his car. What had she been thinking when she started pedaling home? At the very least, she should have stayed at Barney's. Maybe, deep down, she'd wanted Byron to rescue her. She'd guessed he was out at the lodge. She'd seen Liza's T-bird streak past her. *I'm not that kind of woman. I left Barney's because I thought I could get home before the worst of the storm hit. Don't make more of this than there is.*

"You okay?" Byron asked.

"Just wet and cold."

He set her pumpkin on the seat between them and started the car. "What's the pumpkin for?"

"This one, not much. I was checking what Barney had in the way of jack-o'-lantern pumpkins. I do a Halloween party every year. Byron, I'm getting your car all wet."

"It'll have time to dry, not that I'd give a damn if it didn't. I wish I had a blanket or something to give you—"

"We'll be home in just a few minutes."

"Right. You're sure you don't want to go back to the lodge? It's closer."

She looked out the passenger window. "I'm humiliated enough as it is."

Byron sighed. "What the hell's so humiliating about getting caught out in the rain?"

When she didn't answer, he pulled out onto the road, but, mercifully, headed toward town rather than turning back toward Timberlake Lodge. Nora tried to relax, but she couldn't. She was too cold, too tired, too aware of Byron so close beside her. She was used to doing things right. Taking care of herself. She didn't need him. She didn't need *anyone.*

"Thank you for the ride," she said finally.

Byron looked at her, his expression virtually impossible to read. "It wasn't my choice." Then he smiled irreverently. "That's supposed to make you feel better."

"So I won't think you were being nice to me on purpose?"

"Seems to annoy the hell out of you when I try."

She said nothing, uncomfortable with the note of wistfulness she detected in his voice, even as his eyes and smile remained hopelessly irreverent. Instead of trying to explain her jumble of contradictory feelings, she pulled off her drenched sweatshirt. Immediately she regretted what she'd done. The turtleneck underneath wasn't of the highest quality, the thin, pearl-gray fabric becoming translucent when wet. She could see the lines of her lace bra, and the outline of her nipples, hard with the cold, the rain, the awareness of the solid man beside her.

"Nora...a week of this..."

There was no point in denying the obvious any longer. "I know."

They arrived at her house. Byron parked along the curb, and before he had the engine turned off, Nora shot out of the car, unlocked the door and dashed in to her room. She peeled off her wet clothes. Despite her purple fingers and toes and her goose bumps, her body felt as if it were on fire. She couldn't remember anything so erotic as feeling that hot and that cold at the same time, at least not in the past three years. If

Byron Forrester walked into her bedroom right now, she'd pounce. There was no question in her mind.

"Nora," he called from out in the hall, "are you all right?"

"Fine!"

"If there's anything I can do, let me know."

Oh, Lord! She grabbed fresh underwear—the most utilitarian she had—and put on iron-gray drawstring sweatpants that would have made Marilyn Monroe look like a truck driver. Then she got out a black turtleneck and her father's old Black Watch wool hunting shirt and put them on, letting the tails hang down over her hips. She found some wool socks that were about as sexy as organic compost, then combed out her hair. The extremes of hot and cold had melded into a pleasant feeling of dry, cozy warmth.

She found Byron building a fire in the study. Seeing him on one knee, leaning over the birch logs and kindling as he watched the flames take hold, was like striking a match to a drought-stricken prairie. As the fire spread, the flames licking the wood, rising blue-edged and hot, Nora could feel herself begin to burn.

"You're still in your wet clothes," she said.

He climbed to his feet. "I'll go change."

She nodded, stepping out of the doorway so he could get past her without touching her. If he did, she'd go up as fast as the kindling.

But he stopped on the threshold. "It won't work, you know."

"What won't work?" she asked innocently, fearing that she knew what he was talking about.

"The woods-woman look. Believe me, if I wanted you soaked to the bone in a camouflage poncho and the driving rain, I want you now."

And he ducked out fast, before she burst into flame by pure spontaneous combustion. She was so damned hot she had to take off the watchplaid shirt and push up the sleeves of her turtleneck. Who needed a real fire?

She made a pot of coffee and heated up a couple of applesauce-nut muffins she'd stuck in the freezer earlier in the fall, then got out her Halloween tray with the pictures of pumpkins on it, two orange paper napkins and plain white mugs and plates. In a few minutes, she was back in the study, everything nicely arranged.

Byron joined her. She wondered if getting into dry clothes had had a similar effect on him and if he was now more composed. He didn't look as if he were hanging by his fingernails to the last shreds of his self-control. The fire was burning well and good sense seemed restored. Outside, however, the storm raged on.

"Should I call Cliff and Liza?" she asked.

"No, I think they'll figure it out."

"Well...I wouldn't want them to get the wrong idea."

"Nora—"

He broke off, but she'd spotted the knowing concern—the I-know-something-I-wish-I-didn't in his eyes—and prodded him. "What is it?"

He shook his head. "Nothing. Tell me about your Halloween party."

Sitting on the floor, Nora leaned back against her couch and stretched out her decidedly unsexy legs toward the fire. Byron sat cross-legged opposite her. He'd put on dry cords and a dark blue shaker-knit sweater that somehow made her believe he could be the president of an East Coast publishing house. He, too, had skipped shoes. The fire crackled. The study was small, with just a couch, a glass-fronted bookcase, a couple of caned chairs and a tub table. It was where Aunt Ellie had best liked to read.

"About seven years ago," she said, "Aunt Ellie and I decided to have a Halloween party for our neighborhood—adults as well as children. Aunt Ellie always considered Halloween a bizarre custom. She just didn't get trick-or-treating. But she loved bobbing for apples, haunted houses, ghost stories, jack-o'-lanterns. She didn't approve of having a bunch of mercenary kids in dime-store costumes pounding on our door for free candy."

Byron smiled. "And I'm sure her opinion of Halloween was no secret."

"Hardly. She was starting to get real curmudgeonly about the whole thing—to the point of wanting to turn out the lights and pretend we weren't home—until I suggested a party. Only homemade costumes—they didn't have to be fancy—were allowed. I ordered all kinds of materials for the store—face paint, false noses and teeth, hats, sequins, feathers—the works. And we'd do all the old-fashioned stuff, like bobbing for apples, spooky ghost houses, making popcorn balls. It was great fun. Aunt Ellie dressed up as a witch—warty nose, croaking voice, poison herbs and all. For the first two years nobody knew it was her. They all thought she'd gone to visit her friend in Milwaukee when I had my party. She just loved that."

"And what were you?" Byron asked, his eyes on her.

She felt the warmth rise into her cheeks. "A gypsy."

He laughed. "Eleanora Gates, who's never lived anywhere but Tyler, Wisconsin, as a gypsy. That *is* a fantasy. Did you read palms?"

"Of course."

"And have a crystal ball?"

"One year I did. Lars Travis broke it."

Byron was silent for a minute or two, and Nora found herself unable even to guess what he was thinking, yet very much wanting to know. Was he imagining her in her gypsy costume? Remembering past Halloweens when he and Cliff were children? For three years, she'd thought she had him all figured out. To her, he was a wanderer, a cad, a womanizer, a man of talent and vision who would never commit to anything but a fleeting image he could capture on film. Now all bets were off. He might have been some of those things, or none. She didn't know who Byron Sanders Forrester was, what made him tick.

"After Aunt Ellie died," she went on, "I wasn't sure I wanted to continue our Halloween party tradition. But that first Halloween—she'd only been dead seven weeks—I found myself at Barney's buying up pumpkins, and I came home and made jack-o'-lanterns and popcorn balls and ... I don't know, people just showed up. I never sent out a single invitation. It was almost like Aunt Ellie had gotten us together, just to prove we could—or at least I could—carry on without her. I remember putting on my costume and feeling so alone. She was gone." Nora glanced over at Byron, her throat tightening. "You were gone. And there I was, dressing up like a kid for Halloween. But I could feel her spirit with me, telling me to buck up and get on with my life. So I did."

"What costume did you wear that night?" Byron asked.

Nora didn't expect that question. "What?"

"What costume? It's important."

"My gypsy costume. I've worn the same one for years."

He nodded. "Good."

"What were you thinking?"

"I was afraid you'd taken over Aunt Ellie's role as the Halloween witch."

Breaking a warm muffin in half, Nora let Byron's words sink in. Had she considered donning Aunt Ellie's black crepe dress and wax warts? Had she wanted to be Aunt Ellie that night?

"You're like her in many ways," Byron went on, "but you're not her. You're yourself, Nora. You have to live your own life."

"I know that."

"Yes, maybe you do. If you'd worn Aunt Ellie's witch's costume that night—"

She smiled. "I'd still have made a lousy witch. She was taller than me, remember? Besides which, my gypsy costume's a lot more fun to wear than Aunt Ellie's warts and poisons. I get rhinestones, a racy little embroidered top, lots of makeup... it's fun. And believe me, people wondered who the gypsy was for a while, too. I think people thought Aunt Ellie and I both had either gone nuts or had been spirited off by goblins."

Byron poured himself a cup of coffee. "How little and how racy?"

"What? Oh..." She grabbed a small couch pillow and threw it at him, but he caught it with one hand. "You have a nerve, Byron Forrester."

He grinned, unapologetic. "When's your party this year?"

"Tuesday evening."

"If I'm still around, what'll you do with me? I haven't dressed up for Halloween in years. A lot of years."

She gave that one some thought. "Well, you'd make a damned good goblin. Wouldn't even take that much imagination. But I think most likely I'd just dress you up as a skeleton and stick you in a closet. Appropriate, don't you think?"

"Let's not talk about nerve," he said, climbing to his feet.

"Where are you going?"

"Thought I'd run up to the lodge for a little while. It looks as if the weather's breaking— I'd like to let Cliff and Liza know what happened to us."

"Okay."

He hesitated. "Nora, I'm sorry I left the way I did three years ago, with so much unsaid. I let you believe some pretty unpleasant things about me. I thought I was doing the right thing."

"Maybe you were," she said, almost inaudibly.

"I don't know, but I...well, I've been wondering if I shouldn't leave Tyler for now. Come back just in time for the wedding."

"Why?"

"Because of you. Nora, I don't want to mess up your life. I want to respect your choices— I do care about you, you know." He smiled. "Why else would I tease you the way I do?"

She swallowed, her throat tight, and wished she could just go on hating him. But she couldn't. She wasn't sure she ever had. He hadn't been half as mean to her three years ago as they both were pretending. He'd told her he had to leave Tyler. He'd explained he knew she couldn't go with him. He just hadn't explained why he couldn't stay, and had let her believe that she hadn't meant enough to him. And he'd never asked her to go with him. Of course, she hadn't offered.

He left her alone in the study, the fire dying down, his muffin untouched, his coffee still steaming. Nora wiggled her toes inside her socks. She was nice and toasty. With Byron gone, she could do a few things around the house.

She wondered if he'd be back for dinner.

Well, it wasn't that hard to whip up something for two. She was used to it from her days with Aunt Ellie. If he showed up, he showed up. If not ...

If not, she'd eat alone, as she had almost every night for the past three years.

CHAPTER EIGHT

THE CUCKOO CLOCK in the study was striking midnight when Byron tiptoed into Aunt Ellie's old bedroom down the hall from the kitchen. He'd just come in. He had enough damned pumpkins for every man, woman and child in Tyler. Barney, who had to be 105 years old, had known a soft touch when he saw one. Byron had listened to the weather reports. It was going to rain all day tomorrow, and even with Liza's bridal shower in the middle of the afternoon, that made for one hell of a long Sunday ahead. Byron planned on carving a lot of pumpkins.

Cliff had already told him he needed space tomorrow. Liza could play the sweet bride-to-be and unwrap a dozen toasters, but he needed time alone to think. Byron understood. They'd called London from the lodge, talked to their mother. By the time Byron got on the phone, she couldn't stand it anymore and had burst into tears. Cliff knew. She'd held it together for him, but listening to Byron's end of the conversation, he'd figured out what was going on.

"I wish I could undo all the suffering I've caused her," he said when Byron hung up.

"She wishes she could undo what you've suffered. None of us can, Cliff. Let it be enough that we want to."

Cliff had twisted his hands together. "I'm close," he'd said in a choked whisper. "So damned close. If I lose it again..."

But he hadn't finished, retreating out into a very cold, very dark night, and Liza, white-faced, had joined Byron in the kitchen. It was painful to see such a vibrant woman look so worried and scared.

"I'm canceling the wedding," she said. "It's too much for him."

"Don't Liza. Not yet. Let me get out of here and see if he doesn't rally—"

"No...no, Byron, you're just not getting it. It's not you. It's crowds, the prospect of really thinking about the future. Cliff's used to living just for today. He hasn't thought about tomorrow in years, if that makes any sense. I'm making him. With me, he has to think about a big wedding, becoming a part of my family, having a family himself one day. The stress of you and your mother—that's only a small part of what he's going through." She threw up her hands and let them flop down to her sides. "I'm just asking for too much too soon."

"Is there any other way?" Byron had asked, rhetorically. "Half measures don't work in a relationship. It eventually comes to a point of all or nothing."

Liza had looked at him knowingly. "Is that what happened with you and Nora?"

"I promised I wouldn't tell."

She hadn't pushed, instead throwing on her wild serape and heading out to find Cliff. Byron admired her courage, her unshakable love for his brother. They'd already triumphed. The rest—the wedding, the painful Forrester family reunion—was just logistics. When they both saw that, they'd be fine.

Byron had tried pitching Cliff's old tent. It leaked. Then the wind blew it down. And he'd known he wouldn't stay out all night, anyway. He had to go back to Nora's little twenties house with the mums on the porch.

"Nora?"

"So it is you." She sat up in bed, only her silhouette visible in the dark room. He noticed she had a night-light. Living alone didn't come that easily to her. "You're lucky I don't sleep with a gun under my pillow."

"I just wanted to let you know that I'm back."

For a few seconds she didn't speak. Then she said, "Okay."

"Pleasant dreams."

"Thank you." He started out, but she stopped him. "Oh, Byron. I'll make breakfast in the morning. I bought eggs."

He couldn't help a small grin. "Knew I was coming back, did you?"

"No," she said quietly. "No, I really had no idea."

That did it.

He took three long strides across her dhurrie-carpeted floor and grabbed her by the forearm, not hard. She could have pulled away if she'd wanted to.

He drew her toward him, careful not to lose his balance and fall onto the bed. If he did, they were doomed.

In the dim, pale glow of her night-light, her eyes were liquid and luminous, and he recognized the painful loneliness in them, because it was the same agony he'd felt night after night for the past three years. Even as he'd known he was doing what he had to do, even as he'd structured a good life for himself, he'd wake up nights knowing that his life could have been more than it was. It was like that for Nora, too. He knew it. Her life was good. But it could be more than it was, and on dark, lonely nights, she knew it, too.

And so he kissed her.

Her lips tasted of his best dreams, and when she kissed him back, moaned softly against him, he knew he'd wake up in his brother's collapsing, leaking tent. This couldn't be real. He slid his tongue into her mouth, stroked the sharp edges of her teeth. He felt himself hardening. Her tongue circled his, tasting, testing. To steady himself, he grabbed her by the waist. It almost did him in. His fingers dug into the flimsy fabric of her little nightgown, felt the hot, smooth flesh underneath. It was no dream. If he had dreams as real as this, he'd never wake up.

But he made himself let go, stand up straight.

"Next time," he said, his voice hoarse, tortured with wanting, "know I'll be back."

"I SEE YOU FELL for Barney's routine."

Nora was sitting at the kitchen table, watching

Byron bring in his twelfth pumpkin, which he plopped on the counter with all the others. She hadn't seen so damned many pumpkins since *she'd* fallen for Barney's routine.

Byron leaned against the counter, crossing his arms over his muscular chest. "How does it go?"

"He's getting old, doesn't think he'll plant any pumpkins next year."

"He'd hate to see his last crop used for compost," Byron added, grimacing.

Nora grinned. "He uses his pumpkin money—"

"To buy heating oil for winter."

"That's a switch. Last fall it was heart medicine. The routine works best on tourists. He doesn't even try it on townspeople anymore."

"It ever work on you?"

"Once."

"Aunt Ellie?"

"Never. She went to school with Barney, said he tried at lunchtime to sob-story his classmates out of their desserts. He does grow nice pumpkins, though."

With a dubious grunt, Byron turned around and pulled two knives from her magnetic rack. She admired the way he moved. So far, they'd been friendly with each other, if careful to keep plenty of breathing room between them. She hadn't gotten to sleep last night until after dawn. It wasn't because she'd actually regretted having fallen for his charms. She was honest enough with herself to admit she'd wanted him to kiss her. It was, instead, that she'd enjoyed their kiss too damned much. She'd lain awake because she'd wanted more. She hated the wanting, but it was, she thought, extremely difficult to deny.

"They'd look nice lined up on your porch for your Halloween party," Byron said, pointing at the line of small, medium-size and large pumpkins. "I'll even buy the candles for you."

"I thought you weren't going to be here."

He shrugged, not looking at her. "Changed my mind."

She hadn't asked him where he'd gone last night, why he'd come back. "Any particular reason?"

"No place else to go."

"Weak, Byron. Very weak."

He handed her a knife, which, given his deliberately inadequate answer and the cocky, sexy way he looked at her, was brave of him. She set it purposefully on the table and got up and fetched a pumpkin, a smooth, deep orange one of medium size. It would make a perfect jack-o'-lantern. Setting it on the table, she made sure it was steady and sliced into it with her knife.

"We'll need newspapers for the guts," she said. "The recycling bin's just inside the cellar door." He went after them. When he had the cellar door open, she added, "And Byron, you don't have to tell me anything you'd rather not tell me. You're just my houseguest. You're welcome to stay through Liza and Cliff's wedding."

He returned with a stack of newspapers, which he slapped onto the table. "You know," he said in a low voice, his eyes even darker than they'd been last night, "when you go Victorian virgin on me, it just makes me want you more."

"Cad," she said, unable to hold back a smile.

He grinned. "Count on it."

Naturally he chose the biggest pumpkin, but it was slightly misshapen and had a golf-ball-size growth on one side. He patted it as if it were a prize piglet.

Continuing from where she'd stabbed into her pumpkin, Nora carved a neat circle for a lid, which she gently lifted, intensely aware of Byron's eyes on her. She wondered if rich East Coast publishing types ever made jack-o'-lanterns, as kids or as adults. Suddenly she was madly curious about his life, his upbringing, everything about him.

"I had dinner with Cliff and Liza last night," he said abruptly. "Cliff's on edge—he tries not to show it, but it doesn't take a genius to see that I've opened a can of worms by coming here. And I can't just up and leave. I need to be here."

"For his sake?"

"Yeah, even if he doesn't know it. But for my sake, too. We've had a long, hard row to hoe, Cliff and I. It's time we got it done." He ran his fingers over the circumference of his pumpkin, as if he were a surgeon and this a delicate operation. "Our mother's flying in from England on Thursday."

"She lives there?"

"No, she's visiting a friend—a Pierce & Rothchilde author, actually. She hasn't seen Cliff in five years. And in the past three years, I haven't...well, I haven't made her life any easier."

Nora set her pumpkin cap gently on the table. "Byron, I know Cliff's lived in Tyler for years, but he's kept to himself. No one but Alyssa Baron—and now presumably Liza—understands what drove him into his isolated life up at the lodge. As I said before, you don't have to tell me. I just want you to know that I, too, am in the dark."

He nodded, but said nothing.

"Do you know how to carve a pumpkin?" she asked.

"I haven't done one since I was a kid. Why, are there rules?"

"No, but it's one of those things that's not as easy as it looks. My first one usually comes out looking like Frankenstein's monster."

"Well, it's Halloween."

He seemed distracted, studying her with those mesmerizing eyes. She could almost feel the sandpapery roughness of his beard stubble against her cheek, against her breasts. Licking her lips, she scooped out pumpkin guts and seeds with one hand.

"My father was held prisoner and killed in Cambodia. Cliff was there. There was nothing he could do. He ended up staying, got caught up in the Khmer Rouge horrors, the killing. God only knows what all he saw. He did what he could, was almost killed himself, got out." With the tip of his knife, Byron drew a light line around the top of his pumpkin. "Our family hasn't been the same since."

"Your father was in the military?"

"Air Force. Mother was supposed to have fallen for someone who'd have liked to run Pierce & Rothchilde—she could have run it herself but nobody thought of that at the time—but she didn't. We did the Air Force routine for a while when we were young, until Dad volunteered for Vietnam. Then Mother took us to Providence to wait out the war. Only he never came home."

"I'm sorry," Nora said.

"Yeah."

"Does Cliff blame himself?"

"He did."

"And you? Do you blame yourself?"

Byron stabbed into his pumpkin. "I could have done more for both of them."

Using her free hand, Nora scraped pumpkin goo from her palm and fingers, slapping it onto the newspaper. Body Found at Abandoned Lodge, the headline read. "And your mother?" she asked, keeping her voice neutral.

"She's truly an amazing woman. She doesn't blame herself, Cliff, or me—or Dad. She's accepted what happened. Right now, she just wants to see both her sons happy."

Nora smiled. "Who can blame her?"

"At least Cliff's well on his way."

"When my parents died," Nora said, walking over to the sink for a paper towel, "I was absolutely positive it was my fault. I don't think I've ever been as sure of anything in my life. It was illogical—I had nothing to do with planning or executing their boating trip—

but my guilt had nothing to do with logic. Everyone tried to talk me out of how I felt, until I came to live with Aunt Ellie. She just let me feel whatever I felt. In time, the guilt went away."

"Do you still miss them?"

"Yes. The missing never does go away. I wouldn't want it to. I miss Aunt Ellie, too. I always will."

Byron nodded, not with understanding, she thought, but with acceptance. "I think you and my mother would get along."

"I hope to meet her."

"Oh, you will. I plan to stick around until the wedding. I figure," he said carefully, "the gossip about us will only get worse if I keep leaving and coming back. People'll think something really is going on between us. If I stay, maybe they'll realize I'm just a houseguest after all and you're only doing Cliff and Liza a favor by putting me up."

Nora narrowed her eyes. "What gossip?"

"You know small towns."

She scowled. "Well, you don't, Mr. Forrester. I've never been a subject for that sort of gossip in my life, so you needn't worry."

But he seemed worried, hacking at his pumpkin haphazardly, bound to make a mess.

"Byron—is something wrong?"

"No."

"If it's our...our kiss last night, you needn't worry about that, either. I certainly wasn't an unwilling partner, but I was merely...well, I was curious as to how I'd respond should you... should *we* kiss again. But now I know."

He set down his knife and glared at her. "Are you trying to tell me our kiss was a damned *experiment?*"

"Not an experiment. A test."

"Well, did you pass? Did *I* pass?"

She pursed her lips, carefully slicing out the pumpkin's eyes. It was a delicate maneuver and she didn't want to make a mistake. Having Byron Forrester's dark gaze pinned on her didn't help her concentration. "Now, Byron," she said, "let's be adults about this. You know we were bound to kiss, just because of our history. Now it's done with. We know what it'd be like kissing each other again because in a small fit of insanity we've gone ahead and done it. The mystery's over."

"The hell it is." He tore off his pumpkin's cap, which he'd failed to cut clean through in places, but what didn't come easily he just ripped out. "I'll have you know, Nora Gates, that I wasn't wondering what it'd be like to kiss you again."

Now, she thought, who was doing the self-deluding? "You weren't?"

"No."

Then she got his full meaning and felt her knees weaken.

"As far as I'm concerned," he said, "nothing's done with and the biggest mystery yet remains."

"I see," she said primly.

He grinned. "I'm on to you, Miss Gates. You drag out your Victorian virgin act whenever I hit a nerve."

"Let's get these pumpkins carved."

He laughed. "Let's."

She turned the radio to a live broadcast of *Madame Butterfly,* which Byron vetoed, so they compromised on jazz. In the time Nora carved three pumpkins, Byron did two. His first wasn't too bad, just rather uninspired. The second looked like something out of a science fiction movie.

"Kind of grisly, isn't she?" Byron said.

"She?"

"Looks like a woman to me."

Her three, of course, were perfect jack-o'-lanterns. They could have been carved from a mold. She displayed them side by side on the counter.

"Mine have character," Byron said.

"Yours will scare the neighborhood dogs."

"Count on it. By the way, what time is Liza's shower?"

"Oh, God, I almost forgot! I've got to get ready—would you mind cleaning up? Don't worry about the rest of the pumpkins, we can just set them out ... I'm going to be late, and I promised Liza."

Byron coughed. "Nora, wait."

She stopped in the kitchen doorway, listening. All morning she'd felt he had something on his mind, but she decided not to prod him.

"Have a good time."

Whatever it was, he wasn't going to tell her now. "Thank you, I'm sure I will."

She didn't catch his muttered comment as she raced upstairs to get dressed, wishing she'd kept her promise to Liza to find out what her mother had in store for her. But since Liza Baron was the one who'd thrust her future brother-in-law onto her, Nora figured she'd understand.

BYRON KNEW there'd be hell to pay.

While Nora was off at her bridal shower, he considered all the various things he could do to make his life easier when she got back. There had, of course, been no convincing Liza that the gossips were wrong and he and Nora hadn't been lovers. Only under certain circumstances—this one qualifying—did Byron consider a strategic, outright lie noble.

"Liza, that's just gossip," he'd said. "Nora Gates has never wanted a man in her life."

Liza was unpersuaded. "She's never wanted to get *married*. That doesn't mean she doesn't want to have a little sex now and then."

Cliff, judiciously, had kept out of the discussion.

"Lordy Lord," Liza had gone on, clearly delighted, "now I can't *wait* for my bridal shower. If anyone can drag the truth out of Nora, it'll be the quilting ladies."

Given his role in the gossip in question, Byron had believed it was his duty to warn Nora what she was in for, but with their talk about his family, her parents, Aunt Ellie—with her damned perfect jack-o'-lanterns and her gorgeous, haunting gray eyes—he'd skipped any warning. He could have justified his cowardice by claiming that he'd believed Liza was exaggerating and that the quilting ladies—they sounded like an intrepid lot—would exercise good manners. But the truth was, he'd kept his mouth shut because Nora, a hothead from way back, had access to too many knives, several newspapers' worth of pumpkin innards and a whole line of pumpkins. Byron valued his head.

Still, he debated cleaning her refrigerator, making dinner, carving the rest of the pumpkins, even having at the odd thing it might be handy to have a man around to fix. He'd checked for faulty wires to mend, plaster to patch, squeaky hinges to oil, dried up paintbrushes to rejuvenate. But everything in the Gates household was shipshape. Finally he'd said to hell with it and had caught the first quarter of a football game on the ancient television in the study.

At five o'clock the cuckoo was calling the hour and Nora came home screaming bloody murder.

Byron flipped off the game—it was a rout anyway—and pulled his feet off the couch just as Nora stormed into the study.

She looked great. Decidedly annoyed, but gorgeous.

"You heel," she snarled.

She pulled her handwoven chenille scarf from around her neck and threw it at him. Then came her hat, also handwoven, and her peacoat, which she more or less slammed at him because it was too heavy and bulky to really throw. All the while she screamed, "You bastard, you knew!"

What he should have done while she was out, he decided, was nail down everything in the house, given that sooner or later she was bound to run out of clothes to throw at him.

"You *knew* I'd be interrogated at that shower."

Off came a conservative black pump, which missed him by a yard.

"You knew half the damned town thinks I slept with you."

Off came a second black pump, which missed him by a good deal less than a yard.

"You bastard, you knew and you didn't warn me!"

She was down to her sleek two-piece heavy cotton long-over-short knit outfit and black-tinted stockings. "I have no quarrel," Byron said, "with your tossing the rest of your garments at me, but I think it's something you might regret. We do have a certain relentless attraction for each other, you know."

Her hair was wild. "I've been humiliated."

"How so?"

"Inger Hansen...Martha Bauer...Tisha Olsen, Liza—" She gulped for air. "They all know. The whole town...*arrgh!*"

Byron plucked the scarf off a pottery lamp with wildflowers pressed into its shade. "You're sure they know?"

"Oh, yes." Her eyes bored into him; he could feel the holes. "And they do give a damn. They haven't had such a juicy bit of gossip since the body was discovered at Timberlake Lodge. They haven't had such an *amusing* bit of gossip since they used to sit around trying to identify the rich guests Margaret Lindstrom

Ingalls would invite to her wild parties. They *loved* the idea that I might have slept with a reprobate like you!''

Considering he was president of Pierce & Rothchilde, lived in a house on the Providence Benefit Street walking tour, Byron thought her calling him a reprobate was stretching it somewhat. Probably, he thought, Nora knew this, too. "Nora," he said, "you *did* sleep with me."

"I refused to confirm that fact." She folded her arms over her breasts and panted, her anger having required a good deal of exertion. "No one in this town will ever look at me in the same way."

"Hoist by your own petard, m'dear."

She glared at him. "And what's that supposed to mean?"

"It means," he said, "if you hadn't tried to hide our affair, the gossips in town wouldn't have had anything to find out about you. It's not as if they're spreading vicious lies. They're merely spreading the truth. We *did* sleep together." He shrugged. "Actually, as I recall, we seldom slept."

With a panting glare, she blew out of the study.

"So," Byron called, "was everyone relieved to know you're human or what?"

The whole house shook when she slammed her bedroom door.

His answer, he figured.

Always one to take his life in his hands, Byron walked down the hall to her bedroom and tried the door, but, no fool, she'd locked it up tight. "I wish I had it in me to feel sorry for you," he said, "but I don't. You can be mad at me for not having warned you, but if I had, you wouldn't have gone this afternoon, which would have been a mistake. And go ahead and feel humiliated if you want. But I won't feel sorry for you. What people have deduced about us is true."

She yelled, emphatically, "*Was* true."

"If you'd unlock your door," he said, unable to resist, "we could take care of the past tense."

Something hard struck the bedroom side of the mercifully solid wood door.

"Nora, admit it. Ever since you saw me in your dining room the other night you've been thinking about what we had three years ago, how good it was. You wouldn't have wanted to go through life having missed that chance and you know it."

He could hear her pounding across her floor. She tore open her door, her hair sticking out everywhere, her breath coming in gasps. "There's a tent in my garage. Get it and get out."

"You're just upset—"

"No, Byron, I'm not upset. Take a good look at me. Do I *look* upset? No, I look angry. Furious. And not just with you. With myself. You're right. I set myself up for this afternoon. I should have kept my hands off you three years ago, I should have pretended I didn't know who the hell you were. I thought..." She gulped in more air, her voice rasping because she'd been yelling so much. "I thought I was above being a subject of gossip. All that does is make me a better target—a juicier subject—if anyone does find out the slightest irregularity about my life.''

Byron leaned against the doorjamb. ''I'm not sure I like being called an irregularity.''

She almost smiled. He *knew* she did. But then the anger was back, darkening her face, and she was calling him a bastard and banishing him to the garage for her tent.

It had to be a hundred years old. He could see doughboys camped in it on the Western Front. It stank worse than Cliff's did.

''If Mrs. Redbacker could see me now,'' he muttered. Hell, if the Pierce & Rothchilde board could. This was worse than the dartboard on the mahogany paneling. For three years he'd lived on the road, but his van and tent had never smelled.

The rain had finally ended, but it was still damp and chilly outside, and very dark even though it wasn't even six o'clock. He was hungry. But he'd endured worse conditions.

Not that he had any intention of letting Miss Nora off scot-free for her bad temper. Was it *his* damned fault people in town were on to them?

He could have gone to the lodge, or found a motel or roominghouse, or even driven to Milwaukee and stayed in a proper hotel. He did have options. But this wasn't about options: it was about calling Nora's bluff. She couldn't keep hiding behind her hot, secret temper.

Her yard was bordered with flowers and shrubs, and had a nice little birdbath and bird feeders here and there. That left plenty of room for the flea-bitten World War I tent. He held his nose, shook it out and got to work.

In two seconds, Nora's bedroom window popped open. "What do you think you're doing?"

"Pitching the tent."

"Not here!"

"Why not here?"

"You're being deliberately obtuse. I want you off my property and out of my life!"

She'd poked her head out the window, but she'd combed her hair and, he could see, changed into one of her flowing caftans. Her heart just wasn't in her anger anymore.

"Do you, Nora?" he asked.

"No," she said abruptly, and banged her window shut.

He figured that was as good as he'd get in terms of an invitation to come inside again.

But on his way back to her garage with her tent, he ran into Liza Baron. "My God, Byron," she said, startled, "I thought you were a burglar. What're you doing out here?"

"Checking out Nora's antique tent."

"Yuck, it's disgusting."

"No kidding. What's up?"

"Nothing much. Is Nora around? I just wanted to thank her for going out of her way to make the shower such fun. She knew I was dreading it, but she was right on the money—it really was a kick, in large part thanks to her. I've never seen her so animated."

"I was under the impression," Byron said carefully, "that she didn't have a good time."

"Well, that's news to me. She was the life of the party."

Byron could imagine such a thing, even if Nora herself never could. "What about the gossip about her and me?"

"Oh, *that*. Well, she was terrifically good-natured. Inger Hansen did rib her a little unmercifully— I mean, the idea of Nora Gates having a torrid affair with anyone is front-page news in Tyler, but with *you*..." She laughed, clearly loving the notion herself. "People will be talking about that one for years to come."

That, Byron suspected, would come as no surprise to Nora, though not as a fact to be welcomed.

"And I'm not sure Inger really realizes you two actually *slept* together."

"Now, Liza, you never have heard me confirm—"

She waved him off. "Being a man, Byron Forrester, you haven't denied it, either. Come on, I'm not stupid. Neither are most people in town. Gosh, Nora can't think people haven't been speculating about her sex life for *years*. Even before I left town there was talk—"

"I wouldn't tell Nora that if I were you," Byron put in.

"Honestly, Byron, for someone who slept with her, you sure don't have much notion of what Nora Gates is like. She's one of the most mature, level-headed people I know. She's not going to let a little harmless

town gossip upset her, especially when it's true." She
started up the front porch steps. "You coming?"

"Let me get rid of this tent. I'll be along."

And when Nora answered the door, he heard her
laugh and say, "Oh, Liza," as if she were the most
reasonable person in the world and hadn't just bom-
barded her houseguest with half her wardrobe and sent
him out into the cold, cruel night.

Byron stuffed the tent back into its place in the garage where it could spend the next hundred years.
"Oh, sweetheart," he said to himself, "you don't
know it, but all you're doing is raising the stakes."

And the gossips, he thought, be damned.

CHAPTER NINE

MONDAY MORNING Nora did better. Work helped restore her equilibrium. She acted—felt—like a grownup and the formidable businesswoman she was. She treated employees and customers with her customary respect and reserve, and they responded. There was no indication that the gossip circulating in town had penetrated Gates Department Store.

Until Lucille buzzed her from the book department. "Miss Gates, I have a man here who wants to see you."

Her tone suggested it was a *man* man, not a salesman or customer. Since she was at work, removed from the trials going on in her home, Byron Forrester didn't leap onto her list of possibilities. In fact, no one did. For her that was a happy state of affairs. She assumed Lucille herself was reacting to the man's asking to see the boss.

"Who is he?" Nora asked.

"He hasn't given me his name. Let me see . . . Oh, excuse me, sir, Miss Gates hasn't agreed to see you. Sir!" Lucille sighed. "He's on his way up. Shall I call Horace?"

Horace was the daytime security guard, and now that she knew it was Byron Forrester bounding up to her office, Nora imagined what he might tell Horace to get him to back off.

"No," Nora said, "I'll handle this one."

"I thought you might want to," Lucille said, her meaning impossible to miss.

With considerable effort, Nora kept her response professional. Then she buzzed her assistant, Albert Shaw. "Albert, I wanted to let you know that a friend of mine is on his way up. Send him right in, won't you?"

"Is this the brother of that guy up at Timberlake Lodge, the one who's staying with you?" Albert asked.

Despite their many virtues, Nora thought, small towns did have their flaws.

She had just enough time to reapply her lipstick before Byron Forrester strolled into her office, breathtaking in his slouchy jacket, shaker-knit sweater and wool pants. The weekend storm had blown out the mild weather of the end of last week and brought in clear skies and winterlike temperatures. Nora herself had worn a smart steel-blue wool suit to the store.

"'Morning," he said in a drawl that sounded more Georgia than New England.

Nora leaned back in her chair. "Lucille implied that you had an urgent need to see me."

He grinned. "Oh, I have an urgent need, but it's not just to see you."

She sighed. It had been like that since Liza's brief visit last night. Double entendres, teasing remarks, sexy looks. The gloves were off. Byron was making it crystal clear that he wanted to go to bed with her and all she had to do was give the nod and it was done. She'd decided she must have hit him with something in her rampage after all. Or her banishing him to the wilds of Wisconsin, even if he'd tried pitching her tent in her own backyard, had scrambled his brains. Clearly, her anger had lacked its intended effect. Instead of pushing him away, it seemed only to have drawn him to her. He'd seen her at her worst and now seemed to want her more than ever.

Either that, or he was just rising to the challenge she presented.

Well, let him.

Still, if he weren't so damned attractive himself, so sexy and easygoing and yet mysterious, resisting him would have been a hell of a lot easier. As it was, it was fast becoming one of the major challenges of her life. She could feel the ache—a physical longing that was so acute, so real it was almost painful—spreading from between her legs to her breasts, her nipples, her mouth, the tips of her fingers. Every part of her was sensitized, electrified.

And he hadn't even touched her.

"Byron, I'm working. It's a very busy day. What is it you want?"

"Besides to make mad passionate love to you?" His voice was light and teasing, but his eyes were not. "How 'bout spiriting you off to lunch?"

"I can't. I have a meeting."

"In my whole life, I've attended maybe two meetings that couldn't have been postponed or canceled altogether."

"You must be a treat to work for."

He walked over to the window and looked down at the town square, still, in these days of shopping malls, an attractive and active downtown. "I can see Narragansett Bay from my office."

She tried to imagine it. "Must be nice."

"Yeah, it's a great view."

"Do you like your work?" she asked, suddenly very much wanting to know.

"It has its moments." He hadn't looked up from the window. "I don't live for Pierce & Rothchilde. My work is my work, not my life."

If his comment was a dig at her and her commitment to Gates, she couldn't tell. "What about your photography?"

He shrugged. "I haven't picked up a camera in the three months since I ended my leave of absence and took my place at P & R."

"Is that a loss for you?"

"Not for me, no." Looking around at her, he seemed all at once the tall, well-built, well-educated, handsome East Coast blue-blooded executive. "I've felt some pressure from critics to continue—so I can trip up one of these days and they can lambaste me, I think. But I chased all the demons I wanted to chase. The rest are going to stick around forever. We're used to each other."

Nora recalled the photographs in Byron's book, the fathers and sons he'd captured on film. In context with his life, they made even more sense to her—were even more heart-wrenching and, in some ways, optimistic. If Byron Sanders Forrester could look back with such love and hope at a relationship that had ended so painfully, so tragically for himself and particularly for his older brother and father, then, surely, others could look beyond the wounds of their own past to the future. Byron had never been the shallow, insensitive cad she'd tried to make herself believe he was.

"Actually," he went on, "I don't mind being a publishing executive. I'm just not sure I want to continue as a publishing executive at Pierce & Rothchilde."

"Because of your family?"

"No." He smiled at her, moving away from the window. "Because they don't do technothrillers."

She didn't get it.

Byron laughed. "I'll have to introduce you to Henry—I should now say Hank—Murrow one of these days. All I'm saying is that Pierce & Rothchilde has a tendency to believe its own press, always a dangerous thing. They take themselves too seriously. They need to loosen up. It's like your place here. Gates has found a nice balance between quality with a capital Q and keeping its feet planted firmly on the ground. P & R too often focuses narrowly on quality—which becomes elitist. A technothriller, for instance, can have quality."

"With a capital Q?"

"Absolutely." He was warming to his argument now. "Why does Gates carry cotton dusters?"

Nora answered without hesitation. "Because our customers—some of our customers, particularly the elderly women—want and need them."

"And they're good quality, sturdy cotton dusters."

"Sure."

"But they're still cotton dusters. There, you see? I rest my case."

Nora thought she knew what he meant, but Byron Forrester, Harvard M.B.A. or not, did have a unique perspective on business.

"Now," he said, "lunch?"

"I still can't."

"A stubborn woman you are, Eleanora Gates the Younger." He planted his palms on the front edge of her desk and leaned over until his face was mere inches from hers. "Thinking what it'd be like for us to make love on your blotter, aren't you?"

The thought had occurred to her. "Byron..."

"We will." His voice was husky, his eyes liquid and midnight-black. "Some night after the place's closed up we'll come in here, lock the door and make love until dawn."

Then he was gone, and it was several minutes before she could breathe again.

That evening, she came home to a quiet, if not orderly, house. Byron had been cooking. In addition to a sink full of pots and pans, he'd left a note.

I made curried pumpkin soup. It's in the fridge. It's horrid stuff, but don't blame me. I got the

recipe from one of your healthy cookbooks. I'm
off to the lodge for dinner. See you tonight.

B.

He hadn't exaggerated about the soup. It was truly
dreadful. The recipe, however, wasn't the culprit; he'd
used homemade puree that he'd cooked insufficiently
and, worse, had neglected to drain. The soup was
lumpy and stringy, and she found a seed. He'd also put
together a salad, however, that was wonderful.

By seven, she was off to a closed meeting of the
Tyler town council. As usual, it began with an animated discussion of the latest victories of the high
school football team and its chances for a title, then
moved on to what was happening with the Body at the
Lake, hopes for doing something about the deterio-
rated condition of the public library, and—the only
real business at hand—the problems in the police department. Nora did her best to concentrate.

"Belton's giving up its police department," Johnny
Kelsey was saying; Belton was a nearby town, also in
Sugar Creek County. "They've gone to just having a
sheriff's substation. It's saved them a ton of money."

Alyssa Baron, who seemed even more distracted
than Nora, frowned, her hands twisting together in her
lap. Talk of the mysterious body discovered on her
father's land had upset her more than usual. Ordinarily she was sharp-minded, acutely interested in the
affairs of her town. "I don't know if I like the idea of
having to rely on the county for all our police protection. Tyler has always been independent. Nora, what
do you think?"

At the moment, Nora was working up enough interest to give a damn. Just a week ago nothing had compelled her more than every little going-on in Tyler, Wisconsin. "I don't know as we have much choice."

"With Paul retiring," Johnny said, "the timing couldn't be better."

Paul Schmidt was Tyler's longtime police chief. Nora nodded, but she had her reservations. "Has anyone talked to Brick?"

Alyssa winced. Johnny sighed. Sometimes it wasn't easy being on the town council. Tough decisions had to be made. Good people got hurt. Likely enough, Brick Bauer would be one of them. He was the obvious choice to replace Paul Schmidt as Tyler police chief. If Tyler went to a sheriff's substation, Brick would suddenly be working for the county, not the town.

"He's a good man," Alyssa said.

Johnny nodded. "Nobody wants to see Brick get the shaft, but he knows it's not personal."

"Becoming a county employee," Alyssa added thoughtfully, "could actually help his career, I suppose."

But, as it was with Nora, Tyler had always been Brick's first love. She remembered when he'd moved to town; he'd been in high school, a Robert Conrad type a couple of years younger than she. He could have gone to Milwaukee or even Chicago to advance his career, just as Nora could have, if she'd been interested in big department stores. But that wasn't what she'd wanted. What about Brick?

"I know the needs of the town come first," she said. "I'm sure Brick knows that, too."

"But," Alyssa finished, "he's a part of this town and we need to be open, direct and sensitive."

Johnny Kelsey sighed, but nodded in agreement. "Sometimes I wonder why I ever ran for this job. How 'bout you, Nora? You're a born politician." He grinned. "Except you have integrity. No skeletons hanging in your closet."

Obviously, she thought, he hadn't been privy to recent gossip. Feeling her cheeks burn, Nora refused to meet Alyssa Baron's eye.

"Going to run for the state legislature one of these days?" Johnny teased.

Nora laughed. "Now when would I do that?"

"Good to see you smile, kid," he said. "I was beginning to think you were taking this police substation thing too seriously. We'll work it out. Brick won't get the shaft."

The meeting adjourned not long after, the decision on the police department problems temporarily postponed. Alyssa Baron followed Nora outside, where it was dark and downright frigid.

"Can I give you a ride home?" Alyssa asked.

"I don't mind walking. . . ."

"Oh, you'll freeze. Look, my car's right here."

Sensing Alyssa was reluctant to be alone with herself just yet, Nora climbed into the passenger seat of her sister-councillor's expensive car. Alyssa pulled on thin leather driving gloves. She was so different from Liza, Nora thought, that it was almost eerie.

"I know Liza didn't notice yesterday afternoon," Alyssa said, turning on the ignition, "but I did. Nora, I'm sorry if any of this talk about you and Byron Forrester has caused you embarrassment. Liza...it just doesn't occur to her that a woman not much older than herself would be less than amused by such gossip."

Nora was taken aback, but resisted her impulse to deny that anything so silly as local talk could upset her. She was tired of pretending she had no feelings. "Thank you for noticing, Alyssa. You're right— I was embarrassed, but only at first."

Alyssa pulled out into the dark, quiet street. "Then there's no truth to the rumors?"

"About Byron and me? Well, no...I mean, yes, there's truth to them."

Alyssa Baron was silent.

"Three years ago," Nora said, staring out her window, "Byron came to Tyler to make sure Cliff was all right. He didn't intend to contact anyone in town—he just wanted to check on his brother and get out."

"But he met you."

"He told me he was a photographer. One thing led to another and I invited him to dinner. Then he met Aunt Ellie."

Slowing for a turn, Alyssa didn't take her eyes off the road. "The pictures."

Nora exhaled. "For a long time I was convinced he used her."

"I can't imagine anyone taking advantage of Ellie Gates."

"They spent a lot of time together. And I spent a lot of time with Byron. Then he left and a few weeks later Aunt Ellie died."

"How awful for you," Alyssa said with genuine sympathy.

Nora looked at her. "I wasn't thinking just of myself. For the past three years I've told myself I should have seen what Byron was and warned Aunt Ellie, spared her...." She trailed off, unable to finish.

"Spared her what, Nora?"

"Having to spend so much of her last weeks with someone who saw her as quaint, as a subject for a series of photographs that would advance his career. That's what I've thought for the past three years. I'm not sure I was right."

Alyssa almost missed her next turn and had to brake hard, at least by her standards. "Nora, you amaze me sometimes. You have a tendency to look at all the wonderful things Aunt Ellie did for you without even considering the wonderful things you did for her."

"She never wanted marriage or children, but I came along—"

"You came along and enriched her life. She was already close to seventy when your parents died. She had the store and many, many friends, but you were her only close relative. She taught you what she knew about business. Don't you think that gave her tremendous satisfaction and solace? And you gave her constant companionship and true devotion in her old age. You were never a burden, Nora. How many times did she tell me you kept her young? You made her keep moving—she couldn't give up."

"She'd never have given up."

"Maybe. Maybe not."

Nora swallowed, her throat tight. "I used to think she'd live forever."

"At one time or another I think we all thought that of Aunt Ellie," Alyssa said, smiling wistfully. "I remember when I was a little girl— I must have been tiny because Mother was still around. She took me to Gates Department Store to buy handmade chocolate angels Aunt Ellie had special-ordered for Christmas. She was standing behind the glass counter herself and she seemed old even then." Alyssa paused, her expression warm and nostalgic. "Not old, really. Timeless."

They'd come to the house Aunt Ellie had had built for herself, back even before she was officially an old maid. Alyssa pulled her Mercedes alongside the curb.

"Honoring Aunt Ellie," she said, "doesn't mean you have to become her."

"Thank you, Alyssa. You've been awfully kind, considering the stress and strain you must be under. I know I can be hard on people—"

Alyssa laughed softly. "Oh, Nora, you're so much harder on yourself. People in this town look up to you and you try to fulfill all their expectations. But Aunt Ellie dared to be herself. Let that be an example to you." She shifted the car into neutral, her foot on the brake. "I had dinner tonight with Byron, Cliff and

Liza. Actually, Byron and Liza. Cliff didn't stick around."

Nora could hear the concern in her older friend's voice, but withheld comment.

"Liza's my first child to get married. I want her to be happy and to have a memorable wedding." Alyssa hesitated. "And I know she believes in trial by fire. She thinks I've been too protective of Cliff and that he needs to jump feetfirst back into society. But a big church wedding..."

"You're worried Cliff might have a relapse," Nora said.

Alyssa's nod was almost imperceptible. "He hasn't been around people in a long, long time."

"Do you think Byron's being here is a help or a hindrance?"

"I don't know."

"And their mother—she's arriving on Thursday."

"Yes." Alyssa sighed, her foot slipping off the brake; the car rolled forward. "He desperately wants to see her again."

"But..."

"But I'm worried. Liza, the renovations, the—the discovery at the lodge. Now the wedding and Byron... It's a lot for a man who only a few weeks ago most people in Tyler thought was a burned-out recluse beyond redemption."

The past weeks, Nora thought, couldn't have been easy on Alyssa Baron, either, and perhaps she was projecting some of her own anxiety onto her daughter's fiancé. Discovery of the Body, whatever the ul-

timate results, had to have stirred up memories of
Alyssa's mother's departure from Tyler when she was
just a little girl. Nora had lost both her parents at a
young age, but at least she'd known what happened to
them. Alyssa didn't have that small consolation. For
all she knew, Margaret Ingalls could still be alive.

Or, Nora thought dismally, lying on some slab in a
morgue, awaiting identification.

"I'll talk to Byron," she offered.

Alyssa smiled her sweet, nonjudgmental smile. She
was too kind a person, Nora thought, to suffer.
"Thank you."

BYRON HAD A FIRE raging in the study. Nora could feel
its warmth from the doorway. She sank against the
painted doorjamb, and it occurred to her that she'd
never really wanted to live alone. Until she was thirteen, she'd had her parents. Then there'd been Aunt
Ellie. For a few weeks—or days, really—she'd had the
promise of a life with an itinerant photographer. Only
since Byron's departure from Tyler and Aunt Ellie's
death had she lived alone. They'd been fulfilling years.
She'd coped with plumbing problems and a foot of
snow in her driveway and the odd bat swooping into
her bedroom. But she liked coming home to a warm
fire and a warm body in the house.

Spotting her, Byron smiled. "You look done in."

"It's been a long day, but I like to keep busy."

She kicked off her shoes and walked across the thick
carpet in her stocking feet, then hiked up her skirt a bit
and sat cross-legged in front of the fire. Byron had his

shoes off, too. His feet were bare, his toes almost touching the flames. He had his ankles crossed. She noticed the length of his legs, the snug fit of his jeans on the hard muscles of his thighs. He had his shirt pulled out, the bottom wrinkled where it had been tucked in. He'd pushed up his sleeves. There was something inordinately sexy, Nora thought, about the man's forearms.

"I made a couple of long distance calls on your phone," he said. "Seems Pierce & Rothchilde can't get along as swimmingly without me as they believed."

"Do you find that reassuring?"

"Not in the least."

Leaning back on her elbows the way he was, she stretched out her legs, but because they weren't as long as his they didn't quite reach the fire. "Does it worry you, then?"

"Nope." He seemed confident of his answer. "I do my job. So did the woman I replaced. If I stay, I'll continue to do my job. If I leave, someone will take my place. It's a mistake to believe you're indispensable." He shrugged. "It's also arrogant."

"I'll bet your great-grandfather didn't feel that way."

"Good ol' Clifton Pierce? He wasn't nearly as married to the company as his son, my grandfather, Thorton Pierce, was. The old bastard never even retired. Died at his desk."

"Aunt Ellie died at home," Nora said, "but she never officially retired."

"Big difference."

Nora stared at the flickering flames, failing to see his logic.

"Aunt Ellie didn't live to work, Nora. She worked to live. Gates Department Store was her life's work and she loved it, gave it her all. But she also loved Tyler, and you. She had her friends, her hobbies. She was a whole person. That's what my series of photographs on her was all about."

"This," Nora said, not too nastily, "from a man who knew her all of two weeks."

"Two and a half weeks," he corrected amiably.

"She never knew you'd misrepresented yourself."

For a full minute, Byron said nothing. Nora listened to the crackling of the fire and the soft ticking of her cuckoo clock, keeping her eyes on the man stretched out beside her. Finally, he said, "Yes, she did."

"You told her you were Cliff's brother?"

"She guessed. Said we had the same eyes."

Nora rolled over and rose up on her knees, peering into Byron's eyes. "You do. But how would Aunt Ellie have known what Cliff's eyes looked like?"

"She'd seen him a couple of times around town. She was a highly observant woman. She was also a tad suspicious. *And* she'd badgered Alyssa Baron into telling her what she knew about the weirdo living out at her father's abandoned lodge. So I was already neck-deep before I'd even opened my mouth."

Not certain how to react, Nora sat down again. "She never told me a thing."

"Like the younger Eleanora Gates, the older Eleanora Gates didn't repeat gossip or confidences."

It wasn't in Nora to be angry with Aunt Ellie for not having shared with her all she'd known and deduced. But *Byron* could have told her! She glared at him.

He got the message. "Nora, I know what you're thinking. It was up to me to tell you the truth about myself and I didn't, simple as that. If it's any consolation, Aunt Ellie understood my decision to leave Tyler when I did, if not the way I did. Cliff had his demons. I had mine. You had yours. We all needed the past three years. We weren't ready for each other."

"And now?"

"Now," he said, turning to her, his eyes reflecting the orange glow of the fire, "Cliff has found Liza. And I'm not letting him off the hook this time— I'm not backing off, no matter how hard it is for either or us. He's my brother. As for you, Miss Nora..." He smiled, moving closer. "I'm very ready for you."

It was another of his deliberate, incorrigible remarks designed to make her aware—intensely aware— of the way she'd responded to his kiss the other night, the boundless passion they'd shared three years ago. She was not unmoved.

"Is this," she said, refusing to inch away from him even as he inched closer, "your way of distracting me from demanding reimbursement for your phone calls?"

His eyes danced, or else it was the flickering of the flames. "I think you're the one trying to do the distracting."

"Do you miss Providence?"

"No."

"Do you feel the same way about Providence as I do about Tyler?"

"No."

"But you've been there two hundred years," she said.

He laughed, the flames still dancing in his eyes. "I haven't."

"You said the Pierces . . ."

"Actually, the Pierces have been in Providence for more than three hundred years. They've had their house on Benefit Street for only two hundred."

Nora tried to imagine it. "Those are serious roots."

"Cliff and I are the last direct descendants of Clifton Pierce—"

"The founder of Pierce & Rothchilde."

"Cofounder. There are other Pierces in Providence. We both love the Pierce house and I guess Providence will always be home, but I've traveled too much and have had too many varied experiences to sink down 'serious roots' there."

"Or anywhere else?"

He looked at her. "Not necessarily."

She smiled. "There, you see? I have distracted you."

"No," he said in a low voice, touching her mouth with one finger, "you haven't."

His touch, as brief and light as it was, rekindled the desire she'd managed to keep at a slow, quiet burn through her dinner of salad and stringy pumpkin soup and her routine meeting of the Tyler town council. If she'd bypassed the study and gone straight to bed, as common sense had told her to do, she'd have dreamed about him. Now she knew she wouldn't have to rely on dreams.

"That's okay," she said. "I haven't distracted myself, either."

"I wondered."

His lips grazed hers. It was just a small kiss, a taste. It had the effect of a small spark on a very short fuse. Nora sizzled. Unfolding her legs, she sat up straighter than he was, her chest at his eye level. He unbuttoned just one button of her pale lemon silk blouse. She glanced down and could see the lacy edge of her bra, her breasts straining against its stretchy fabric.

"Byron, I don't want to dream about you tonight."

He looked up at her. He was propped up on one elbow, turned on his side, his head at a different angle, so that the flames no longer danced in his eyes. "What do you want?"

With a hand that trembled only slightly, she unbuttoned three more buttons on her blouse. They were small buttons, shaped like pearls, and not that difficult to work. In a few seconds, she slipped the blouse from her shoulders. She could feel the silk drop onto her hips and the heat of the fire on her exposed skin, which glowed in the orange light. Her nipples were hard against her lace bra. She reached around to unclasp it, but Byron stopped her, instead reaching around himself. With one hand, he unfastened the hook. The fabric fell loose. He slipped one strap off her shoulder and then the other, until her breasts were free. She shook the bra off her arms and watched him watching her.

"You have your answer," she whispered.

And he rose onto his knees, his mouth, already open, reaching hers. His tongue was hot, wet, insistent. She got to her knees as well. He caught her breasts with his palms, moaned softly into her mouth as his tongue plunged deeper. Slowly, he moved his hands down her sides, around to the small of her back. She pressed herself against him, feeling the warmth of his shirt against her bare breasts. Now she, too, moaned.

"I never thought this would happen to me again," she whispered. "Not twice in one lifetime."

He answered with her name, spoken hotly against her mouth as his hands slipped into the waist of her skirt, sliding inside her underpants and stockings, down lower until he was cupping her buttocks, lifting her against him. His fingers went lower, deeper, probing, exploring.

They melted together to the floor.

"I want to see all of you," he said hoarsely. "To touch you everywhere."

Happy to comply, she unzipped her skirt in back, arching up slightly, but then he seized the hem and slowly, erotically, pulled the skirt down over her hips, her thighs, her ankles. He cast it aside. Breathing hard, he made shorter work of her panty hose. She lay on the carpet in just her lace bikini underpants, her feet very close to the fire. She doubted she looked much like a stern, Victorian old maid.

"I thought I'd never want you more than I did three years ago," Byron said, his voice low, hoarse with the desire that made him hard and taut all over. "But I do. Nora, there's never been anyone in my life even remotely like you. I knew when I left Tyler I'd never forget you—and I never did. I never will."

She helped him with his own clothes then, lifting his shirt over his head, resisting the sweet agony of pressing her breasts to his chest. First things first. He wasn't wearing a belt with his jeans. They came off with little effort. Underneath he wore deep purple stretch underpants not much bigger than her own; they barely contained him.

"I thought all East Coast blue bloods wore striped boxers," she said.

"Not this East Coast blue blood."

And in a matter of seconds, he wore nothing at all.

Hooking his thumbs into the elastic waist of her underpants, he slid them down her thighs, over her knees, down her shins, her ankles and off.

He looked at her for a long time, seeing all of her. And he touched her, tentatively at first, as if making certain they hadn't plunged together into the same dream. Nora had never experienced anything so deliciously erotic. And he did what he'd said he'd wanted to do, touching her everywhere.

After that, he tasted her everywhere.

And she him.

Then she was drawing him onto her, into her, and because it had been so, so long, it hurt a little, but it was a welcome hurting, and he held back just long enough, although she could see that it was an effort. But then there was no holding back. It was as if the fire at their feet had spread over them, consumed them, until they were red-hot coals, burning everything they touched.

It was a long, long time before they burned down.

When they did, Nora gathered up her scattered clothes and dashed to her bedroom, leaving Byron dead asleep in the study.

She looked at her reflection in her antique mirror. At her love-swollen lips and reddened breasts, at the places where she could still feel his touch on her.

"Some old maid you make," she said, not lightly at all.

And she locked her door, so as not to tempt fate or a Rhode Islander in the form of Byron Sanders Forrester.

CHAPTER TEN

NORA AWOKE to the clanging of pipes, the hissing of her radiator and a warm haze enveloping her. In a few minutes she was sweating under her quilt. In another minute, she was on her feet, pulling on her robe and stomping to the kitchen. She stopped at the thermostat in the hall.

"Seventy-two!"

Incredulous, she found Byron in the kitchen. Even as it struck her how oddly right he looked at her counter, she noticed he had on running shorts and a Boston Marathon T-shirt. No shoes, no socks. He smiled a good-morning at her and cracked an egg on the side of her medium-size stainless steel bowl.

"I've *never* had the thermostat up that high, even in the dead of winter," she told him. "I'm surprised the furnace didn't blow up."

Byron began whistling some obnoxiously cheerful tune. "You really are such a genial soul in the morning. As far as I'm concerned, Miss Nora, if you leave a man sleeping stark naked on your study floor with your thermostat set at a notch above frigid—"

"Sixty is a perfectly reasonable nighttime setting."

"Tell that to my vitals."

He'd cracked another two eggs into the bowl. That made at least three. Was he expecting guests for breakfast? Just what other liberties did he intend to take with her home?

"If," he went on blithely, "you'd tossed a quilt over me or put another log on the fire, I might have resisted the impulse to turn up the heat to a humane level."

"I don't mind you turning up the heat, but seventy-two?"

He cracked another egg into the bowl. "It's a nice round number, guaranteed to thaw certain frozen body parts. And I didn't turn *up* the heat. I turned it *on*. A fine but critical distinction."

"Easterners," Nora said, and sat down at the table, since it didn't look as if Byron needed any help just yet. If the kitchen had been any warmer, she'd have needed a fan. "What are you making?"

"A frittata."

"A glorified omelet. How many eggs are you using?"

"Enough. I'm not using all the yolks."

"Are your frittatas better than your pumpkin soup?" she asked dubiously.

He grinned. "My frittatas will melt in your mouth."

It wasn't an exaggeration. While he worked his miracles with her eggs, she made toast and coffee, breaking out her mocha java beans, and set the table with Aunt Ellie's best English stoneware breakfast dishes. Nora was warm in her chamois robe, so she went back to her bedroom and changed into her lightweight waffle-weave cotton robe, which, ever the optimist regarding Wisconsin weather, she hadn't put away yet for the season.

"I'll let you have your way with my thermostat until I head off to work," she told Byron upon her return to the kitchen for cleanup.

His dark eyebrows went up. "Oh?"

"Byron! Are you going to act like an eighth-grader again today? I can't say anything without your twisting it around into something dirty."

"What's so dirty about any of my remarks?"

"You know what I mean."

He squirted way too much dishwashing liquid into her sink. "Are you going Victorian virgin on me again?"

"Now that," she said, almost under her breath, "would be a neat trick, wouldn't it?"

And after cleanup, they ended up making love, laughing and teasing each other, on the lace coverlet of the bed in the front guest room. Byron spirited her there while she was supposed to be getting ready for work, on the pretext that the radiator didn't work. She had a look. It worked fine.

"It was probably slow heating up," she said, "because it hasn't been on since early spring. I like a cool house."

"Do tell. Instead of turning up the heat I should have crawled into bed with you at dawn. Let you warm up my cold body parts."

She shrugged. "It would have been cheaper."

He crossed his arms over his chest. "I tried, you know. Your door was locked. Sort of like closing the barn door after the cows've gotten out, wouldn't you say?"

"More like," she said, "after the bull had been on a rampage."

At which point he'd pounced, flinging her onto the bed and tickling her unmercifully, until she was howling with laughter, screaming for him to stop before the neighbors called the police and Brick Bauer himself came to see what was up. "Then I'd have to vote against the sheriff's substation to keep him quiet, and there goes my reputation...."

Byron had silenced her laughter.

Quite efficiently.

And made her late for work for the first time in twenty years. When she told him, he applauded. "On your way out," he said, "turn down the heat. It's hotter'n hell in here."

He did have a way of getting her to not take life—and herself—too seriously. Given the tragedies of his own life, it was a remarkable gift.

It was just her luck to run into Inger Hansen in the Gates Department Store parking lot. "I was just coming in to look for something for Liza for her wedding," she said, peering closely at Nora. "You look flushed, Nora. Are you ill?"

"No! Really, I—I ate a big breakfast."

And she held back a silly giggle, imagining what immature, crude, *funny* rejoinder Byron Forrester would have ready. He was, she thought, a decidedly unsettling influence on her life. And a potentially wonderful *part* of her life. But she couldn't think about romance and such now. There was a Thanksgiving window to plan, the Christmas season to prepare for—plenty of work to be done.

On her way up to her office, however, she stopped at the book section to see what Gates carried from Pierce & Rothchilde.

Not a single title.

She and Byron were, she thought, hardly for the first time, from very different worlds.

"SO," CLIFF SAID, "you're setting her up for a broken heart all over again."

Byron could feel his brother's tension. Cliff was standing in front of him on the veranda, where he'd gone with a cup of coffee. They'd spent the morning and early part of the afternoon together in the lodge, which, when the renovations were complete, would be an incredible place. Mostly they'd talked about the past. And the implications of having discovered a body on the premises. On the surface, Cliff was avoiding speculation until he had concrete information. But underneath, like so many in Tyler, he was worried. If the body *was* that of Margaret Lindstrom Ingalls, how had it gotten there? What did his future grandfather-in-law know? How would his future mother-in-law, a sensitive and perhaps somewhat emotionally fragile woman, react? And Liza, Byron thought. How would Cliff's future wife react? Could they continue to live at the lodge where her grandmother might have been murdered?

Then there was Cliff himself. He'd already seen far too much murder and destruction, far too many families torn apart. With his big church wedding just days away, he had to be feeling the stress.

It was easier, Byron realized, for Cliff to focus on his younger brother's somewhat suspicious love life.

"Cliff, she's an adult," Byron said patiently. "She doesn't need your protection. And I *do* care about her."

Cliff looked around at him, his face unyielding, even ravaged, speaking volumes about how difficult the transition from recluse to ordinary human being still was for him. That he couldn't have done it without Liza's unconditional love—and his unconditional love for her—was crystal clear. "Nora Gates has to live in this town after you've gone. So do I."

Byron sighed. He had no good response, if only because he'd stopped believing in crystal balls. He didn't know what the future would bring. He did know, however, that he'd never loved anyone—now or three years ago—as much as he loved Nora Gates. But was love enough?

Cliff looked out toward the lake. It was a bright, clear, crisp Wisconsin afternoon. The weekend rain had whipped most of the remaining leaves from the trees, leaving them suddenly bare, their gray branches and trunks outlined in sharp focus against an achingly cloudless sky. Only clusters of rust-colored leaves and a few fading yellows clung to the odd tree. In town, more leaves had held on through the wind and rain. But it was very cold. Before he left Nora's house, however, Byron had lowered the thermostat, not to sixty, but to a reasonable sixty-five.

"I don't know," Cliff said, squinting at the sparkling lake. Coming up next to him, Byron could see the pronounced lines at the corners of his brother's eyes. They were eyes, he thought, that had seen too damned much of humanity's dark side. "Sometimes I think Forrester men are destined to break the hearts of the women they love."

Byron tensed. "Cliff, don't."

"Look at Mother. How she's suffered for having loved Dad."

"She married a military man. There was a war. They knew what they were doing. Cliff, you're not Dad. Liza isn't—"

But Cliff turned abruptly, the strain he was under, just for an instant, rising to the surface. "Liza and I are forever. That doesn't mean I won't break her heart. And you, Brother. You're more like Dad than you want to admit. I'm like the Pierces. I like to sink roots. Tyler's a good place. I can stay. But you? You like to wander."

"I've done my wandering."

"Have you?"

"For three years."

"Now you're back at Pierce & Rothchilde. And you hate it."

Byron said nothing.

Cliff's mouth twitched. "Mrs. Redbacker still there?"

"She'll go out like Grandpa Thorton."

"Feetfirst," Cliff said.

"I like the job. I've got weekends for wandering."

"You still take pictures?"

Byron shrugged. "Always."

His brother's only response was a small nod as he sipped his coffee, still steaming faintly.

"I don't think," Byron said, choosing his words with care, "that Nora will regret what's happened between us, regardless of what the future brings. And it's not just what I want and who I am, you know. It's also a matter of what she wants and who she is."

Cliff kept his coffee mug close to his mouth. "And right now you contradict what she thinks she wants and who she thinks she is."

"In a nutshell, Brother," Byron said, "that's it."

WHEN NORA CAME HOME from the store a couple of hours early to prepare for her Halloween party that evening, she found Byron in her bedroom checking out his glow-in-the-dark skeleton costume in her full-length mirror.

"Good Lord," she said, "where did you find *that?*"

"That's classified information."

There was nothing like it at Gates. It was a black knit unitard—including feet—with a skeleton outlined on the fabric in white fluorescent paint. He looked positively eerie.

"I have white face paint, too," he said.

"Gross."

"There's a hood and a mask, but they're a bit much, don't you think?"

He held them up. They were more than a bit much, so he received no argument from her. All day, she'd worked hard and diligently to keep in mind that she was a woman who didn't focus exclusively on the moment. She always kept in mind the past and the future—where she'd been, where she was going. When she was with Byron Forrester, the past seemed unimportant and the future elusive, something that would take care of itself. But that was dangerous thinking, she'd told herself. And it wasn't her.

But he was so damned sexy in his sleek skeleton costume.

"Ahh," he said with considerable relish, "if only the Pierce & Rothchilde board could see me now."

His hair was wild and dark, and he had plaster dust in his cuticles, a couple of scraped knuckles. He'd spent the day, she remembered, at the lodge with Cliff. She found it strange, yet curiously right, that two brothers from the East had ended up in Tyler, Wisconsin. One definitely to stay, the other probably not.

But she wouldn't think about Byron's leaving right now.

"Any calls to Rhode Island today?"

"Only from. Seems my pal Hank Murrow was a bit premature in gloating about his technothriller megacontract. Now he wants us to buy some dreary tome he's written."

"It's not good?"

"Oh, no. I'm sure it's great."

Nora made no pretense of understanding the publishing industry, or Byron Forrester's attitude toward it. "What about his technothriller?"

"Who knows? It's not what P & R does." He pulled at the neckline of his skeleton suit. "God, I'm about to suffocate in this thing. It's like being encased in a giant rubber band. How was the store today?"

"Busy."

"Gearing up for the Christmas rush already?"

She nodded, unable—or at least damned unwilling—to take her eyes off him. She'd worn a navy wool gabardine coatdress with chunky silver jewelry to the store, distracted periodically all day by images of Byron slipping it off her when she got home. Now here he was in her bedroom.

"The party's not for another three hours," she said.

Naturally he read more meaning into her statement than she'd intended. "Oh?"

"I was just reminding you—"

"In case I didn't want to run around in my glow-in-the-dark skeleton costume for the next three hours or in case I had other plans in mind?"

She snapped her mouth shut. "I just thought you might get hot." Then she added, because he was determined to give her no rest, "In your skeleton suit."

"It is a bit close. Here, give me a hand—there's an invisible zipper in the back. Stand aside, though. When I peel this thing off it'll snap back down to Ken doll-size."

He did have a point.

He'd also neglected to tell her how little he had on underneath his costume. Not that there'd been much mystery.

"Are you blushing?" he asked, highly entertained.

"Men have no modesty."

"Mustn't generalize. Besides, there's nothing here you haven't seen ... aha, so that's it! You're not the least embarrassed, Miss Nora. That's pure *lust* I see in those beautiful gray eyes of yours." He slid his arms around her and drew her close. "You are beautiful, you know."

"No one's ever told me—"

"That's because they were afraid you'd clobber them if they did. You do have a temper."

"Only with you." He had her in such a tight embrace she could do nothing with her arms except slip them around him; he had a strong, smooth back. "You seem to bring out...not the worst in me, I think, but whatever it is I'm feeling, good, bad, or indifferent. I'm afraid I'm not very good at censoring myself when I'm around you."

"That's good, isn't it?" he asked seriously.

"It's not like me— I'm usually more controlled. But yes, I think it's good. I don't hold anything back when I'm with you. I just can't seem to be ... well, circumspect."

"I'm glad."

"And you?"

He smiled. "What you see is what you get."

She knew it was true. Even three years ago, when he'd neglected to tell her the whole truth of who he was and why he'd come to Tyler, he still had been his own person. Most of her negative feelings toward him for the past years had stemmed not from what he'd done or said, but from what he'd let her—deliberately or otherwise—believe about him, from her own suppositions, deductions, prejudices. He was more centered now, more balanced, but the irreverent sense of humor was still there, the sexiness, the energy, the optimism. He'd needed those three years on his own. So had she. But he was still the Byron she'd loved three years ago. And he'd loved her. She was sure of that now.

"I'm not holding back on you," he said, without her prompting. His smile had faded, in its place an expression of warmth and gravity. "I've never known anyone like you. I've never felt for anyone what I feel for you. I doubt I ever will."

She draped her arms over his hard, bare shoulders. She could feel her lips part, inviting him, but she didn't wait for his response. Instead she tilted back her head and kissed him lightly on the chin. "The first time I saw you on the street outside Gates," she said in a low voice, "I knew you'd change my life. It was just there, a certain knowledge. I didn't know how or why or in what way, but I knew you were meant to be standing out there on that sidewalk while I was doing that window. And I don't even believe in fate."

"I felt the same way."

She nodded. "I believe you."

"Nora—"

"Byron, I want you to know that I do trust you. I'm not saying I know what's going to happen to us. I don't know where we'll go from here. But I do know that the past—what I used to think about you—what I *needed* to think..." She paused, wishing she could be more articulate, wishing she could explain how certain and yet mixed-up she felt. "I just believe you now."

His arms tightened around her, and he seemed unable to speak. Their mouths were very close. She let her tongue flick against the edges of his teeth, into his mouth.

And he responded, in action if not in words. Lifting her, he carried her to the bed. Halfway there her shoes fell off. He kissed her deeply, his tongue plunging far into her mouth, its sensual rhythm a promise of what was to come, a promise of much more than sex. Her dress was hiked up to midthigh. When he laid her on the bed, it hiked up to her waist.

Finally, he managed to whisper her name. It was enough.

She assumed he'd start by removing her dress, or stand back so that she could, but he didn't. Already his eyes were dusky with passion. He peeled off her panty hose, purposefully taking her underpants with them this time. The air in the bedroom was cool on her overheated skin. She didn't object.

Starting at her ankles, he slid his hands, alternating between his fingertips and palms, up the insides of her legs. She ached with anticipation. A small moan escaped when he came to her inner thighs, betraying her longing. He paused just for a moment. She was almost overwhelmed with a need that was sensual, earthy, so very real.

He touched his fingers to where she was dark and moist. She arched for him, cried out for him not to stop, but he drew back, all the way to her ankles again, were he followed the same trail with his tongue, until he was back to where she was wet and dark and aching, and this time he stayed. In seconds she was a volcano erupting, spilling out molten lava, and at some point he dispensed with his scrap of underpants, entering her with a heat that matched her own.

"I love you," he whispered. "I think I always have."

And she believed him.

Finally, when they became aware of the world again, Nora noticed the clock. "My party!"

They had to scramble. Together they lined up the jack-o'-lanterns they'd made on the front porch and got them lit, put the spooky music on the stereo, tucked ghosts and goblins and shrunken heads here and there, filled a tub with water for apple-bobbing, loaded bowls with mountains of treats. At last Byron sauntered off to put on his skeleton costume, and she retreated to her bedroom, where she quickly smoothed out her bed and put on her layers of makeup, her jewelry and the filmy, gaudy fabric.

"Good God!" Byron said, staring at her when she joined him in the living room. "How many years have you been dressing like that?"

"It's the same costume I always wear. My rendition of a gypsy—"

"Well, if there's a single person left in Tyler who still believes your Victorian virgin act after seeing you in this getup, I'll swear you're as pure as the virgin snow myself."

"What? I'm *not* a gypsy." She laughed, loving how he teased her—how he refused to take her too seriously. "It's sort of a sexy costume, I realize, especially for me, but—"

"Sort of?"

If the proverbial doorbell hadn't rung, in another minute there'd have been a gypsy and a glow-in-the-dark skeleton making love on the living room floor.

By six-thirty, Nora's house was packed. People who didn't ordinarily come to her annual Halloween party took advantage of her open invitation and showed up. She figured most of the newcomers had stopped in to get a glimpse—quite literally—of the skeleton in her closet. Byron seemed to enjoy popping out of the entry closet, scaring the daylights out of little kids. Then, of course, charming them.

People came and went; others lingered. Nora tried introducing Byron as her houseguest, who'd be staying through Cliff and Liza's wedding on Saturday, but he refused to say he was anything but a skeleton in her closet. It made for many widened eyes.

"You always have this many people at this thing?" he asked, pulling her aside.

"Not half. Everyone wants to see what you look like. It's not easy to tell with the face paint. The clingy costume doesn't leave much of the rest of you to the imagination."

He grunted. "I should have dressed as a pirate and kidnapped you, given them all something to talk about."

"They have plenty to talk about as it is."

His eyes turned serious. "Do you care?"

She smiled. "If talk's the only punishment, it's well worth the crimes I've committed."

"And to think," he said, laughing, "we've only just begun our crime spree."

Later, when the little kids had gone home, Nora put on the cassette of *Night on Bald Mountain* and broke out the hot mulled cider and the pumpkin rolls—no strings or seeds included—she'd made ahead and frozen. They were filled with layers of cream and nuts, then sprinkled with sifted powdered sugar. They'd been Aunt Ellie's favorite. Nora also had her biggest pottery bowl brimming with warm cinnamon applesauce.

Into this quieter, homey part of her Halloween festivities, Liza Baron walked, pale and scared, wearing a huge, patched denim jacket that had to be Cliff's. Someone started to tease her about not wearing a costume. But she didn't smile in her vivacious way, and her big eyes wouldn't focus. Nora quickly set down her tray of mugs filled with steaming cider.

But Byron was already on his glow-in-the-dark feet, grabbing his future sister-in-law as she stumbled into the music room. "Liza, what's wrong?"

She looked at him, the tears spilling down her white cheeks. "It's Cliff." She almost collapsed, but Byron was there. "He's gone."

CHAPTER ELEVEN

BYRON TOOK the next flight East.

He'd told Liza—and Nora—that he thought he knew where his brother was headed.

When his plane touched down at Logan Airport in Boston, he got his car out of long-term parking and drove to Providence, arriving very late. It seemed he'd been gone for years, yet it had been less than a week. He called Nora from the kitchen phone in the Pierce house on Benefit Street, half-expecing his grandfather to sneak around the corner and whack him with his cane for slouching. Thorton Pierce had been a brilliant publisher and a formidable grandfather. He had never taken—or, to be fair, tried to take—Richard Forrester's place. He'd made no secret of his mystification over his son-in-law's choice of a military career, particularly when there was a war on.

Nora picked up on the first ring.

"Any word from Cliff?" Bryon asked, just in case.

"None."

"I didn't expect there would be. Is Liza with you?"

"Yes. Alyssa talked her out of staying at the lodge alone, especially . . . well, you know."

The mysterious dead body discovered on the premises. It had to give anyone, even the irrepressible Liza Baron, pause. Byron nodded grimly, aware of his own solitude in the elegant town house. It was well after midnight, but Nora sounded fresh and alert, one of Tyler, Wisconsin's rock-solid citizens, a responsible woman who could be counted on in an emergency. In addition to wanting to make love to her night and day, Byron did also admire her.

"There's nothing more I can do tonight," he told her.

"I know," she said, more for his sake, he felt, than for hers. "Cliff's a grown man. It's not as if he's likely to be in any danger."

Liza, in fact, had given no indication whatever that Cliff had flipped out. Despite the strain he'd seen in his brother earlier in the day, Byron was inclined to believe her assessment. But what Liza hadn't articulated—and what he knew she most feared—was that Cliff Forrester had up and left her the same way, for the same reasons, that he had left Rhode Island and his mother and brother so many years before. *Liza and I are forever. That doesn't mean I won't break her heart.* Cliff's words of less than twenty-four hours ago.

But Byron thought he knew, finally, something that Cliff, even after his years of isolation, was only beginning to figure out. His stress and need and fears in these days before his marriage to the woman he loved weren't about cold feet. They weren't about his reluctance to face crowds or his fear of flipping out and hurting someone, even Liza.

No, Byron thought, looking in his refrigerator for something to eat. He found a shriveled apple and a beer. He chose the beer. It hissed when he unscrewed the cap.

Cliff's stress and need and fears were about Colonel Richard Forrester of the United States Air Force. They were about a man who'd died in captivity a long, long way from home and about the son who'd tried— and almost died—to save him. Ultimately, they were about confronting who Clifton Pierce Forrester had been, as a brother and a son, as a boy and a young man. They were about all of those things, Byron knew, because he was there himelf, coming to terms, at last, with the past. Accepting what was.

He sipped his beer, but it didn't taste right, and he broke out the last of his grandfather's private stock of brandy and poured himself a glass. He went up to the top floor of the grand, historic house, where he had his studio. Or, more accurately, what was supposed to be his studio. Since his return to Pierce & Rothchilde, he'd had precious little time for photography or anything else.

Aunt Ellie, he thought for no particular reason, would have loved the sweeping staircases, the eclectic furnishings that reflected the best in American craftsmanship, from the 1790s when the Pierces were shipbuilders, to the 1990s when they were publishers. Byron didn't know what they'd be in the year 2000.

"Snooty publishers," Aunt Ellie had called Pierce & Rothchilde in her outspoken manner. She loathed anything in herself or anyone else that smacked of elitism.

The house was warm. Upon leaving for Wisconsin, Byron hadn't thought to turn the heat down from its usual sixty-eight-degree setting. Now...well, it was obvious to him that nothing would ever be the same. Like his last trip to Tyler, Wisconsin, this one had changed him forever.

In his studio, Aunt Ellie grinned her toothy grin from behind a glass-fronted counter on the first floor of Gates Department Store. Beside her, smiling demurely, was her grandniece and namesake, Nora. Byron had had the picture blown up and framed. It was his favorite of all the shots he'd taken that hot Wisconsin August, one he'd held back from the series the Chicago paper had published just before Aunt Ellie's death, lauching the photographic career of Byron Sanders. Eleanora Gates had seldom left Tyler in her long lifetime, but she'd seen so much, knew so much. *The best gift you can give someone you love is the gift of being your whole self. Don't give yourself to Nora in pieces, Byron. She can't put you back together. No one can but you. If you ask that of her, you'll destroy yourself. And you'll destroy her.*

He raised his brandy snifter to her. "You were a wise and kind woman, Miss Eleanora Gates."

And he dialed Mrs. Redbacker's home number, because it was Tuesday night. She'd be with her mother, alternating as she did with her siblings to keep the elderly lady out of a nursing home, and he was guaranteed to get her message machine. Which he did. He left instructions for her, then finished his brandy in the company of Aunt Ellie and her grandniece, and went downstairs.

In his mail—delivered by a housekeeper he hadn't yet mentioned to Nora—he found a thick padded envelope that looked suspiciously like a manuscript. Didn't anyone know the difference between a publisher and an editor these days? He didn't have time to *read*.

"Aw, gee."

It was Henry "Hank" Murrow's technothriller. There was a note attached. "Thought you might want to have a look to see how stupid New York publishers really are."

Having nothing better to do until morning and knowing he'd never sleep, Byron started to read. After page three he knew that New York publishers weren't nearly as stupid as ol' Hank wanted to believe. But he did keep reading.

At least worldwide mayhem was a distraction from thinking about Cliff.

And Nora Gates.

"Oh, Nora," he whispered, hoping for a dose of her pragmatism and can-do spirit. He'd need them.

LIZA PACED back and forth from the living room, through the music room, down the hall to the kitchen and back until dawn, then collapsed for a few hours on the study couch. When Nora asked if she needed anything, she pulled in her lips in a look of pure Ingalls stubbornness. "The bastard could've left me a note."

Never had Nora seen anyone as worried about someone and yet as strangely confident that everything, in the end, would be fine. She'd watched Liza's initial panic settle into a slow burn of frustration. But whatever Cliff's agenda, his love for Liza Baron was a given. That was settled. Nora considered it bizarre. Cliff Forrester had cut out on Liza just days before their wedding, she might for all she *really* knew never see him again—and yet there was no doubt in her mind that he loved her. Then what the devil was love? Who needed it?

Love, Nora had thought uncomfortably as she dragged herself off to bed, was a peculiar thing. But she'd known that for years. Look at how she felt about Byron. It was the most mixed-up jumble of feelings any person could possibly want to endure. Her hopes and longings and needs and dreams all suddenly seemed to revolve around that dark-eyed Easterner, and made for lots of tossing and turning. She ached for him. She hurt for him. She wanted for him. She wanted him to be happy, to be everything he could be, needed to be. He had definitely turned her world upside down.

But life was easier when her world was right side up.

In the morning, she called Albert first thing and told him she wouldn't be in today. "I'm not surprised," he said. "I had coffee at the diner this morning and heard that Cliff Forrester had bailed out on Liza Baron. Word is she's hiding out at your place."

"She's not hiding. She's staying with me until we know more."

"Then the rumors are true?"

Too late, Nora realized she'd been had. She was in the awkward position—one she usually studiously avoided—of having to comment on gossip instead of merely hearing it. She'd seldom confirmed or denied a Tyler rumor. "Albert, you know I don't comment on other people's personal affairs."

"Well," he said, undeterred, "at least tell me if the wedding's still on. Will folks be lining up at the door to return wedding gifts?"

"They shouldn't be," Nora said crisply, changing the subject before hanging up in relief a few minutes later.

If only Byron would call again. She and Liza needed information. An update. Any scrap of fresh news they could hang on to. But the phone was annoyingly silent. And she couldn't call him. He'd neglected to give her his Providence number and it was unlisted. She'd tried Rhode Island information even before she'd called the store.

Liza had come into the kitchen. Her hair was tangled and sticking out at odd angles, and her eyes, ordinarily so clear and bright, were puffy and red from insufficient sleep. She'd borrowed a flannel nightgown from Nora that came to well above her ankles. She was barefoot, but Nora wasn't worried, since she'd kept the thermostat at whatever "humane" temperature Byron had settled on.

"Good morning," Liza said.

"'Morning. Coffee?"

She smiled weakly. "Just inject it directly into my veins. Anything new?"

Nora shook her head.

"What's that I smell?"

"Corn muffins."

"Nora, you didn't have to—"

"I was up early. It gave me something to do." While waiting for the phone to ring, she thought, but she was unwilling to let Liza know the extent of her own emotional involvement in the Forrester brothers' goings-on.

Liza sat at the table, and Nora brought her a mug of steaming coffee. The way things were going, she'd get used to having company for breakfast and would never want to go back to oatmeal alone with CNN and the *Tyler Citizen*.

"I *hate* waiting," Liza said suddenly, visibly squeezing her coffee cup, her impatience nearly palpable.

"It's not my long suit, either."

"Why the hell would Cliff go to Rhode Island?"

"Byron could be wrong—"

"But he's not. You know he's not." She exhaled, setting her mug down hard. "Cliff's told me zip about his life in Rhode Island. I've got the highlights, but he hasn't talked a whole lot about what his childhood was like, what he did *before* he went to Southeast Asia.

He's got stuff to settle with his family and I...well, I'm not part of that."

Nora poured herself a cup of coffee, took a sip. "Do you regret having invited Byron and Mrs. Forrester?"

Liza shook her head adamantly. "No, this had to come out and get done sooner or later. And you know me—better sooner than later. What that family's been through can't have been easy. Cliff's taking a big step. I wish I were a part of it, but...if we're going to be everything we want to be to each other, he's got to do it all, come to terms with all he's got to come to terms with. I can't dictate what he needs to do and doesn't need to do. I just hope..." She sighed, blowing on her coffee, not meeting Nora's eyes. "I just hope he hasn't run away because of this big wedding we've—*I've*—got planned. I would've thought he'd tell me if it was too much."

"Surely he would have," Nora said.

"Yeah, I guess. But everything's moved so fast..." She shrugged, her words coming in bursts, her concentration not at its best. "If it's Rhode Island...you know, if his family's been there for hundreds of years and he wants to go back there to live, I'm game."

"You'd move East?"

"Sure."

"But your needs and wants count, too."

"Yeah. They do. They just don't happen to include living in Tyler forever and ever. I mean, I can. It'd be great. But I can leave, too. If Cliff *has* to be somewhere, that's okay by me. I've been thinking he has to be at the lodge. Now maybe I'm wrong." She frowned. "Am I making sense? It's like you, Nora. You *have* to be in Tyler. I don't know what Byron wants, but I'll bet he doesn't need to be in Providence the way you need to be in Tyler."

Nora wasn't sure she liked the implications of what Liza was saying, which were that she was inflexible and stuck in her ways. But she focused on the other implication. "Liza, I know you think that Byron and I . . . that we . . ."

Liza's grin, even with her disheveled appearance, held some of its old devil-may-care spirit. "Oh, give it up, Nora. You and Byron *are*. It's so obvious."

The oven timer buzzed, and Nora, glad for the distraction, got out the muffins, dumping them onto an old, bent cooling rack Aunt Ellie had had forever. She got out the butter and honey, heaped the muffins onto a platter, and brought them to the table, where she sat across from Liza.

"You couldn't live in Rhode Island, could you?" Liza asked.

"I've never even been there."

"What do you think Cliff's up to?"

Nora shrugged. "Marriage is a milestone. No matter how willingly one goes into it, it's got to make anyone think about the past—where one's been. I'd guess Cliff's making his peace, with whatever drove him to Timberlake Lodge in the first place, the choices he's made, what he's done. Not just in Southeast Asia. Before that."

Dropping a piping-hot muffin onto her plate, Liza asked softly, "You don't think he's running?"

"No, frankly, I don't."

She dipped her spoon into the honey. "Maybe I've asked too much of him too soon."

"No more," Nora said confidently, "than he's asked of you or either of you has asked of yourself."

Liza nodded, not so much in agreement as in acknowledgment that she understood what Nora was trying to say, and she looked thoughtful, contemplating Nora's words.

Then she said, "You know, the bastard *could* have left me a note."

Nora smiled. "Yes, he could have. And Byron could have called again by now."

Liza watched the honey drip from her spoon onto her split muffin. "I've never been to Rhode Island, either."

Nora got up, tore a scrap of paper from the notepad by her phone, sat back down and pushed it across the table to Liza.

"What's this?" Liza asked.

"The times of today's flights from Milwaukee to Boston and Providence."

This time, Liza's smile reached her sparkling eyes. "You, Miss Gates, are far more devious than you look."

IT WAS A CLEAR, sharply cold New England morning in late autumn. As he walked onto the quiet, isolated stretch of Nantucket Island beach, Byron could smell the salt in the air, feel it on his skin. The wind off the Atlantic penetrated his bones. In the distance, the sea gulls swooped and croaked. These, he thought, would always be the sights and smells and sounds of home. Which was why he'd known his brother would come here.

He could see Cliff walking slowly along the ocean's edge, his shoulders hunched against the cold.

Byron hesitated, then moved across the white sand. And in his mind, he could see two small boys and their father running across the sand, discovering tide pools, scooping up shells, chasing waves. He could hear the father's laughter. It was clear and strong and filled with love and hope. The two boys responded with hoots and squeals. For the boys and their father, and their mother who would join them later for a clam-bake, Nantucket was a retreat, a place of peace and beauty where they could be together without the pressures of the outside world—of war, family, commerce, reputation. On Nantucket, they preferred to live simply, in harmony with the rhythms of the sun and the tide.

Then Byron was standing beside his brother, and he could see that the two boys had become men. And he knew that the father was gone and had been for too long. Cliff didn't look at him. He didn't speak. He and Byron continued along the beach together.

Finally, Cliff said, "We all did our best."

"Yes," Byron said, "we did."

"It wasn't enough to save Dad."

"No. There was never any way it could be. But he knew that. He didn't expect it."

Cliff nodded, looking out at the choppy ocean that was so impossibly blue, so impossibly beautiful, under the cloudless sky. "I know he knew."

For a while longer, they walked in silence.

Then Cliff said, "I couldn't save everyone I wanted to save in Cambodia."

"You saved more than most, Cliff. More than anyone could have asked you to save."

Cliff's gaze cut toward his younger brother; the bright sunlight revealed every line, every scar, a harsh reminder of the years that had passed, the time they'd lost. "Until Liza, I'm not sure I ever really understood what it must have been like for Mother to lose both of us, Dad and me."

"She didn't lose you, Cliff."

"I know that now. I didn't for a long time."

They walked into the wet sand where a wave had receded, making footprints that wouldn't last. Cliff seemed unaware of the cold. Byron zipped up his leather jacket.

"You'd knew I'd be here?" Cliff asked.

"Yeah."

He nodded, not needing to know how Byron had known. It was enough that he had. "We were all at our best here. I had to come before I walked down the aisle on Saturday. I had to know I could."

They started back across the empty beach.

A woman was coming toward them, over the same ground Byron had come, moving slowly, uncertainly.

Her head was wrapped in a flowing challis scarf against the increasingly fierce wind. If it didn't die down, Byron thought, the plane he'd chartered would be grounded and even the ferry wouldn't run.

But then, beside him, Cliff whispered hoarsely, "Mother."

And she recognized him, too, and hesitated, and Byron could feel his brother's pain that his own mother would hold back when she saw him. But, for a time, that was what he'd wanted, what he'd needed. Now it wasn't.

He grinned suddenly and waved.

Even with the wind, Byron could hear their mother's cry of happiness and relief. Cliff was moving faster. Byron hung back. This was their moment.

Their mother's scarf had come undone, trailing down her back, and she wasn't the young woman who'd tried to explain to her sons their father's sense of duty when he'd gone back to Vietnam for yet another tour, who'd tried to give them hope and stability in their grandfather's historic house in Providence during those difficult years, first of absence, then of uncertainty, finally of loss. Anne Forrester had grown older since her husband had gone off to war, never to come home, even to be buried. But she'd retained her strength and courage and humor. Byron could sense those qualities, even as he saw tears glistening on her cheeks.

Then Cliff caught up with her, and he held her, and both mother and firstborn son were still and silent, and crying, in the autumn wind.

"HOLY COW," Liza Baron said as she and Nora stood in the reception area of the very sedate, very plush Providence offices of Pierce & Rothchilde, Publishers. "Cliff wasn't kidding when he said his family were East Coast mucky-mucks."

Nora doubted those had been Cliff's exact words, but Liza did have a point. She couldn't imagine a better symbol of East Coast blue bloods than the beautiful brownstone headquarters of one of the most prestigious publishing houses in the country. Mrs. Redbacker, Byron's intrepid secretary, came out to greet them, reluctantly bringing them back to the offices of the president.

"Mr. Forrester is away this week," Mrs. Redbacker said.

Liza, in her serape and leggings and much more herself now that she was *doing* something, spoke up. "I know. He went to Wisconsin for his brother's wedding. I'm his almost sister-in-law."

Mrs. Redbacker nodded, as if outrageous Liza Baron was about what she'd expected. Nora, in a more conservative outfit of wool pants and plaid blazer, took in the antique furnishings, the computer, the fax machine, the steely-eyed portraits of Clifton Rutherford Pierce, Cofounder, and Thorton Pierce, Past President, above the marble fireplace mantel. And for three years she'd thought Gates Department Store was as close as Byron had come to corporate America. She gritted her teeth. The man did have a way of setting her off.

"So Byron hasn't been around today?" Liza asked.

Mrs. Redbacker sniffed. "No, he hasn't. And I'm sorry, but I don't expect him."

Liza frowned, in no mood for anyone to tell her anything she didn't want to hear. They'd checked at the airport in Milwaukee and then again in Providence—she'd vetoed flying into the bigger airport in Boston, which was farther away—but there was no word, anywhere, from either Byron or Cliff. Not at the lodge, not at her mother's, not on Nora's message machine, not at the store. This did not sit well with Liza. It was sitting less and less well with Nora.

Nora tore her gaze from the two Pierce portraits and smiled at Mrs. Redbacker as she would at a dissatisfied Gates customer. "That is a surprise," she said calmly, "because Mr. Forrester—Byron—asked us to meet him in his office."

She glanced at Liza, hoping her friend would realize what she wanted: she had to see Byron's office. She might never get another chance. And it could tell her so much about this man who'd wormed his way into her life, into her mind and heart. She wanted to know everything about him, regardless of what the future held.

"He did?" Mrs. Redbacker asked, not expecting an answer. "Well, I suppose it's entirely possible."

Her tone was unmistakable; she thought she'd make a better president of Pierce & Rothchilde, Publishers, than Clifton Pierce's great-grandson and Thorton Pierce's grandson did. Possibly she thought almost anyone would. There was no rancor in her voice, just the long-suffering of a secretary devoted to her company more than to a particular personality slated at birth to run it. Mrs. Redbacker seemed not to resent or dislike Byron Forrester as much as she simply believed he wasn't where he belonged. Nora had employees herself who were more loyal to Gates and its meaning to the community than to her personally. And Aunt Ellie's longtime personal secretary had retired just before her boss fell ill, at which point Nora had hired a full-fledged assistant in Albert Shaw. Not that it would have mattered; most people regarded her as another Aunt Ellie.

Clearly Byron was not another Clifton or Thorton Pierce.

Which Nora found curiously heartening.

She decided to intervene. "Byron and I are old friends."

Mrs. Redbacker narrowed her eyes. "Oh?"

"He did a series of photographs on my great-aunt three years ago," Nora said, trying to stick to the truth as much as possible. "He's an award-winning photographer, you know."

"I'm aware of that." Mrs. Redbacker's tone was a little too sharp for Nora's tastes. It wouldn't be easy to get past her. She narrowed her eyes. "What did you say your name was?"

"I didn't, but it's Nora. Nora Gates."

Liza warmed to the project. "We're here to pick up something for Byron from his office. It's a special gift for Cliff. His brother. You know—"

"Yes," Mrs. Redbacker said. "I know all about Cliff Forrester."

Liza snorted. "You don't believe us!"

Mrs. Redbacker sighed. "To be perfectly honest, I don't know what to believe. Mr. Forrester—Mr. Byron Forrester—did leave something in his office for Miss Gates. But I understood I was to send it to her." The very experienced secretary, clearly out of her element, turned to Nora. "If you're Nora Gates of Gates Department Store, Tyler, Wisconsin."

"I am."

"Well, then, come along. It's a photograph of an elderly woman—your great-aunt, I believe—and some girl. I'll show it to you and you can decide if you want to take it with you or have it sent to Wisconsin."

Liza was grinning. "Yeah, that'd be great."

Nora, however, found herself unable to speak, and silently followed Liza and Mrs. Redbacker into the elegant office of the president of Pierce & Rothchilde, Publishers.

"MY PERSONALITY was probably more suited to running this place than yours," Cliff said as he and Byron headed down the cream-colored corridor to the office occupied by a Pierce for most of the past century. "But it wasn't meant to be."

"It's not a bad job."

"It wasn't a job to Grandfather. It was a passion— the way Gates is for Nora."

Byron nodded. "That's to be respected, unless it interferes with a person living a full life. Anyway, my passions lie elsewhere."

"Photography," Cliff speculated.

"For a few years, yes. But I don't want to make a job of it. I like it as something I can do when the muse strikes, so to speak."

They'd come to his office.

In the outer room, Mrs. Redbacker was speaking to a slightly paunchy security guard. "I don't believe they're in any way dangerous, but they...well, they just won't *leave*. They insist Mr. Forrester is bound to show up sooner or later. One or the other Mr. Forrester, they say. They keep dialing his home but get no answer. If they did, I suspect they'd go harass him there. Why, I do believe they'll *sleep* here if he doesn't return. And it's after five now!"

"I'll talk to them," the guard said.

Cliff hung back, amused. "Sounds like you've got company. Do your thing, Brother."

Imagining boycotters and protesters of various descriptions—someone could be found to disapprove of virtually any book on any given publisher's list—Byron stepped forward, trying to look presidential. "What's up, Mrs. Redbacker?"

She was clearly flustered, an increasingly frequent state during his three-month tenure at Pierce & Rothchilde. "Oh, I'm so *glad* you're here." Which had to be a first. "Early this afternoooon two women barged in here. One claimed to be your brother's fiancée and the other seemed quite respectable and normal at first, and I...well, I fell for their act, I must admit. They're in your office now. They've been there for hours, and they won't leave. They...they're playing *darts*, Mr. Forrester."

"Darts?" Byron repeated.

Behind him, Cliff said, "Liza couldn't hit the side of a barn."

Byron grunted. "I'll bet Nora could take the eyes out of a bull at a hundred feet."

"Ol' Granddaddy Pierce is probably doing flips in his grave."

"Both ol' Granddaddy Pierces," Byron said.

"Think we should leave 'em to security?" his brother asked.

"It's a thought."

Then his office door swung open, and a dart came flying out, landing with a precise thwack on Mrs. Redbacker's bulletin board, just inches from Byron's head.

"I think," Cliff said, coming up beside him, "your lady's pissed off."

"Mine? *You're* the one who skipped out on your fiancée three days before your wedding."

Then another dart whizzed out of the inner sanctum of the president of Pierce & Rothchilde, Publishers. It thwacked against the wall near enough to Cliff for him to know he was the intended target, but the plaster wouldn't hold it and it fell onto the floor.

Mrs. Redbacker had ducked behind her desk. The security guard was looking to Byron for guidance. With some effort, he remembered he *was* the boss. He grabbed the dart off the bulletin board. Cliff got the idea and snatched up the one on the floor.

Apparently the two interlopers in Byron's office got the idea, too, and slammed the door shut.

"You two can go on home," Byron told his secretary and security guard.

He and Cliff waited until the two had retreated, Mrs. Redbacker with a frosty good-night, the guard without a word.

Then, darts in hand, the two brothers took their grandfathers' office in a frontal assault.

CLIFF ADMITTED he should have left Liza a note. He said he should have called. He said he loved her with all his heart and soul.

She relinquished her cache of darts.

Byron allowed he should have called with an update, as promised, although he figured his bumpy flight to Nantucket and his absorption with his mother and brother a good excuse for not doing so. So as not to irritate Nora further, he didn't mention anything about loving her.

She did not, however, relinquish her cache of darts. And she seemed to have the much bigger cache.

"I ought," she told Byron, "to pin your stinking hide to your mahogany paneling."

"Me? What'd I do?"

With great exaggeration, she let her gaze fall on the framed photo of her and Aunt Ellie looking like two peas in a pod, a photo Mrs. Redbacker was *supposed* to have wrapped and sent via overnight express by now. Of course, she'd had to cope with a sit-in most of the afternoon.

"What's the problem?" Byron asked, really not sure.

"You've had this picture for *three years?*"

Clearly she wasn't pleased. "Yes."

"On your studio wall?"

"Not the whole time. I only had it framed and hung on my studio wall three months ago, when I came off my leave of absence from P & R."

"It's a picture of Aunt Ellie," she said stonily. "Part of your series on her."

"Yes—"

"I never saw it."

"No—"

"I'm in it."

Byron considered that obvious and decided he'd better not comment.

Nora was rigid, darts clenched in her fist. "What," she said angrily, "if you'd walked into *my* house and found a picture of you and Aunt Ellie on *my* wall and I said, yeah, I've had it hanging around for *three damned years* but it's just a picture of Aunt Ellie and I never even noticed you."

Thick-skulled Yankee though he might be, Byron finally got it. "Nora, you—"

"Obviously," she interrupted, really angry now, "I've never had the impact on you and your life that you've had on mine."

"Nora, if you're suggesting you don't mean as much to me as I mean to you, you—"

"I said impact, Byron. I said nothing about whether it was a positive or negative impact."

She was definitely not in a mood to have him say anything more about loving her, which he most definitely did.

"How could you have had that picture for *three years?*"

And, not a woman to hold back anything from him, as she'd pointed out, she started pitching darts at nothing in particular—not even aiming at him—and he and Cliff and Liza all ducked, Byron knowing he'd never get through to her while she was throwing-things mad.

At which point Anne Forrester walked into his office, looking fresh and happier than he'd seen her in years. She and her sons had agreed to meet at P & R and then go out to dinner as a family, for the first time since Cliff had left for Southeast Asia so many years ago.

"Mother," Byron said, "I'd have warned you, but—"

"You must be Liza," she said to Nora, smiling. "I heard you were a live wire."

Nora was clearly mortified. She set down the rest of her darts on Byron's desk.

"No, Mother," Cliff said, trying not to laugh, "*this* is Liza."

And Liza, who, unlike Nora, could never stay mad for long, rushed out of hiding to greet her fiancé's mother. Anne covered for her mistake with her usual good grace, giving Byron a look out of the corner of her eye. It was one of those I'm-your-mother looks. *Who is this woman and what have you done to make her so mad?*

This time, Byron knew the answer. He'd fallen in love with her, was what he'd done. Madly, passionately, forever.

And she'd fallen in love with him. Maybe just as madly, surely just as passionately, and possibly even forever.

By Nora Gates's account, definitely a crime punishable by darts.

CHAPTER TWELVE

ON FRIDAY MORNING, Gates Department Store went on a low-level alert as Anne Forrester paid a visit. By eleven o'clock Nora had word that not since Margaret Ingalls, had Gates sold so much "pricey stuff," as Albert put it, to one person in a single hour. By noon a debate was raging whether the wealthy East Coast blue blood had beaten the missing Chicago socialite's record, taking into account inflation. The mother of the town's recluse, Mrs. Mickelson reported, had even purchased a set of Wisconsin place mats.

When Nora returned from her midday sweep of the three floors of her department store, she found Byron Forrester with his size elevens propped up on her rosewood desk.

"I think I'll buy you a dartboard for your office," he said.

He was never going to let her forget perhaps the most embarrassing moment of her entire life. Cliff, Liza, Anne Forrester—they'd all seen her out of control. Since attacking Byron in his own office with his own darts, Nora had become more subdued, shell-shocked from her peek at his life in Providence. He'd put them all up at the Pierce town house on Wednesday night, calling in his housekeeper to make dinner, change beds, put out fresh towels. Quite sure of himself, Byron had shown Nora his studio, his darkroom, a part of his soul, and she'd realized, with a deep pang of emotion she didn't understand, that he and his family had stronger roots in the East than she did in Tyler. For three years she'd thought of him as an itinerant photographer, rootless, uncommitted, a wanderer and a rake. But that wasn't the real Byron Sanders Forrester.

On Thursday morning, they'd all flown back to Wisconsin. Liza, proving herself truly Judson Ingalls's granddaughter, grumbled about how much money all this flying around was costing. Like Nora, Cliff was quieter and more contemplative. Anne Forrester was radiant and gracious; Nora had liked her immediately. In Milwaukee, Cliff and Liza had headed for Tyler in his pickup, which he'd left in the airport lot. Nora had driven home alone. Byron had rented another car and driven back to Tyler with his mother, whom Nora, thinking it was a sensible idea, had invited to stay with her.

"I won't be distracted," Byron had told her as she'd left the airport.

"I'm just trying to be helpful."

"No, you're not. You're just trying to avoid being alone with me before the wedding. Doesn't matter. There's always after the wedding."

"What about your nonrefundable ticket home on Sunday?"

He'd smiled. "I can absorb the loss."

Good son that he was, he'd moved to the back bedroom, which Nora had set up for her younger guests, and let his mother have the front bedroom. No sleeping naked in the study, no predawn visits to Nora's room. Setting her alarm, Nora had gotten up early and made oatmeal and fresh apple muffins, which went over well with Anne Forrester. Byron had picked the raisins out of his oatmeal.

Now, in his charcoal-gray turtleneck, wool trousers and his herringbone jacket, he removed his feet from her desk. "This place hasn't changed since Aunt Ellie's day."

"There was no need," Nora said, remaining standing behind her desk.

"If it ain't broke, don't fix it?"

"Precisely."

He nodded, his eyes resting on her in a probing way, reminding her of his photographer's acuity, and their mad sessions of lovemaking. In another minute, she'd have no choice but to sit down. "Perhaps I should have had a little more of that attitude when I took over at Pierce & Rothchilde. I wanted to put my stamp on the place."

She shrugged. "That's a normal impulse, I think."

"Of course, the reverse can be true—you can be too afraid of change."

She'd thought he'd go on, but he didn't. She had nothing to add. The silence between them, however, was uncomfortable. *I have to remain strong. I have to remember who I am.*

"What'd you think of Providence?" he asked casually.

Too casually, Nora thought. He wanted to know. He wanted to talk, to listen, to understand. Finally, she had to sit. "I had no idea . . . it's obvious you and your family have deep roots there. When you went on the road three years ago . . ." She sighed, wishing she could articulate her still-jumbled feelings. "It must have been a difficult choice."

"To leave my dartboard and barracuda of a secretary?"

"Well, your executive style may be a bit unusual, but—"

"But I'm a Pierce," he finished for her.

She nodded. "Yes, and your family's been in Providence for generations. That means something."

"What?"

"That's not for me to say."

"Bingo. It's not. It's for me to say. I'm not just half Pierce. I'm also half Forrester."

"Pierce & Rothchilde is an important company."

"So's Gates."

"In Tyler, yes. But Pierce & Rothchilde has a wide impact. It's recognized internationally as a quality publishing company and—"

"So?"

"So it's *important*."

"What, you want to run it?"

She groaned. "No! Byron, I'm trying to be serious."

"Okay." He nodded at her and paused a few seconds before going on, "I care about P & R, but I don't need to run it. I can continue to sit on the board and I'll still own stock, but it doesn't matter to me if I remain president—and I daresay it doesn't matter to most of the people under me. Just because a Pierce almost always has sat in the president's office doesn't mean one always must. If Mother wants, she can take over. She says she's too old, but that's hogwash."

"Then you don't feel obligated to stay on?"

"I did at one time. I don't anymore."

Looking away, Nora said in a low voice, "You think I feel obligated to run Gates."

"No, I don't," Byron said gently. "My grandfather instilled a sense of obligation in me. He hadn't had a son himself, Mother married the wrong man and God forbid a Pierce woman should do something as distasteful as work. Cliff...well, you know what happened to him. So there was me. It wasn't the same for you, Nora. That's one of the things so precious and wonderful about Aunt Ellie—she didn't make you feel you *had* to take over Gates when she was gone. You're here by choice."

Nora looked around her, at the simple, tasteful furnishings Aunt Ellie had bought so long ago, at the framed pictures of Gates Department Store in its early days. She could hear the traffic down on the town square and smell autumn in the cool air coming through her window, which she'd cracked open despite the gray, blustery weather.

"And you love Tyler," Byron said.

She nodded.

"You don't see me sitting on the Providence city council."

"But..."

"But we've been there three hundred years. Sorry, love, but I just don't feel the burden of that. We moved around a lot when we were kids—why the hell do you think my mother married someone in the military?"

Then Albert buzzed, telling Nora that Anne Forrester had finished her shopping. "I've arranged to have her purchases delivered directly to your house."

Had she actually beaten Margaret Ingalls's record?

"Well!" Anne said, coming into Nora's office, looking slightly flushed and very content after her Wisconsin shopping spree. "What a delightful store you have here, Nora. I'm afraid I left Rhode Island in such a whirlwind, and then with having been in London, I had a number of things I needed. I'm so relieved I could find everything here. Byron, have you gotten your brother a wedding gift yet?"

Byron grinned at her. "My presence isn't enough?"

She pursed her lips, obviously accustomed to her younger son's sense of humor. "I bought them a dozen Waterford goblets—Liza did have them marked in her bridal registry. It's difficult after all these years to imagine Cliff sitting down to a set table, but I suppose..." She shrugged, smiling. "Liza Baron does have a way with him."

With that, both Byron and Nora could agree. Nora said, "I'm glad you liked Gates. If there's anything else we can do for you, don't hesitate to ask."

"Oh, you've done far too much already. And it's truly a wonderful store. We're off to Timberlake Lodge for lunch. Won't you join us, Nora?"

Nora didn't give herself a chance to think, but shook her head immediately. "I have a million errands to run—and I need to be back here at one for a meeting. But thank you. Have a good time."

Anne Forrester rushed along, but Byron lingered. He shut Nora's office door and walked back to her desk, leaning over it. "You can't avoid me," he said. "You can't distract me. And I won't leave Tyler until I know you don't want me in your life, because, Miss Eleanora Gates, I very much want to be in yours."

Then, with Albert buzzing her, he kissed her hard on the mouth, and it was just as well her lipstick had rubbed off hours ago or Anne Forrester and Albert and everybody at Gates would have known everything. Which, she thought, might have been just as well.

"ARE YOU GOING to tell me what's going on between you and Nora Gates?" Anne Forrester asked her younger son, following him onto the porch of Timberlake Lodge.

Byron shrugged. "It's tough to explain."

His mother gave him a small smile. "In other words, no, you're not going to tell me."

Inside, the lodge was warm and surprisingly cozy, with a fire going in the kitchen fireplace. Amid the renovations, Liza and Cliff had put together a lunch of curried corn chowder, fresh sourdough bread and carrot-raisin salad. Byron could smell apple pie baking in the oven. Alyssa Baron was there, and Liza's sister, Amanda, and her brother, Jeffrey. Judson Ingalls was noticeably absent. The lodge, Byron remembered, wasn't his favorite place. But it couldn't have been easy for Alyssa, who'd lost her mother at such a young age, to be there, either.

"I should have had a rehearsal dinner," Anne whispered to Byron.

"Cliff would have croaked."

"As my dear father would have said, this wedding is all so *irregular.*" She smiled broadly. "But I don't give a damn. It's so obvious Cliff is happier than he's ever been." Then her smile faded, and she turned to Byron, her eyes narrowed. "Now if you'll get your life straightened out, I'll be a contented woman."

Byron grinned. "Once a mother, always a mother."

"Nora Gates—you'd better do right by her, Byron Sanders Forrester. While I was shopping I overheard talk about you two. Quite a considerable amount of talk."

"Don't tell Nora. She likes to think she's above being a subject of gossip."

Anne Forrester sniffed in her upper-crust way. "That only makes her a juicier target, I'm afraid. I gather her romantic life—or lack thereof—has been a topic of quite considerable speculation over the years.

She's something of an independent sort, rather like her great-aunt, but at least several elderly ladies in the fabric department—have you seen the range of calicos Gates carries?—think that Nora is avoiding romantic entanglements whereas Aunt Ellie simply wasn't interested.''

Mercifully, Liza spotted them and burst forward, taking her future mother-in-law by the hand and introducing her to her family, thus sparing Byron, a grown man, from having to listen to his mother discuss what people of Tyler were saying about him and the would-be old maid owner of Gates Department Store behind their backs. He certainly wasn't going to corrobortate any of the gossip. First, it wasn't his place. Second, Nora would likely have his hide. Third, they'd find out soon enough. In due time, the people of Tyler—the whole world—would know how much he loved Nora Gates. He was willing to tell them right now. But he respected Nora's ambivalence, her fears, her resistance to change, her need to make that decision for herself. He respected her enough to let her decide when she wanted to admit to the world that she loved him. Because she did. Byron *knew* she did.

CLIFF WAS NOWHERE to be seen. After saying his hellos and being introduced all around, Byron found his older brother out on the veranda.

"I can't wait for this circus to be over," Cliff muttered.

Byron could sense his discomfort. "Going to get through it?"

"If it's what Liza wants. I've already gotten what I want—my life back."

If his brother seemed more at peace after his excursion to Rhode Island, it was also clear to Byron that he didn't enjoy being in the public eye, that the people-activity of his wedding—being something of a spectacle, the burned-out recluse marrying Judson Ingalls's granddaughter—continued to take its toll. He wasn't in danger of flipping out. He just didn't *like* what was happening.

"Sometimes," he said, "I feel like grabbing her and getting the hell out of here."

"Hey, you guys," Liza called from the door, "lunch is on."

Byron clapped a hand on his brother's shoulder. "Tomorrow morning it'll all be over."

Cliff nodded grimly. "My tux arrived this morning. Can you imagine?"

Byron couldn't. But it wasn't his place to tell his brother and future sister-in-law that they were going about their wedding all wrong, trying to please everyone but themselves. And when it came to romantic advice, Byron supposed he did lack a certain credibility.

At least, he thought somewhat more optimistically, for the time being. Who knew what tomorrow would bring?

FRIDAY NIGHT was quiet, cool and rainy, and Nora spent it deliberately alone, before a fire in her study. She'd made herself a cup of hot cocoa and had dug out one of her favorite Agatha Christie mysteries, featuring the indomitable Miss Marple. Byron and Anne Forrester had taken Cliff and Liza and Liza's family to dinner. They'd invited Nora to join them. She'd declined with thanks, on the grounds that she had piano students. But she was not a Forrester. She was not a Baron. She was not an Ingalls. She was not a member of the wedding party. There was no reason Miss Manners would support her presence at the dinner, except as Byron's date.

Alone in her study, Nora tried to get in touch with the life she'd had since Aunt Ellie died, before Byron's second visit to Tyler. Peaceful evenings. Independence. Freedom. Time and space to think and reflect.

The cuckoo clock struck ten, and she counted each cuckoo as she blew on her steaming cocoa, feeling its warmth on her fingertips and mouth. It was almost erotic. A reminder, if a strange and unexpected one, of making love with Byron on her study floor.

"Independence doesn't mean solitude," Aunt Ellie had lectured more than once over the years. *"I'm an independent woman—but so was your mother, who was married and had a child. I might not be married, and I have no children, but I'm not alone. Even before you came to live with me, Nora, I never considered myself someone who 'lives alone.' I have too many friends and neighbors—I'm too involved with people—to feel isolated."*

Even after three years, Nora missed her great-aunt's wisdom and solid presence.

But it was her mother, now, who came to her mind. She'd been a quiet, hardworking woman who'd died far, far too young. In her grief, Nora had wanted never to inflict the kind of loss she'd endured on anyone. Life with Aunt Ellie only reaffirmed her determination never to marry, never to have children, never to let anyone get close enough to be hurt.

Someone pounded on her front door, startling her from her introspective mood. She went into the entry.

It was Liza, smiling tentatively, nervously. "No emergency—the Forrester clan's splitting a bottle of champagne before the festivities tomorrow. I ducked out. Nora, I need a favor. Actually, it's more than a favor."

"Sure."

"Be my bridesmaid tomorrow."

Leave it to Liza Baron not to beat around the bush. Taken by surpirse, Nora invited her back to the study, where she threw a log on the fire while Liza, with her usual restless energy, paced.

"Look," Liza said, "you're the best friend I have in Tyler right now. I wasn't going to bother with a bridesmaid—my sister didn't mind being spared—but you've been so incredible, I'm not sure Cliff or I would have made it through this week without you. I know I brought a lot of this stress and strain on myself by inviting the Forresters and opting for a big wedding, but I'm glad I did. I have no regrets. And I'm so grateful for all you've done. You've been there for me."

Nora wasn't so sure she'd been there for anyone this past week, including herself, but she didn't argue. "I'm very flattered, Liza, but I don't have a dress—"

"You own the best store in town, Nora."

"Yes, but—"

"But it's short notice and you don't do much on short notice." Liza stopped pacing a moment and smiled. "Remember what you said? Bridesmaids are about sisterhood. Nora, please. I want you to be by my side tomorrow morning."

Nora sighed, touched by Liza's offer of real friendship. Then she, too, smiled. "What color should I wear?"

Liza being Liza, she had an answer. "Got anything in burgundy?"

AT TEN O'CLOCK Saturday morning—just an hour before his wedding—Clifton Pierce Forrester was out at the lodge woodpile in a tattered plaid flannel shirt and patched jeans. Byron, in a navy summer suit himself, found him. "Mother says you vetoed the tux."

Cliff steadied a chunk of wood on the block, heaved his ax up high, then swung it down sharply splitting the wood neatly in two. "I tried it on. Looked like an ass. Tuxes aren't me, Brother."

Neither, Byron thought, were big weddings with hundreds of invited guests. "You own a suit?"

He picked up the two halves of cordwood, tossed them onto his growing pile. "Nope."

"Then what're you going to wear?"

"Clean clothes."

His brother, Byron could see, had withdrawn into himself to a perilous degree. "Cliff, what's going on?"

He set down his ax. Sweat poured down his temples and stuck his shirt to his back. Last night's showers had moved east, leaving southeastern Wisconsin under clear skies with warmer-than-average temperatures. Cliff and Liza couldn't have asked for a more perfect wedding day.

"I'm okay," Cliff said. "Guess I'd better get cleaned up, huh?"

"I guess so."

"Marrying Liza's what I want more than anything else in the world. If I have to do it in front of a crowd, then so be it."

In his mind, Byron had the bare inklings of an argument, but before it could take shape, Anne Forrester showed up at the woodpile. She was in her version of a mother-of-the-groom dress, meaning she'd opted for a plain blue wool dress instead of her usual tweed suit and had put on her best gold earrings. "There you two are. Cliff, I wanted to give you your wedding present. It's something . . . well, I'll let it speak for itself."

She handed him a small, flat, battered case that Byron doubted contained a dozen Waterford goblets.

Inside were about two dozen seashells, most of them broken, none of them worth a nickel.

"They're the ones you and Byron and Dad and I collected on vacations on Nantucket when you two were little boys," Ann said unnecessarily. "I wanted

you to have something tangible of your childhood—
something that would have meaning for you—to keep
with you here in Wisconsin."

Cliff struggled visibly to retain his composure.
"Thanks."

His mother laughed. "You're welcome."

And Byron's argument—his idea—took shape. He
waited for his mother to go back inside. Then, walking slowly back to the lodge with Cliff, he and his
brother talked, poured out their hearts, and plotted,
coconspirators—really brothers—once more.

Alyssa Baron greeted Nora at the front door of
her beautiful Victorian home on Elm Street, where
Liza, bowing to tradition, had decided to get ready.
Wearing a slim, silver-gray sheath with a matching
beaded jacket, Alyssa looked radiant, calmer than
she'd been in the weeks since the body was uncovered
at her father's lodge.

"You look so wonderful!" she said warmly to
Nora, who was dressed in a lovely burgundy silk dress
she'd worn the night she was elected to the Tyler town
council. "The orchids just arrived," she said, "and
Amanda and Jeffrey and Dad are meeting us at the
church." But she licked her lips, a hint of worry
creeping into her eyes. "Liza's upstairs. I—I've never
seen her so reflective. You know it's more like her just
to plunge ahead. Nora... Nora, if this wedding isn't
what she wants, if she's doing it for my sake, please tell
her she's making a mistake. I only want what she
wants. I mean that. I trust her."

"Isn't it a little late to be worrying if a big wedding's really what Liza and Cliff want?"

"No," Alyssa said, suddenly very sure of herself. "No, it's not too late."

"But people are already arriving at the church and the reception—" Nora broke off. "I'll talk to Liza."

Upstairs, Liza had put on her hand-sewn wedding dress, made from fifteen yards of silk organza and five-inch-wide lace that Gates had special-ordered for her from Paris. She was staring out the window overlooking her mother's backyard, fingering a simple clamshell she'd strung around her neck. "Cliff brought it from Nantucket with him. It's just a worthless shell—it isn't even pretty. But it's a part of who he is, where he's come from. God, I never thought I'd find anyone I love as much as I love him. I want...I want today to reflect who we are together and all that we can become. That sounds corny, I know, but it's true."

"Liza, it's ten o'clock," Nora said firmly. "You have to decide. It's up to you. Cliff is going to do what you want. If you want to go through with this big wedding, then let's get a move on. If not, then let's think of alternatives. Traditionally, weddings are much more the bride's responsibility."

"Mother—"

"Forget Alyssa. She wants what you want. She's told you, she's told me. Believe her."

Liza bit her bottom lip. Tears shone in her beautiful black-lashed eyes. "I want *her* to be happy, Nora. She seems so alone—and with all I've put her through over the years with my little rebellions, and now with this damned body stirring up painful memories...and Dad..." She exhaled sharply. "I just want to make up for some of what she's had to suffer."

"Then do it, Liza. Do it by having the wedding you want to have, because *that's* what your mother wants for you. That's what will help make her happy."

Turning back to the window, Liza said, "Last night I dreamed Cliff and I were married at the Lake—just him and me, you, our two families. It felt so right. It's where we met, where he's spent so many years healing. I'm not...we're not your traditional wedding types."

"Don't you think your mother and everyone else in town knows that?" Nora asked, realizing time was a-wasting and it was high time a decision was made.

"Cliff shouldn't have to be a spectacle, even if he gladly would for me. And it's such a beautiful day."

"Yes, it is."

"People are already arriving at the church."

"This isn't their wedding. It's yours."

Then Alyssa Baron was standing in the bedroom door, looking very maternal. "I've called Jeffrey. He said he can grab the preacher and meet us at the lodge. Amanda will get my father. They're waiting by the phone for me to give the word. What's it to be?"

Liza broke into a huge smile and ran to her mother, hugging her, even as Cliff Forrester, looking like a derelict, showed up in the doorway and announced that he wanted to get married at the lodge.

"Well, then," Liza said, laughing, "let's get a move on."

IT WAS ENTIRELY appropriate, somehow, that Liza Baron and Clifton Pierce Forrester were married in a short ceremony on the banks of Timber Lake, with a rotting dock in the foreground, a partially renovated lodge in the background. Liza wore her wedding gown, and Cliff, looking absolutely stunning, had put on the handsome tuxedo his bride had picked out for him.

It was one of the most beautiful and touching Wisconsin weddings Nora had ever attended. She stood beside Byron, slipped her hand into his, not caring if anyone saw, and cried. She always cried, if very discreetly, at weddings. This time she wasn't so discreet. She knew what she wanted, she knew who she was. If word got around Tyler that Nora Gates cried at weddings, well, that was fine with her.

Even Judson Ingalls admitted the lodge had been the right choice for his youngest grandchild. "But how're we going to explain this to all those folks waiting at the church?"

Byron stepped forward. "Nora and I will handle it."

They took her car, and Nora drove fast—ten miles over the speed limit, which, given her position in town as a business and community leader, she hated to do. But she wanted to get to the church not too much after the eleven o'clock ceremony was scheduled to begin. *And when this is settled, I'm going to tell Byron I want ours to be the next Tyler wedding.* She was suddenly very sure that was what she wanted. As sure as she'd been that warm August day when she'd been working on the back-to-school window at Gates and had spotted Byron for the first time and known he would change her life.

"Shame to let a good wedding go to waste," Byron said casually.

A chill went through Nora. Was he thinking what she was thinking? "Cliff and Liza will make an appearance at the reception. That will help. People will understand."

"I'm sure they will, but everyone loves a wedding. No question a lot of folks are going to be disappointed."

She gripped the steering wheel, taking a sharp curve. "Well, we can't cook up a replacement in the next five minutes."

Her heart was pounding. Because she knew they could.

Byron was silent. Then he said softly, "We could."

Nora nearly drove off the road. "Who?"

"Don't be dense, Nora. You know I'm talking about us."

"Us," she repeated.

He shrugged, confident, every inch of him a man she didn't want to live without. "Why not?"

"Because..." She pulled over to the side of the road, a few yards from Barney's pumpkin patch. She swallowed, but like Byron, she was suddenly confident, absolutely sure of herself and what she wanted. "No reason that I can think of."

"Do you love me?" he asked softly, his eyes penetrating all the way to her soul.

"Yes, Byron. Oh, yes, I love you. You've known that for a long time. You knew before I did."

He smiled, but she could see the relief—and the pleasure—in his dark eyes. "I knew before you'd *admit* you loved me. Nora...Eleanora Gates the Younger, I do love you. I always will. There's no going back." Then his smile broadened into a grin. "So let's get married."

"I've never done anything so impulsive in my life—"

"It's not impulsive. It's been three years in the coming. Look, we've got a church full of people—we won't even have to send out invitations. My mother's here, my brother, my sister-in-law. Couldn't be easier."

"You're serious?"

His smile vanished. "Yes."

"But Byron, where will we live? What will you do? What will *I* do?"

He sighed, hunching down in his seat, not looking the least bit worried about those particulars. "I'll remain on the Pierce & Rothchilde board. I called the appropriate parties this morning and resigned as president. I have a new idea for a series of photographs, but it'll take some time to accomplish—it won't, however, require a great deal of travel."

"No living in a tent?"

"I wouldn't ask a woman who needs her oatmeal and raisins every morning to spend the next umpteen years wandering from place to place and sleeping in a tent. Besides, that's not what I want."

"So you'll be a photographer—"

"As an avocation. I don't see it as my work. I'm also thinking about writing a book, teaming up with Henry Murrow."

"The literary novelist?"

"Yeah." Byron seemed very comfortable with the idea. "We're going to collaborate on a technothriller. He's tried one on his own, but it needs a ring of authenticity I can help provide, being my father's son and an ex-Air Force officer myself."

Nora didn't move. "A what?"

He laughed. "You sound so shocked. Yes, it's how I spent a part of my youth. I didn't make a career of it. I went to Harvard after I got out, then to Pierce & Rothchilde. Then I came to Tyler, Wisconsin, and met you and Aunt Ellie, and everything changed. I became a photographer and worked through what I needed to with regard to my past."

Nora felt a warm breeze against her cheek. "You're sure this is what you want?"

"Yes."

"We haven't...there's so much we don't know about each other, about our pasts."

"Well, we have to have stories to tell each other on cold Wisconsin nights. We know the important things, Nora. We know we love each other and that that's not going to change."

But she was staring at him, making sure. "Then you don't need to live in Rhode Island?"

"I haven't made that clear by now? No, I do not need to live in Rhode Island. It'll always be home. I'm sure I'll whisk you off periodically to Nantucket and visits to Benefit Street, but I'm already feeling as if Tyler's my home. I've followed in a lot of people's footsteps. When I came here three years ago, Aunt Ellie helped me realize I needed to find my own path so I could make my own footsteps. I've done that. Now I want to do it with you, Nora— I want us to find a place where our paths come together and become wide enough for us both to walk."

"We have," she said, as confident as he.

In five minutes, they were at the church in downtown Tyler. Byron jumped out while Nora went to park the car. When she came to the front door, Liza Baron Forrester was already there, handing her a bouquet of orchids.

"What're you doing here?" Nora asked.

"Are you kidding? I wouldn't miss this for anything."

Nora frowned. "I smell a plot."

"No one's ever said you were a dummy."

"Byron?"

"He's been thinking about international espionage—you should have heard him and Cliff plotting murder and mayhem last night over dinner, not to mention the millions they could make writing technothrillers. Though getting Tyler's own self-declared spinster up the aisle must've taxed him more than figuring out how to blow up the world."

"Liza . . ."

"Come on," she said, grinning, "we've got a packed house anxious for a wedding."

"Do they know what's going on?"

"Oh, they'll figure it out. People have been wondering for years when and if you'll ever get married. I think there are several pools going in town."

Two weeks ago, Nora would have been mortified. Now she laughed. "But, Liza, this was supposed to be your day—"

"It still is. But I want it to be your day, too." She tucked the second bouquet of orchids in front of her. "This time I'd rather not be the center of attention. You've always been there for everyone in Tyler, Nora. It's your turn to let us give you a party. Now, how 'bout I serve as your matron of honor?" She made a face. "What a yucky term. Any defense?"

"None. Let's abolish it. Just be my friend."

"Let's be sisters," Liza said, hugging her, and she whispered, "You're not alone anymore, Nora Gates."

And as she started up the aisle, Nora knew that she wasn't alone; indeed, had never been alone. Tyler was her family. Up ahead, Anne Forrester, looking as if she'd expected as much from her two sons, was in the front pew, waiting. Cliff Forrester moved next to his brother at the altar. The organ began to play, the crowd rose, and nobody seemed to bat an eye when it proved to be Nora Gates instead of Liza Baron who was the bride.

When she got close enough to Byron that he could hear her, Nora muttered, "You've been plotting this for *hours*."

"Nope." And he produced an antique ring from his pocket. "Belonged to my Great-grandmother Sanders. I've been plotting this for days. I didn't know it'd be this morning, but I knew it would happen."

"What about a marriage certificate?"

"Already talked to the minister. He says we can get one Monday morning."

Nora was grinning. "I love you, Byron."

"Yeah. I love you, too. But I think what everyone's waiting to hear are a few I do's."

And they did, in a Wisconsin wedding that would surely go down in Tyler history.

EPILOGUE

ON A SNOWY MORNING a few weeks after the Forrester brothers had given Tyler a fresh jolt of gossip with their surprise marriages to two prominent town citizens, Nora was working on one of her famous Christmas window displays when she spotted Byron in the street. Her heartbeat quickened. Snowflakes were gathering on his dark hair. He waved at her and flicked a snowflake in her direction, always ready to tease.

She loved him totally. He'd continued to prove himself a man of excitement, surprise and change. He'd already talked to Joe Santori—Tyler's most eligible bachelor—about turning part of the garage into a studio for himself. The little twenties house was fast becoming not Aunt Ellie's, not Nora's, but a comfortable blend of the tastes and spirits of the woman who'd built it, the lonely girl who'd found herself there, the man who'd found love there. Together, Nora and Byron were becoming renowned as hosts. She was getting to know his friends from the East and all over; he was getting to know her friends from Tyler and the world of Wisconsin retail. That weekend,

Henry Morrow—Hank, as he now preferred to be called—was coming to discuss technothrillers.

Byron pointed to the entrance to Gates Department Store, indicating that he was coming inside. Nora finished what she was working on and joined him.

He was already on a stepladder, hanging the photograph of Aunt Ellie and Nora above the glass-fronted perfume counter where he'd taken it. Looking at the image of herself from three years ago, Nora realized Aunt Ellie had been right to encourage Byron to leave Tyler then. He'd needed the time, but so had she. Those three years had made today—and their future together—possible.

Byron climbed down and stood next to his wife. "Johnny Kelsey stopped by the store earlier," she told him. "Word's going out—they've identified the body found at the lodge as an adult female. Her size isn't inconsistent with Margaret Ingalls's."

"Does Liza know?" Byron asked seriously.

"I'm going out to the lodge now. I'll tell her myself."

He nodded. "I'll go with you. Thank God she has Cliff! With all he's faced, he can help her get through whatever she has to in the next weeks or months."

Nora looked up at the smiling face of her plain, beautiful great-aunt. "Aunt Ellie admired Margaret for being her own woman, even at the risk of having people disapprove of her."

"I wonder what she'd have said about this latest news."

"First things first," Nora said, quoting the woman who'd helped raise her, who'd guided her into adulthood and had helped her find her true self, even if she hadn't lived to see it all happen. She slipped her arm around her husband's solid waist, overwhelmed, as she still so often was, by how much she loved him, how tremendously lucky she was. "And she'd insist that Tyler's strong enough to face the truth."

"Your Aunt Ellie was a wise woman."

"She was," Nora said, "herself."

And now,
an exciting preview of

MONKEY WRENCH

by Nancy Martin

the fourth installment of the
Tyler series

Television celebrity Susannah Atkins returns
to Tyler to take care of her elderly grandmother, Rose, who has decided that Joe
Santori is the most likely candidate as a husband for her spinsterish granddaughter. Joe,
a building contractor who sings opera on the
roof while he pounds nails, isn't exactly Susannah's cup of tea. But the sparks fly when
Joe and Susannah are alone together. While
they sort things out, Joe and Susannah learn
that opposites do indeed attract!

CHAPTER ONE

"THAT'S A WRAP!" the director called. "Have a merry Christmas, everybody!"

Susannah Atkins blew a sigh of relief and stepped out of the spotlight that brilliantly illuminated the kitchen set of "Oh, Susannah!," the daytime household hints program that was her claim to fame. Untying the strings of her apron, she draped it around the neck of her favorite cameraman, Rafael, and playfully tugged him close.

"Thanks for rescuing me when I missed my cue. And happy holidays, Rafe."

"Same to you, superstar."

Susannah laughed and gave the young man a kiss on his bearded cheek. Around them, the rest of the crew and production staff of "Oh, Susannah!" were calling cheery farewells and "see you next years" to each other. It was a pleasant sight. After six exciting years of working together, the team had become a close-knit family, not one of those squabbling gangs Susannah heard horror stories about when she visited other stations. Everyone connected with "Oh, Susannah!" was genuinely fond of the others, and Susannah felt a swell of pride at the thought. A relaxed and professional attitude of the star sometimes made all the difference.

The show's burly director, Pete Willard, made a detour around a camera to say goodbye to Susannah personally. "That's a good show, Suz," he said, pushing his glasses onto the top of his slightly balding head—a sure sign he was finished working for the day. He pinched the bridge of his nose to alleviate his chronic headache. "You headed someplace exciting for the holidays?" It was almost two weeks before Christmas. Somehow the taping schedule had worked out so that Susannah had nearly three full weeks of glorious free time before she had to be back at work.

Susannah grinned and began to rub the director's tense shoulders—the best way she knew to ease Pete's stress. "The Caribbean. I can hardly wait. We've got a condo right on the ocean."

The director groaned as she rubbed. "Sounds wonderful. I'd give my right arm to get out of Wisconsin this winter, but the kids...well, they think it's not Christmas without snow."

"I hear Santa visits beach houses, too."

"Yeah, well, tell that to my two-year-old! You don't know how lucky you are not having any kids, Susannah."

She kept her smile in place and released his neck. "I'll think of you on Christmas Eve when I'm dancing to steel drums—"

"And I'll be putting together that damned dollhouse I bought for my Jennifer. Ah, that feels great. You're the best masseuse I know, Susannah. Must be that Swedish ancestry of yours." Pete looked far from dismayed at the prospect of spending his holiday piecing together a toy for his child. He patted Susannah's arm and said, "Have a great time. Just don't get sunburned! We'll need that pretty face of yours back in front of the camera on January second!"

"I'll be here," Susannah called over her shoulder, half-wishing she could be worrying about something other than her face this Christmas.

But she banished the thought quickly and waded into the studio audience—her faithful fans.

The audience always waited patiently for their favorite local star after the show taping. And Susannah had been careful from the beginning not to play the prima donna. Even in a city the size of Milwaukee, it never hurt to hang on to those small-town values that her public seemed to appreciate most. Susannah signed autographs and allowed her picture to be taken a dozen times.

"Miss? Susannah?" An elderly man tugged at her sleeve. "I really got a kick out of your pumpkin pie recipe. Who else but you would have thought of adding summer squash and pecans? You ought to write a book!"

"Oh, it's just an old family recipe of mine. I enjoyed the chance to share it."

"Would you mind signing my program?" he asked flirtatiously. "I want to prove to the guys at the bowling alley that I really talked to you."

"For a pumpkin pie lover, anything! How shall I write the inscription?"

"To Hank," coached the old man, leaning close. "What a hunk. With love, Susannah."

Susannah cheerfully obeyed. She liked the relaxed and genuine affection of her fans. It made up for a lot of things—things Susannah tried not to think about. After half an hour, she finally tore herself away and headed for her office, a small, unpretentious cubicle tucked at the end of a narrow corridor near the studio.

In the office, which was jammed with so many books and gadgets it looked like the lair of a mad wizard, stood Susannah's young secretary, Josie. Nearly six feet tall in her flat shoes and always dressed to the nines, glamorous Josie looked more like an up-and-coming television star than Susannah, who left her clothing choices to the studio wardrobe department and wore jeans in her off-hours. Josie always looked elegant despite her youth. Susannah, on the other hand, looked elegant only when somebody else dressed her. Otherwise, she preferred to use her energy on more creative endeavors.

Despite their differences in personal style, Josie and Susannah were a perfect team. With a schedule as hectic as Susannah's was, she needed a good secretary more than she needed anything else. And Josie was worth her weight in gold. Her limitless energy had often saved Susannah when her own resources got low. With the telephone receiver pinned to her ear as Susannah pushed through the door, Josie was saying sweetly, "I'm sorry, sir, Miss Atkins is still taping a show in the studio. I can't interrupt."

Susannah mouthed, "Who is it?"

Josie shrugged elaborately and said into the phone, "I'm sorry, sir, but unless it's an emergency, I can't...yes, yes. All right, I'll double-check. I'll put you on hold for a minute, all right?"

Susannah was also thankful that Josie was unbelievably organized—a quality Susannah herself lacked almost entirely. And Josie took inordinate pride in her ability to fend off the hundreds of hopeful male viewers who called the station every week on the chance of getting in touch with "Oh, Susannah!" herself. The young black woman had turned the gentle letdown into an art form.

"Who is it this time?" Susannah asked, sliding into the comfortable swivel chair behind her antique desk. "Another senator who wants to meet me for lunch, like yesterday? Or someone trying to sell his mother's recipe for goulash?"

"Neither," Josie said, lighting a cigarette one-handed, obviously in no rush to get back to the caller waiting on the other end of the line. "He's a nobody. But he's got a voice that makes my blood tingle." She blew smoke and waggled her dark eyebrows lasciviously. "You know, the low and rumbly kind, a cross between Darth Vader and...oh, somebody sexy. Kevin Kline, maybe. Trouble is, the ones with great voices always turn out to be four feet tall with overbearing mothers."

"Josie!" Susannah laughed and kicked off her shoes. She put her stocking feet on the desk, noting lackadaisically that she had a run in her panty hose already, and leaned back in her chair to relax. "Do you mean to say you actually meet some of the men who call for me?"

Josie sniffed aloofly. "In the interest of science, that's all. Somebody ought to do a study on guys who call television stations. It might as well be me. One of the perks of my job is getting your castoffs. It's in my contract."

"Yeah, right. I think my contract says I *can't* date men who call here."

"You don't date anybody, honey," Josie remarked. "'cept old Roger, and he hardly counts."

"What's wrong with Roger?"

Josie shrugged. "Too nice."

"Too *nice?*"

With a grin, Josie tapped cigarette ash into a seashell sitting on the desk, "You deserve more excitement. Want me to line up an appointment with this guy?" She wiggled the receiver. "Maybe his face matches his voice."

"I doubt it. Better get rid of him."

"Chicken. But you're the boss." Josie punched the hold button with one of her long, enameled fingernails. "Hello? Still there, sir? Good. Look, I'm sorry, but I can't seem to locate Miss Atkins at the moment. I could . . . yes, I can take your name."

Susannah closed her eyes and listened with only half an ear while Josie reached for a pad and pencil from her desk and began scribbling. "Will you spell that for me, please? S-A-N-T-O-R-I. Yes, I got it. Now, can I

ask what this is in reference to, Mr. Santori? Who?
From Tyler?''

Susannah sat up straight. "Tyler?"

Josie's gaze met Susannah's, communicating a new
message altogether, and she said into the telephone,
"Yes, I know Tyler is Miss Atkins's hometown. Who?
Oh, you mean Miss Atkins's grandmother? Is something wrong?"

Susannah didn't waste another instant. She reached
for the receiver and took it from Josie's hand.
"Hello?" she said briskly as soon as she clamped it to
her ear. "This is Susannah Atkins. Is my grandmother all right?"

A wonderfully melodic male voice said, "I thought
you couldn't come to the phone."

"I'm here now. What's wrong?"

"Nothing's wrong," he said soothingly. "I'm butting in, that's all. I think you ought to come home for
Christmas."

"Home? Why? Is my grandmother ill? Or—"

"Take it easy. She's not sick. At least, not yet."

"What's that supposed to mean?" Susannah found
she could hardly breathe. Her grandmother was the
most important person in her life, and the thought of
Rose sick or in trouble was horrifying. Susannah's
hand clutched the receiver with a clammy grip.
"Please tell me what's wrong."

"Look, I don't want you to get all upset, Miss Atkins, okay? Your grandmother's not sick—at least she
claims she isn't. But...well, in my opinion, she hasn't
been up to snuff lately."

"Oh, dear heaven."

"It's not bad," the man assured her. "But she's disappointed that you're not coming home for the holidays, and I . . . well, I don't believe she's feeling as good as she pretends. I got to think—if it was me, I'd want somebody to call before I went away on a trip. And I'd want to check for myself. You're going to a beach, I hear."

Susannah frowned and tried to control her emotions. "My plane leaves tomorrow. I was going to see her when I got back, but—"

"Do you have time to drive out here this afternoon? You could take a look at her yourself before you go."

"Let me check my book."

"Your book?"

Most people did not understand Susannah's total reliance on the small, leather-bound datebook she kept within reach at every waking moment. With her many appointments and her ousy work schedule, Susannah's life was very complicated. She had many obligations and responsibilities. What made things worse was her mental weakness concerning dates and times. Though talented in a hundred different ways, she absolutely could not keep her life on track without writing down every detail. Fortunately, Josie kept a duplicate book so that, between the two of them, Susannah ran on schedule.

But the man said peevishly, "You can't squeeze in a couple of hours for your own grandmother?"

"Of course I can," she retorted. But there were things to juggle, no doubt—like a public appearance at a department store that Susannah had promised to make that very afternoon. As she flipped open her datebook, her eye fell on the appointment at once.

Josie was checking her version of Susannah's schedule, too. In an undertone, she said, "I'll cancel the department store, if you want."

"They'll understand a family emergency."

"But listen," Josie said. "The store's on your way to Tyler. Why not drop in, make the appearance a short one and buy yourself that bathing suit you need for your trip?"

"I'm not sure," Susannah murmured uneasily.

"You could be in and out of the store in twenty minutes. I'll go along and make sure it goes smoothly."

"I really must get a bathing suit."

"May I suggest a bikini?" said the dry male voice in her ear. "In pink, maybe."

Susannah had forgotten that her voice was audible to her caller, but he probably hadn't heard Josie's side of the conversation. "Oh, sorry—"

"You look good in pink," he continued sarcastically. "A pink bikini sounds like the perfect choice. It'll make you forget all about your grandmother, I'm sure. Sorry to have bothered you Miss—"

"Wait! That's not it at all. I'm just checking my schedule. Of course I'll come. I just have to make a quick stop along the way, that's all."

"For the bikini. All right, go ahead." Tartly, he added, "The right bathing suit might do you a world of good, in fact."

"I beg your pardon?"

"A lady as straitlaced as you seem on television—a lady who has to check her book before she goes home for a visit—well, that's a lady who needs loosening up, I'd say. Get a hot-pink bikini, Miss Atkins."

He was probably right, Susannah thought. Maybe her life *was* pretty strict, and she had allowed herself to forget the things that were truly important—like grandmothers and bathing suits. She found herself nodding in agreement.

Besides, it was hard not to be seduced by that marvelous voice. Glad he couldn't see her smile, Susannah said, "I'm hardly the bikini type."

"Who says so?"

"*I* say so."

"That's too bad." There was a slight pause, during which he must have decided he'd flown off the handle. His voice dropped another half octave and on that new note he said, "Maybe you ought to try something out of character for once."

"I like my character the way it is."

"An occasional change can be healthy. Buy a bikini and see what happens."

Susannah couldn't hold back her laugh. "Are you always so free with your advice?"

He laughed, too, and the tension eased. "When it's needed. And I think it's definitely needed in this case.

I'll tell your grandmother that you're coming today, all right?''

"Fine." Susannah hesitated, then impulsively asked, "Who are you, anyway? A friend of my grandmother?''

"Yep," said the voice. "I'm Joe Santori."

"Well, I'm warning you, Joe Santori. My grandmother is going to be mad at you. She doesn't like people interfering."

"I can take it," he replied with a laugh.

He hung up without another word, leaving Susannah to stare, smiling, at the humming receiver. For a friend of her grandmother, he sounded very young indeed. Maybe he was one of those little old fellows who hung around Tyler's retirement home. She frowned again, trying to place his name. Was Joe Santori one of the old coots who played gin rummy every day at the hardware store? Or one of the gentlemen who sang in the church choir?

He didn't *sound* like an old man. Far from it. With that low, sexy voice, he could be—

"Well?" asked Josie, interrupting Susannah's runaway thoughts. "Who was he?"

"I haven't the faintest idea," Susannah replied, cradling the phone. "But I'm going to find out."

THE DEPARTMENT STORE was mobbed with Christmas shoppers, but Susannah and Josie managed to slip into the resort-wear section for a swimsuit before making Susannah's quick appearance in kitchen appliances where she had promised to demonstrate a new brand of food processor. She apologized to the store manager for cutting her stay short, but the woman was completely understanding.

"I look after my grandparents, too," she said sympathetically. "Sometimes I have to drop everything to take them to the doctor's office or to the grocery store. It's exasperating, but I wouldn't trade them for any promotion in the world."

"Thanks," Susannah said, relieved that she'd found a human being to deal with. "I'll make it up to you, I promise."

The manager smiled. "I'll hold you to that! Our customers love 'Oh, Susannah!'"

Josie took the manager aside to schedule another appearance, and Susannah began her presentation. It was fun and lighthearted, and she even managed to sell a few food processors to people who had gathered around the demonstration table to watch her chop, grind and puree.

Then Josie stepped in and broke up the event, making apologies on Susannah's behalf and hurrying her out of the store.

"You know how to get home to Tyler, right?" Josie asked, bundling her into her car in the parking lot. "You want me to follow you as far as the interstate?"

"I may be an organizational cripple," Susannah shot back cheerfully, "but I can find my way home."

"Okay. Then you'll come back early tomorrow, right? You need time to finish packing for your trip. I'll phone Roger to tell him what's happening."

"Thanks. What would I do without you, Josie?"

"You'd be a dismal failure, I'm sure," Josie said with a grin, kissing Susannah's cheek as they hugged. "Either that, or you'd be a network star making millions. Maybe I'm just holding you back."

"You're holding me together. Someday it will be your turn, you know."

"I can't wait. One more thing. You'll need this." Josie handed over the small suitcase she insisted Susannah always keep ready in her office, packed with a few essentials and a change of clothes. "Don't go off to Tyler unprepared."

"Oh, Josie, you're a lifesaver. And I appreciate it more than you can imagine. Give Marlon a smooch for me."

Marlon was Josie's temperamental cat. Josie laughed. They parted then, with Josie turning her car back to the city and Susannah heading west.

The drive to Tyler normally took more than an hour, but Susannah lost track of time and was surprised to find the sunlight slanting over the horizon when she finally pulled her station wagon into the town limits of Tyler, Wisconsin.

Tyler looked as pretty as a Christmas card, covered with snow that sparkled in the last flicker of afternoon light. Picturesque trails of smoke wisped from the chimneys of the neatly kept houses on Elm Street. The steeple of the Methodist Church pointed heavenward from a thatch of spruce trees, with snowflakes settling gently on the fluffy green branches.

Susannah's chest felt tight as she drew up to the curb in front of the tall Victorian house on the corner of Elm and Third streets. No matter how many years had passed since she'd left her hometown for college, she always got a pang of pleasure when she returned.

Pleasure mixed with regret. Susannah often thought of Tyler as the life she'd left behind. The lovely town was quiet, yet full of good people who lived rich, full lives. Tyler had a lot to offer. But even though she visited occasionally, Susannah had turned her back on it somewhere along the line. She had never meant to abandon her roots completely. Sometimes a hot career in the big city paled by comparison.

Her grandmother's house, with its gracefully curving front porch, its scalloped trim and its twin turrets, looked as welcoming as ever. Susannah knew every nook and cranny in the house, having lived with her grandmother after the deaths of her parents. Nothing had changed, as far as Susannah could see. It was comforting to know that life stayed the same in Tyler.

When she opened the car door, she could hear the soft croon of Bing Crosby singing Christmas carols from the loudspeakers in front of Gates Department Store, just a few blocks away. Across the street, Mr. Connelly was stringing colored lights in his shrubbery while his two small children watched, bundled in identical yellow snowsuits with pompoms on their hats. The children looked away from their father long enough to give Susannah happy waves of greeting.

"In the air there's a feeling of Christmas," Susannah murmured, reaching into the back seat for her overnight case and a gaily wrapped jar of peach chutney she'd brought along to give to her grandmother. It was an old family custom to bring little gifts when visiting. Then she straightened and inhaled the fragrant scent of wood smoke that hung in the air. "That's the way life is in Tyler—it's always like Christmas. Oh, I almost wish I wasn't going to spend the holidays in the Caribbean!"

"Maybe you can get a refund," said the same wonderfully masculine voice Susannah had heard on the telephone.

She spun around, fully expecting to come face-to-face with one of her grandmother's friends—an old man with a cane, perhaps, or loose dentures. A lot of men came to visit Rose Atkins, because she was so lively for her age. Her vigor seemed contagious. But standing in front of Susannah on the snow-encrusted sidewalk was no withered senior citizen with a gleam in his eye. Far from it.

He was tall and lanky, with amazing shoulders, coal-black mischievous eyes full of improper suggestions, plus curly dark hair that tickled his ears and the back of his strong neck. His clothes were rough—a rumpled old parka over jeans, a faded flannel work shirt and heavy boots suitable for hiking the Klondike. The parka was unzipped enough to reveal a low-slung tool belt worn with the panache of a gunslinger.

"Let me guess," said Susannah when she could control her vocal cords. "Mr. Busybody Santori?"

His wide mouth quirked into a wry grin. He had a strong Italian face with prominent cheekbones, expressive brows and velvety black eyes that communicated volumes. "Am I going to get a lecture from you, too, Miss Atkins?"

"That would be cruel," Susannah shot back, smiling. "I bet my grandmother has chewed you up one side and down the other already."

"I'm still licking my wounds, in fact."

"She was angry at you for calling me?"

"Furious," Joe Santori pronounced. "She says I have spoiled your vacation by suggesting you come home, and I'll never be forgiven."

"It's not as bad as that," Susannah replied, hefting her suitcase out of the car and slamming the door with her other hand. "I'm sure I'll still be able to catch my plane. I'll bet she's mostly angry that you interfered. My grandmother prides herself on her independence."

"She has a right to be proud." Joe took her overnight case without asking and slung the strap effortlessly over one shoulder. "But we all need a little help now and then."

Looking up at him, Susannah doubted that Joe Santori believed his own words. He looked like a man who'd rather die than ask for help himself. The arrogance that showed plainly in his face was tempered only by his lopsided grin. Obviously, he was perfectly at ease conducting the lives of people around him and felt justified telephoning a complete stranger to come home to check on a sick relative.

But there was something else in Joe Santori's expression, too—something Susannah felt she could trust. Along with his natural self-confidence, he seemed to radiate honesty. He had a few flecks of gray in his dark hair, and the laugh lines around his eyes also seemed to bespeak a certain amount of tragedy along with amusement. He had an interesting face. A trustworthy face.

"Tell me the truth," Susannah said, coming directly to the point and knowing she could rely on him. "Is my grandmother really sick?"

Joe shrugged and responded just as bluntly. "I can't tell. I've known her for a couple of years, but only as an acquaintance. I started doing some work on her house earlier this month, and Rose seemed pretty perky then. But now…well, I can't tell what's wrong, exactly. Maybe she's just feeling blue."

Susannah shook her head, concerned anew. "Not before Christmas. It's her favorite season. My Granny Rose loves getting ready for parties and…well, everything."

"Don't jump to conclusions before you've seen her," Joe cautioned, his voice low and quieting. He put one hand on Susannah's shoulder to steady her and said with a grin, "Maybe you'll take one look at your grandmother and decide to belt me for dragging you to Tyler on a wild-goose chase."

Susannah appreciated his kindness. She didn't feel like belting him at all.

Joe looked down at Susannah Atkins and couldn't imagine her belting anyone. She was so small, for starters. On television, she looked average in size, but in person she was quite dainty. Her body concealed by a flowing, camel-hair coat, belted casually around a slim waist and long enough to show slim ankles encased in trim black boots. But Joe was familiar enough with "Oh, Susannah!," the popular television show that came on after the noon news every day to know that Miss Susannah Atkins had a body worthy of great admiration.

And while she was pretty on the small screen, Joe hadn't been prepared for how exquisitely beautiful she was in real life. She had a delicate face with a sharp chin, pointed nose and thickly lashed blue eyes that were deep-set and luminous. Her shoulder-length blond hair was smooth and glossy, pulled back into a raspberry-colored beret that exactly matched the shade of her lipstick. With her quirky little mouth and those expressive blue eyes, she looked darling—just ready for someone to come along and muss her up a little.

With a lilting laugh, she said, "I don't believe in belting people, Mr. Santori. I leave that to my grandmother. Has she ever told you the story of when she chased a burglar with a frying pan?"

She was charming, Joe decided. "There are burglars in Tyler?"

"No, it was just a teenage boy trying to sell encyclopedias, but Granny Rose didn't like the way he seemed to be casing the joint and she decided he was a burglar. Rather than call the police, she chased him for a block, waving a frying pan." Susannah turned and led the way up the sidewalk to her grandmother's house, saying, "As it turned out, he *was* a fraud. Granny Rose investigated the company he worked for and found it was a very shady outfit. Single-handed, she chased them out of the state."

Joe suspected Susannah was every bit as stubborn as her grandmother. He said, "Rose is independent, all right. I'm glad I don't have to tangle with her anymore. Maybe you can handle her."

"She doesn't need to be 'handled,' I'm sure," Susannah replied.

"Taken care of, then," Joe corrected.

"No," she said, mounting the porch steps. "Not that, either. The Atkins women don't abide people trying to control them. We like our freedom."

Joe stopped on the top step. "There's a difference between freedom and plane foolishness. Your grandmother needs supervision, Miss Atkins."

Susannah paused and turned to face him, lifting one narrow eyebrow as she studied Joe again. "Are you one of those macho fellows who wants to be in charge of everyone, Mr. Santori?"

"Hell, no, but—"

She smiled. "I bet you're the sole breadwinner in your family, and your word is law at home. Am I right?"

"Yes, but—"

"Then you're not used to women like my grandmother. She was the child of an immigrant farmer who built their house with his own two hands, and she worked hard all her life, Mr. Santori. Her husband died when she was still young, and she's outlasted her children, too, earning a meager livelihood but living a very full life. Don't think you can come in and start bossing her around now."

"Listen, Miss Atkins—"

"And you can't boss me around, either."

Joe's comeback was cut off by the sudden opening of the front door, and in another instant, they were joined on the porch by Rose Atkins herself, a feisty old woman in blue jeans and sneakers. She was just as diminutive as her granddaughter, and must have been every bit as beautiful in her day, her blue eyes sparkling.

"What's going on out here?" Rose demanded. "Are you two talking about me?"

"Yes," Susannah replied at once, kissing her grandmother before saying smoothly, "Mr. Santori tells me you're furious with him, Granny Rose."

"I am," Rose snapped, glowering at Joe and folding her arms over her sweatshirt, which was imprinted with a *Far Side* cartoon concerning Holstein cows. "He's poking his nose in things he has no business poking into, and if he's ruined your vacation, Suzie, I'll never speak to him again."

"You have to speak to me," Joe replied calmly. "I'm not finished fixing up your back porch, and you can't stop yourself from checking up on me every five minutes."

"I want the job done right!"

"So you hired the best man to do it!"

"I hired you because you're the most entertaining carpenter I know, but I didn't plan on paying you money to butt into my personal affairs."

"I won't bill you for butting in."

Susannah began to laugh. "You two sound like a couple of toddlers who need naps. Granny Rose, I brought you some chutney I made in the fall. Invite Joe inside for a snack and we'll settle this once and for all."

Rose looked sulky. "He can come in, I suppose. But we're not going to talk about me."

"Well, it's a start."

Rose sent Susannah a glance that was suddenly glimmering with purpose. "Maybe we should talk about you."

"Me?"

"Joe, what do you think of a woman who is so busy being glamorous that she hasn't time to find a husband and start a family?"

"Granny Rose—!"

"It's a crying shame," Joe said, laughing.

"I have spent a lot of time trying to find the right man for my granddaughter, but she's very fussy, not to mention more disorganized than..." Rose snapped her fingers. "Good heavens! I don't know why it didn't occur to me before."

"What are you talking about, Granny Rose?"

"You and Joe, of course. Despite some rather obvious superficial differences, I suspect you'd make a perfect couple."

"A perfect—? *Granny Rose!*"

"Why, of course! Joe is so bossy and you're such a fool with keeping track of things that...why, you're ideal for each other!"

Joe began to laugh at Susannah's expression—a pink-cheeked, blue-eyed combination of mortification and profound fury. The glamorous television star in her stylish beret looked appalled at the thought of being half a couple with a blue-collar carpenter. She swung on Joe with fire in her eyes, as if blaming him for the sudden turn of events.

Joe was still laughing. "It looks like your grandmother's not the only one who resents interference, Miss Suzie."

"I never—I didn't—"

"Come inside, Joe" Rose commanded. "I want you to get to know my granddaughter."

It was a command Joe couldn't resist. He stepped inside the house on the heels of Susannah Atkins, the most beautiful little hothead he'd ever laid eyes on.